SPLITTING HEIRS

ALSO BY DIANE MICHAELS

Novels

Ellen the Harpist
Ellen at Sea
Ellen the Bride
Pet Peeves

Novellas

King & Queen of the Bouncy Castle
King & Queen of the Roller Derby
King & Queen of the Bowling Alley
King & Queen of the Poker Game
King & Queen of the Carnival

Short Stories

Watching the Grass Grow

Wedding Ceremony Music Guide

From Here Comes the Bride to There Go the Grooms

Visit dianemichaelsbooksandharp.com/books to view
sheet music for harp.

SPLITTING HEIRS

Book 1 of the
Empire State of Mind series

Diane Michaels

ArrowHeart Press

This is a work of fiction. Names, places, and events are either fictional or used fictitiously. Any similarity to real people, living or dead, or to actual events is coincidental and not intended by the author.

ArrowHeart Press

First paperback edition: June 2020

The author acknowledges the trademark status and owners of products referenced in this work of fiction, which have been used without permission and to which the author is not associated.

ISBN 978-1-7351022-1-4

To David Michaels
Not if I see you first.

CONTENTS

CHAPTER ONE
STELLA!

You can have your Colin Firth emerging from Pemberley's lake, his sheer shirt clinging to his manly chest. You can have your men in uniform, too. Neither vision is enough to ruffle my petticoats. But ruffle they do when a man of no more than forty approaches me.

With each stride, he commands my heart to accelerate until it matches his pace. The fabric of his bespoke suit rustles in the rhythm of a military tattoo. His fingers plunge into his glossy, black locks, but they rake a diffident path. His footfall grows hesitant as he draws closer to me. With a shy grin, he bites his bottom lip. Does he doubt his power of seduction?

Cocking his head to the side, he stutters through his introduction. His green eyes glitter with hope. As words tumble from his plump, red lips, I hold my breath until my chest tingles.

He captivated me the moment I noticed him, but I don't want to give the impression of being too eager. Silent and still, I savor my dominance over him, waiting for him

1

to form his question, the very proposition lying at the core of my deepest desire. He pauses for a moment, teasing me. My self-control falters. A second before I leap toward him in a burst of lustful impatience, he asks, "Would you agree to list my four-bedroom, three-bath penthouse on Central Park West?"

It goes without saying that his kitchen boasts state-of-the-art appliances, that the ceilings soar twelve feet above the original wood floors, that the dressing room is larger than the size of the average one-bedroom apartment in New York City, that—

"Lauren!" my mother screeches. I pull my feet off the top of my desk and rearrange a pile of paperwork next to my laptop. I hope to appear too busy to endure interruptions issued from the kitchenette of our family's real estate office. Put a different way, I don't want my mother to catch me in another daydream.

"What?" I yell.

My mom returns to her desk, clutching a mug of coffee. Purplish-red lip prints cling to its white rim. "No need to shout. I'm right here." She lowers herself into her chair, bracing her heels against the floor protector. With a bend of her knees, she scoots the chair into position at her desk. The chair squeaks when she swivels toward me. "When are you leaving to meet with your new client?"

"I told Mrs. Ramos I'd meet her at four-thirty. And after our appointment, I'm going to Emma's."

My mom checks her watch. "You should leave soon if you're going to walk. Unless you were planning on taking a cab? I hope you don't waste your money on a cab. You haven't made your commission yet."

Or any commission in seven months. I should don a pair of fairy wings and prance my way to 72nd Street since I may finally have a listing. Even the potential to sell an unrenovated, four hundred and fifty-square-foot studio apartment should thrill me. But five years after earning my real estate license online, I'm still waiting for the big kahuna.

I make a show of flipping through the files on my desk, pretending I would be tearing myself from a vital task were I to heed her advice and leave now. I tap the file folder on my desk to neaten its contents. "Everything here should keep until Monday. Maybe I will head out now. I'm in the mood for a walk."

My mother pushes herself away from her desk, the wheels of her chair clattering against the plastic. Pressing her hands on the armrests, she rises. "Come here. Let me fix your bow."

I stand stock-still while she fiddles with the oversized bow at the neck of my blouse. She and I are practically twins, bows and all. Her blouse is royal blue, whereas mine is bright pink, and both of us are wearing simple black pantsuits.

I peer at my phone, checking my lipstick with my camera app. "Any final tips for me?"

She flicks the hair from my shoulders. "Put Mrs. Ramos at ease. She needs to trust you with her baby. You'll do fine. I have faith in you."

"Thanks, Mom!" I give her a quick squeeze goodbye.

Her cloying Black Opium perfume, still clinging to me when I leave the office, engages in a head-to-head battle with the blast of fetid steam venting out of a manhole. As if I needed any reminders I don't yet work in my dream version of New York City.

My head spins with worry after I leave Mrs. Ramos's apartment. How she'll find homes for the shopping bags, shoes, stacks of magazines, and unidentifiable clutter littering every available surface in her home before our first open house next Saturday stumps me. I heave a sigh as I enter Central Park.

Emma lives a world away from the chaotic, claustrophobic mouse house I just left. I count on the half-hour walk along my favorite paths in the park to yank me away from dwelling on my sad, little career and into a penthouse apartment larger than even my daydreams.

While I stand in a puddle of sunlight on Bow Bridge, a wisp of a breeze lifts a few strands of my hair. The two towers of the San Remo shimmer above my reflection on the surface of The Lake. I smooth my dark tresses and elongate my neck with a swanlike lift of my chin. With the gesture, I hope to bring to life my fabulous broker alter ego.

Untethered from my desk in the tiny, dingy storefront office located nowhere near the multi-million dollar properties I long to sell, I lap up the enticing promise of New York City. The hint of spring in the early April air and the luxury buildings peeking over the tops of the trees make me believe it won't be long before I attain my goals.

At the foot of the bridge, a woman wrapped in an oversized and tattered orange cardigan asks me if I have any spare change. She has the kindest face, which inspires me to help her. I offer her a Starbucks card I keep forgetting to use. We part, a smile lingering on my face as I continue to walk. An unoccupied green bench with a view of The Lake beckons me to veer away from my intended path.

The quiet at the center of the bustling city along with the view transport me to another era. I remember skipping ahead of my Great Aunt Donna with my cousin Emma, both of us decked out in fancy dresses and too-tight shoes and humming music from the ballet we had seen at Lincoln Center. While our aunt rested on a bench, Emma and I scoured the bramble for rocks and twigs to throw into the water.

I slip deep in my memories, listening to past conversations with my two favorite relatives only to resurface with a start. A tug on my pant leg followed by the chill left in the wake of a cold, wet lapping sensation on my shin sends me to my feet. A miniature poodle with strawberry-blond curls wags a stump of a tail at me. Three larger dogs crane their heads toward me, hoping to get in on the action. The four leashes strain in the hands of a frazzled man who has lost control of the situation.

"Stella, no! Robert, Jane, and Gizmo, don't let her lead you astray. Stop right now!"

The man's expression, like the messy crop of medium-brown hair flopping into his eyes while he snaps on the leashes, is in a state of disarray. He straightens his back and sweeps his hair aside. His eyes meet mine. My heart also obeys his command, coming to a halt. The kindness behind his brown eyes lures me in until I take a second look. He shakes his head, equally surprised to see me. "Lauren?"

If you had asked me in high school which of my classmates would grow up to be a dog walker — and not be good at it — I would not have hesitated to say, "Johnny Skeegs."

Everybody went to school with a Johnny Skeegs. He's the guy who sat in the last row with a textbook standing upright on his desk, behind which he would snooze. The student no teacher could rile or embarrass for turning in an assignment late. The boy who, despite having nothing to recommend himself, was impossible to ignore. He was lanky and had mastered the art of leaning against his locker à la James Dean. Some people found his calm, easy manner magnetic. My friends and I *loathed* Johnny Skeegs. Especially because of what he did in our sophomore year.

I straighten the bottom edge of my jacket and tuck my hair behind my ears. What are the odds I could get away with denying we've ever met? I sigh. No bookie with any sense of decency would let a client bet on me pulling off such a stunt.

"Johnny, right? That's quite a pack." I bend to scratch the poodle's head, avoiding Johnny's eyes lest I again mistake him for someone I wouldn't mind knowing. "Funny, I was thinking about my great-aunt a minute ago. She always said she wanted a strawberry-blond poodle."

What are you doing, Lauren? Don't share personal details with him. Bad girl!

He crouches, wrapping his arms around the largest of the mutts.

Aw! No. Not *aw*. Damn him for displaying such tenderness!

"Must be a sign. Did she ever adopt a dog?" he asks.

"I don't know. We've been out of touch for years." Guilt washes over me. "I need to call her."

Oh, Lauren! Stop telling him your whole life story, I yell at myself.

The other three dogs mob Johnny, insisting he shower them with affection, too. After giving each of their heads a pat, he rises and stares meaningfully into my eyes. I avert them when my heart thumps faster. He clears his throat. "You should call her. I bet it would mean a lot to her to hear from you."

The muscles in my butt clench with an effort capable of crushing a lump of coal caught between my cheeks into a diamond. This is what I get for revealing personal information: Johnny effing Skeegs telling me to call my Aunt Donna. And looking like he cares.

I listen to my inner schoolmarm, who is screaming a warning about him being trouble. She's right. I need to escape. "Yeah. Well, nice seeing you."

"You, too. Are you on your way home from the office?"

"Not yet. I have one more appointment today. You know how real estate is." Of course, he wouldn't know. "Listings all over the City; demanding clients to meet." Little white lies can't hurt me.

"Sounds like you've done well for yourself." Johnny loops the leashes around his hand and pulls them taut. Three of the dogs sit at his feet. The poodle goes rogue and sniffs under my pant leg again.

With enough passion to wow a director during auditions for a new production of *A Streetcar Named Desire*,

Johnny cries, "Stella!"

I don't want him to warn her away from me because he thinks I'm a dog hater. I wave my hands. "Don't worry about—" A warm trickle slithers down my left foot, interrupting my speech. It strengthens into a stream. The ball of my foot squishes in the puddle forming inside my shoe. "Stupid dog!" I pull away from the miscreant, glaring at her with ill intent. "Can't you control your dogs?" I bark at Johnny.

His face contorts in the effort of holding back a laugh. It doesn't matter. His eyes give him away, dancing and sparkling with amusement. "She's not mine. I'm just the dog walker. They say a dog peeing on you is a sign that she likes you." He raises an eyebrow, hoping I'll submit to the humor of the situation. Fat chance.

Johnny digs through the pockets of his field jacket, producing a roll of poop bags. "These won't be of any use, will they?"

I give him the blankest of stares. Four years at the same academically challenging school as me, and he can't tell the difference between solids and liquids?

He stuffs the bags back into his pocket. "I'm really sorry. I should have apologized first. What can I do?" His eyes are no longer laughing at me. They've grown darker with concern. I don't trust him even a tiny bit, though. He has to be loving every second of putting me in such a miserable position.

"Unless you have hand sanitizer, a multi-pack of paper towels, and a pair of ladies' size-seven shoes, you've done enough." I check my phone. I have thirteen minutes to rid myself of the Eau du Subway Station soiling my foot before I'm due at Emma's. I need a plan. Escaping Johnny Skeegs is definitely step number one.

CHAPTER TWO
PIRATE TATTOOS AND BALLET

I step out of the elevator into the foyer of Emma's apartment. I could not be more poorly matched to my surroundings. Three-foot squares of black and white marble tiles form a harlequin pattern on the floor. A sculpture by Erté of a woman holding a fan, a dainty foot peeking out beneath the folds of her gown, rests on a black metal and walnut art deco console table. I am the statue's foil with a new pair of flip-flops in my hand and a peed-upon foot below.

"Emma, I am not yet fit to step into your house. I'm headed straight for the bathroom in the servant's wing. See you in a couple of minutes," I yell from the entrance.

Entering the kitchen via the butler's pantry, I stop in my tracks. A woman in chef's whites is chopping herbs. I sneak across the room, praying she won't notice me. Oh, I hope I haven't interrupted a dinner party!

I fill the tub in the guest bathroom with six inches of scalding water and remove the handheld shower from its holder. Gingerly dunking my foot into the steaming water, I uncap the shower gel and take a whiff. The ultra-luxurious orange and bergamot product was never intended for a purpose so vile.

Five minutes of relentless scrubbing later, I don the flip-flops I bought on my way to Emma's apartment to replace the shoes Johnny's dog offended, which are now en route to the incinerator. I'm as ready to face the public as I ever will be.

My cousin and Troi, her best friend, lounge like concubines on the sectional in her sitting room. Two floor-to-ceiling windows offer a wide-angle view of the luxury apartments across Central Park I had gawked at before the Johnny incident. I don't wait for an invitation to fill the remaining blue-rimmed margarita glass on the coffee table from the pitcher beside it. Let the countdown to numbing my brain commence.

"Where are your manners? And your taste?" Troi clucks his tongue, eyeing my full glass and footwear with disdain.

"This from a man resting his feet on seven hundred-dollars a yard Scalamadre silk damask?" I hold my palm to his face to shush him.

"Girl, get a manicure before you assault me." He grasps my hand to examine the chipped polish and fraying cuticles I desperately want to hide from him.

Emma swings her legs from the couch. "Will the two of you call a truce already? If you can't behave, I will banish you both."

Troi and I air kiss each other and giggle. He and Emma are a package deal. To love her is to love him. And I love them both. Our habit of throwing shade is too old for me to remember its origins and too fun to abandon.

I sit next to Emma and wrap her in a tight hug. Strands of her straight blonde hair snake through my fingers. I suck in a whiff of her perfume. Le Chevrefeuille, which means honeysuckle. The fresh, green scent of the flower stems balance the sweetness of the blossom. It captures her to perfection, reminding me of the first version of

Emma I knew, my cousin from Queens.

She always was too refined for Rego Park, but like her signature scent, she didn't put on airs or overwhelm me with her sophistication. Marrying a billionaire didn't change her; it simply allowed her to fund her desired lifestyle. I'm not jealous. I don't need anything *this* fancy. But fancier than what I have sure would be nice.

It embarrasses me to be sitting next to her in my current state. "For the record, the flip-flops were an act of desperation."

Troi holds the back of his hand to his forehead in a swoon. "Honey, blouses with bows the size of Texas are desperate. I don't even know where to begin with the things on your feet."

"If you must know, a dog peed on my foot on the way here."

Troi doubles over with laughter. Were it not for the seething anger I have toward him for finding my tragedy so mirthful, I would worry about whether the wheezing sound he's emitting means he is in danger of losing his oxygen supply.

Emma does her best to suppress a laugh. "That is awful!"

"You don't know the half of it." As much as it pains me to tell them the story, I hastily walk them through the basic details of my interaction with the rude poodle, leaving out the fact that I know the dog's handler.

Johnny freaking Skeegs. We could not be less alike. I'm driven. Results are everything to me, whether I receive an A after laboring over a homework assignment or field a ton of calls because I ran a perfectly crafted ad for a rental apartment. Admiring my efforts gives me a little thrill. What's more, I don't hate it when others admire my efforts. I suppose that makes me a suck-up. But who's the victim when I try to please people?

Perhaps that's why Johnny annoyed the crap out of me in school. He never tried. Earning a teacher's praise wasn't on his agenda. And he never sweated when he got in trouble.

A part of me couldn't resist imagining my life were I to emulate him rather than strive to make people proud of me. The ground disappeared from beneath my feet when I tried imitating his state of mind, sending me into free-fall. I blamed him for everything that could have gone wrong were I to have actually applied his philosophy to any of my efforts. It taught me he was trouble, and I needed to avoid him at all costs. And for ten years, I had succeeded.

Troi never stops laughing during the tale. I bet he's not the only one. Johnny probably loves that he humiliated a former straight-A student who has a respectable job (read: not a dog walker). The only way an unambitious guy can survive is by sabotaging the competition. With floppy, Daniel Radcliffe-like hair and the smoldering eyes of Aiden Turner, no one will ever suspect him to be the cad he is. It's not fair.

While I curse out Johnny in my mind, the chef places a heaping tray of nachos on the coffee table. I sit on my hands until we're alone again, counting my blessings that the mystery chef is here for us rather than for a formal gathering of Emma's husband's colleagues.

Neither Emma nor Troi would deign to eat anything this caloric or messy in public. In the absence of anyone important, they don't rely on self-control. Our plates overflowing with handmade chips topped with ingredients unlikely to appear on an Applebee's menu, we feast in silence for a minute.

I lick a smear of ancho pepper and truffle-dusted guacamole from the cuff of my blouse. Guess I won't get a second wearing out of it.

"Since when do you have a chef?" I ask.

Emma presses her hand to her lips and raises a finger for me to wait. With a dramatic swallow, she says, "Augusta comes with the building. Another resident forgot to tell her they had canceled this evening's cocktail party.

When I ran into Augusta in the lobby, she was mumbling to herself about the International Culinary Center needing to add a class on how to handle entitled clients. I offered a solution for how to use the groceries she had bought. My neighbor's loss is our gain."

Troi nods. "Gain is right on the nose. I can feel my waistline expanding with every bite." He helps himself to another fistful of nachos, obviously not as intimidated by the calories as he claims. Besides, fat bounces off Troi's washboard abs like a check from a broke huckster.

Emma snickers. "We deserve to show ourselves a little love."

"As in love handles." I pat my belly, which on my skinniest days is at best a one-pack.

"Please. You don't have love handles. You have—" Troi taps his fingertips together and searches the intricate plasterwork on the ceiling for inspiration. "—coldly indifferent knobs."

I wrinkle my nose at him, my eyes scrunched with judgmental confusion. "I beg your pardon?"

"It's a joke, honey. Lighten up."

"You kid yourself if you think you're funny. And, given my inability to prevent myself from shoving food into my gaping mouth, lightening up is not in my future." To prove my point, I refill my plate.

Emma places hers on the table with a bang. "That does it. I'm making an appointment with my trainer for tomorrow. You're spending the night with us, right, Lauren?"

"Can't. I'm taking a client to look at an apartment tomorrow."

"Busy, busy! You're well on your way to becoming Aunt Donna's clone."

I whip my head toward her, blinking dramatically. "So weird for you to say that! She keeps coming up. It must mean we have to go visit her soon. I went to our spot in Central Park today. Remember how she always said when she could slow down, she planned to adopt a miniature poodle?"

With a nod, Emma says, "And she wanted to name it…" She wrinkles her forehead. "What was it? Oh, yeah. Stella. She said it would be a hoot to cry out for the dog like from that play."

I shudder, remembering Johnny's plaintive admonition of the dog right before it soiled my feet. He must feel so smug. Because he had yelled at the dog beforehand, he must figure he's in the clear since he tried to prevent the accident. The jerk. A jerk who, for a brief moment, radiated compassion and warmth in his expression. I harrumph. The Johnny I know wouldn't show such sensitivity.

I say, "So, I left one detail out of the story about my hostile encounter with a dog. It was a strawberry-blond mini poodle named — get this — Stella!"

Emma sniffs. "Weird indeed. You weren't far from Aunt Donna's apartment. Maybe she did finally adopt her dream dog. I wouldn't know. It has been at least two years since I last talked to her. I guess you've been out of touch with her, too?"

I hang my head. "We're terrible people. I love Aunt Donna. Just because she and my mom had a horrible fight doesn't mean I hate her, too. Enough already. After I finish my apartment tour tomorrow, I'm calling her to make a date."

Emma scoots forward on the couch. "We should relive our childhood and go to the ballet."

"Perfect. She's not getting any younger. We have to make the most of whatever life she has left. My mother doesn't need to know, of course."

"Aren't you a little old to be sneaking around behind your mother's back?" Troi asks.

"Clearly, you don't know my mother." I roll my eyes at him before turning back toward Emma. "You and I always had such a blast with Aunt Donna."

"Do you remember when she snuck boxes of Cracker Jacks into Lincoln Center for us?"

I shriek, dribbling a glob of guacamole onto my thigh. I won't get away with wearing my suit a second time before cleaning it, either. "Your prize was a packet of pirate-themed temporary tattoos. I was so jealous, I tried to grab them from you. I batted them from your hands, and they flew under the seat in front of you."

"I don't remember fighting over them. I only remember trying to show them to you."

A stab of shame pierces my chest. This is so Emma. She may have dropped the prize because of my greed, but she's too sweet to remember the whole story. I shake away my guilt. "Aunt Donna crawled around in the tiny space between the seats. I remember laughing because her butt was in the air. Didn't matter why; butts are funny."

"Amen, sister. Butts *are* funny." Troi high-fives me. "Did she find the tattoos?"

Emma says, "She did. We went to her apartment after the ballet, and the three of us decorated our faces with pirate tattoos."

"I have to meet this woman. If I promise to provide a sheet of temporary tattoos, will you two bring me with you the next time you visit your auntie?"

I crunch what I command to be my last tortilla chip. "You got it. She'll love you. OK. I've eaten my last mouthful. I need to head back to the West Side."

As if I had set an alarm, my phone buzzes. It's my mom. While I debate answering it, Emma's phone rings, too. She answers hers. "Hey, Dad. What's up?"

I follow her lead and answer mine. "Mom, I'm still at Emma's. I promise I won't stay out too late since I have an appointment tomorrow."

"I'm not calling to check up on you. We're out, too. I thought you'd like to know that your Aunt Donna died this evening."

CHAPTER THREE
THE DECEASED IS READY FOR
HER CLOSE-UP

Emma and I stare at each, wide-eyed. A tear drips onto my phone. "You heard the news?"

"Yeah. I'm in shock."

Troi looks from one sad face to the other. "Would someone fill me in, please?"

Emma and I speak at the same time and stop when we hear the cacophony. I gesture for her to continue.

When she finishes explaining what happened, he wraps his long arms around the two of us in a comforting hug. "I'm so sorry! What a loss! You don't need me here. I bet the two of you want to be alone to remember your aunt."

After kissing Emma on the head, he walks to his room.

When we're alone, I throw my arms around my cousin, squeezing her for dear life. "I can't believe it. We were just laughing about her butt. I should have visited her this afternoon when I was near her apartment. I suck!"

Emma sighs gently and says, "I'm right there with you. But we shouldn't dwell on the guilt. We've fallen out of a pattern of visiting her because our family dynamic is, uh, complicated. For you, especially."

"I know, right? It's against house rules even to mention Aunt Donna's name to my mother. It was easy to sneak off to visit her in an act of rebellion when I was still in school, but now? Life gets in the way."

Emma smirks. "You were *such* a rebel. I'm surprised visits with a doting great-aunt didn't land you in juvie."

I ignore the ribbing, returning to our previous topic. "She cared for me. For us. I wish I knew why my mother hated her. I should have forced her to tell me the reason. Then I could have made my own decision regarding Aunt Donna. What if, when I heard the story, I hadn't taken my mother's side?"

"Your mother may never have forgiven you. Given the choice between being loyal to her or to Aunt Donna, I know you picked the right side. Like I said, now's not the time to wallow in guilt for having neglected our aunt. I'm in the same boat. Worse. Who would care if I had maintained a strong relationship with her? Not my father. He and Aunt Donna weren't close. Yet I haven't visited her in the past couple of years. We can't alter what's done."

"You're right. But I hate picturing her dying without having her family with her. My mother didn't tell me how it happened. Did your father say anything?"

"He mentioned the dog walker was with her when she had a heart attack. I think she went fast. None of us even knew she had a heart condition. Maybe she didn't. Her business partner is making the arrangements. The funeral's at our old church in Rego Park on Wednesday. No wake."

"So we're facing a Piccolo family reunion in a few days."

The idea of my relatives gathering together sends shivers across every inch of my skin. While my mother's feud with her aunt may be the most significant crack in our family tree, you'll also find a whopping case of a virulent disease ready to fell this once majestic tree. Well, majestic may be a bit of a stretch.

Aunt Donna was the oldest of three siblings. In the middle was my Great Uncle Albert, word of whose death four years ago didn't reach us until nearly a year after his funeral. And the youngest, my Grandpa Joe, died six years before I was born, leaving behind my mother, her older brother Curtis, and her younger sister Simone. My grandparents had been deepwater fishing in the Bahamas. According to witnesses on a second boat, someone on my grandparent's tour boat had gotten into a Hemmingway-esque battle with an enormous fish. The boat capsized, much to the delight of the circling sharks. The local authorities didn't find any survivors.

The sole remaining member of Aunt Donna's generation is Shirley, Albert's second wife. She and Great Uncle Albert met during a chair aerobics class at the Rego Park Senior Center in 2008. He and his first wife, Ethel, didn't have kids. Even in my earliest memories, they were dour old people. Emma, my brother Daniel, my cousin Stew, and I dutifully visited them every year the day after Christmas to collect envelopes stuffed — if stuffed is the right word — with ten one-dollar bills so weathered, no vending machine would accept them.

Albert definitely had a type. His Christmas largess ended once Shirley became the new Mrs. Piccolo. On her wedding day, she examined the four miscreant teens who shared a strand or two of DNA with her husband and opted out. Her creepy son Gerald was all the family she needed besides her new husband/knee lift partner. We haven't seen either of them since before Uncle Albert died.

"Most of the family spends Christmas together. How different could her funeral be?" Emma asks.

"You think Shirley and Gerald will come?"

"It would be nice of them to honor Aunt Donna."

"I bet they will. With Aunt Donna's fortune up for grabs, everyone's going to trip over each other to prove they deserve to be well rewarded in the will."

"That's mighty cynical of you, Lauren."

I scrunch my nose. Emma's propensity for sweetness won't change my mind, not when it comes to my family. "I can't help it. You and I were the most attentive of her relatives, and we hadn't been in touch with her for years. What can her death possibly mean to the rest of the family? I'm counting on my mother to bring her tap shoes for a little dance number on her grave. Aunt Simone will wring out a river of fake tears, all the while putting half the Harry Winston catalog on her wish list. And Shirley will insist that her dear son Gerald deserves the entire estate."

"It's a funeral for a lovely woman, for goodness' sake. I doubt they'll behave badly under such circumstances, especially in the old neighborhood church."

An image of Aunt Shirley smacking the rest of the family out of the way with her handbag and falling in a sobbing heap alongside the casket, underscored by my mother singing a chorus of *Ding Dong! The Witch is Dead* pops into my head. I understand why Emma called me cynical. But she could be right. Perhaps my cynicism is unwarranted. How bad could the funeral be?

It's worse than I imagined. My mother had drilled me repeatedly last night on my responsibility to adhere to her schedule. Ever the dutiful daughter, I am in their apartment, ready to leave before the appointed departure time.

Through the closed door of my parents' bedroom, I hear my father talking my mother into attending the funeral. If I'm not mistaken, he is promising her a lollipop if she'll put on her shoes. I can't say for sure because I can't discern the consonants of his words over the clatter of hangers my mother keeps bashing together in her closet.

My mother finally opens the bedroom door, waves of angry disappointment splashing on her brow. "Lauren, why are you standing around like we have all the time in the world? Get a move on. We're leaving in three minutes."

Now is probably not the right moment to mention that I, unlike her, been ready to leave for the last twelve minutes.

We catch the 3 train to Times Square. I count only eleven asides from my mother on how undeserving her aunt is of my mom's appearance at the funeral. Not bad for a fourteen-minute subway ride.

My father goes rogue when we make the transfer to the R train. "Richard!" My mother's voice cuts through the din of the subway station, drowning out even the cranked-up speaker amplifying three children singing *Sucker* by the Jonas Brothers in an approximation of unison. Half of Manhattan shifts its attention to my mom. The only person who doesn't respond to the scream is my father.

My mother and I stop at the stairs leading to the subway platform and scan the station for my father. I catch sight of him at a newsstand. His elbow resting on the magazines displayed on the counter, he shares a guffaw with the man handing him his change.

Following my gaze, my mother locks eyes on my dad. "Richard!" she bellows again. He glances at her, startled to be summoned.

Brandishing a pack of gum — as if its very existence in his hand will make everything right with his wife — he jogs toward us. "Here I am, Zara. No need to panic. I had the most interesting conversation with Said. Now there's a man with an interesting story. Boy, I'm glad I had a hankering for a stick of gum. Hopefully, I'll be able to find him again to hear the rest of his story the next time—"

No stranger to the skin-dissolving qualities of my mother's most potent glare, he hastily abandons his conversation, shoves the pack of gum into the inside pocket of his blazer, and hustles down the stairs with us. Wisely, he keeps mum about the fascinating kiosk man while the train clatters its way to Queens.

My mother's tantrums and my father's penchant for going off-road didn't impact our arrival time. Years of aunt-related anger reaching its boiling point couldn't prevent my mother from tacking on an extra hour this morning to make sure any delay we might encounter on our journey from the Upper West Side wouldn't render us late. No matter that we've made this trip countless times in my lifetime, always arriving way too early. The only mourners who had gathered at the church before us today were my mother's sister, brother-in-law, and two of my cousins. And a photographer.

Um really? A photographer? At a funeral?

Half a block away from the church, I spy my step-uncle Brock leaning against the front door to the church with an air of boredom clearly staged for the camera. His gray suit is several shades lighter than the death-becomes-us wardrobe my parents and I are wearing. Call me fashion-illiterate (Troi has on several occasions), but I'm not convinced the insouciant bit of ankle showing between his brown shoe and the cuff of his pants is on point for a funeral.

My cousins Stew and Marc don't share my opinion on mourner-appropriate wardrobe choices. Each is sporting the same ensemble as my uncle. Twelve-year-old Marc is the perfect mini-me of his father, from his dirty-blond banker's haircut to his studiously casual pose on the railing of the stairs.

Stew, by contrast, has the comfort level with his ensemble one would expect from a golden retriever puppy forced to wear rain boots. I wait for him to explode out of it. Despite his squirming, he doesn't send scorched fabric flying every which way. An epic wardrobe malfunction is not out of the question in the near future, however.

Aunt Simone consults with the photographer. They hunch over a piece of paper. She points to it. He nods. Lifting her head, she calls out, "Hi, Zara," before returning to her conversation with the photographer.

"What's she wearing?" my mother whispers to me, gesturing toward her sister with her elbow.

Simone's dress is gorgeous. Made from dusky blue silk, it drapes as only a dress affordable to someone with an Emma-sized budget can drape. Aunt Simone isn't in Emma's financial league.

The floor-length gown stays on her body thanks to a pair of thin straps tied behind her neck in a bow that cascades the length of her fully exposed back. I answer my mom, "The dress is pretty, but is sideboob the right look for a funeral?"

"Oh, Lauren." My mother marches away, leaving me to ponder whether I've offended her with my slangy mention of female anatomy or if my spot-on observation led to her subsequent disappointment in her sister. Either way, with Aunt Simone in my mother's sights, I'm free from my mother for the first time in over an hour.

I take my chances with any potential explosive danger on the suit front to get the scoop on the photo shoot from my cousin. "Hi, Stew!" I give him a quick hug. Pretty impressive that what I guess is a brand-new suit already reeks of pot.

My mother often gloats over having a son who earned his Ph.D. in Biomedical Science from Columbia University versus one who has mastered little beyond the physics of a bong. As the less-favored child in our household, I sympathize with Stew. He may be a few steps closer to being my kindred spirit than my older brother Daniel is, but his lack of ambition reminds me of Johnny, making *closer* a relative term.

"Oh, hey, there, Lauren. So. Aunt Donna." He fiddles with the button on his jacket, behind which his gut threatens to make a daring escape.

"Yeah, I know. What a bummer." I adjust my pocketbook strap on my shoulder.

What a bummer hardly captures the level of pain I'm

feeling. Dealing with the Zara of it all has prevented me from sorting through my emotions over losing my great aunt, though. I'll focus on the hurt soon enough.

I scan my cousin from head to toe. "What's the deal with your outfit?"

He wipes his fingertips the length of his thighs. Jerking his neck from left to right, he assesses the suit. "Mom made us wear them. We were going to have some family portraits done later, but she figured we'd look like roadkill if we wore them all day, so we're doing the pictures now. We didn't use to do stuff like this when we lived here in Queens. I miss the old days. Aw, crap. Gotta run. Looks like it's time for another round of photos." He runs to join his mother and his twins on the steps for a new pose.

A black Bentley limo slides in front of the church. I breathe a sigh of relief. The cavalry is here.

CHAPTER FOUR
GREETINGS FROM SIBERIA

The driver opens the curbside passenger door. From the knee-length black skirt of a conservative suit to the pointy toe of a shoe of perfectly understated elegance, the occupant emerging from the car offers Aunt Simone a personal TED talk on the topic of dressing to mourn. Emma stands, taking her husband Brandon's hand to mount the curb. Troi, decked out in a sincere, charcoal-gray suit, makes a stronger case for ankle gap than Uncle Brock does. Last out of the car is my Uncle Curtis. He straightens his navy blazer over his green and blue striped polo shirt, letting its hem fall against his jeans.

My dad makes a beeline for his brother-in-law. My mother sweeps Emma into her arms while Aunt Simone and her husband fangirl all over our resident billionaire.

Troi and I exchange air kisses. He breaks tradition. Instead of finishing the greeting with an insult, he pulls me to his chest. "Lauren, I'm so sorry. The way you and Emma described your relationship with your aunt, you must be hurting something bad right now."

"Thank you. Your sympathy means a lot to me."

"I'm here for—" Aunt Simone and company pull Troi's attention from me. The family reassembles to vogue in front of the church doors. Their quartet has grown by one. Judging from Brandon's expression, he still hasn't processed the reason Aunt Simone has dragged him up the stairs.

Troi does a double take. "Wait. What's with the photographer? Is he a wedding photographer who moonlights at funerals? I can just hear his banter. 'OK. Everyone from Grandma Ethel's bridge club line up. Prove to me you're having the time of your lives. Betty, could you show us a little leg like you want to cheer up Bill since he's feeling down, what with his wife dying and all?'"

I laugh despite myself. Emma, having greeted everyone who is not posing for the camera, joins the two of us. "Aunt Simone seems to be taking the situation badly."

I nod in slow motion. "I know. The grief is destroying her. At least she'll have photographic evidence of her heartache."

My uncle wraps his arm around my waist.

"Hey, Uncle Curtis. When did you get in?" I ask.

"Yesterday. Stayed with my baby girl last night. I'd love to catch up with everyone later, but I have to dash right after the burial. I have a three o'clock flight back to Vegas. Should make it just in time to catch the Diana Ross show at the Wynn. Wouldn't want to miss it. My tickets cost me a fortune."

I give some serious thought to the idea of renting out my family as professional mourners. They add just the right touch to a funeral.

My father taps me on my shoulder. "Your mother summoned you. She wants to make sure we can save seats for your brother and Genevieve before the church gets crowded."

"But—" I gesture to the decided lack of a crowd gathered outside the church. My father flips his palms upward and purses his lips. Neither of us wants to mess

24

with my mother when she's in a mood.

Inside, a guitarist and a violinist play light background music. My mother sits alone in the front pew. I half-expect her to scamper into the choir loft, armed with a BB gun and ready to wreak havoc. Perhaps she's going with spit-balls, thus explaining the choice of a close-range seat. I climb over her legs, settling beside her on the wooden pew.

"Well, here you are at last. I've had a word with the priest. He says there will be no eulogies. Nor will the family process with the casket. Aunt Donna planned her own funeral."

"You weren't intending on speaking, were you?"

Mom pats her handbag conspiratorially. Thank goodness my great-aunt had the foresight to prevent my mother from telling the congregation how she really feels about the deceased.

My mother shoves me with her hip. "Move to the other end of the pew. I want to save the seats closest to the aisle for Daniel and Genevieve." She scowls at me when my eyelids sag with hurt. "Oh, Lauren. You and I see each other pretty much every day. Give your dear mother the chance to spend a moment with your brother and his fiancée, whose lives are so full, they rarely have the time to visit."

"Fine." I scoot my pocketbook toward the Siberian wing of the family pew to save my seat and walk up the side aisle to find Emma and Troi.

"Lauren," a man seated next to the aisle calls out in a hushed voice.

You're kidding, right? What did I do to deserve this? "What are you doing here, Johnny?" I ask through clenched teeth.

He stands and offers me his hand. I give it a limp shake.

"Donna was my landlord. I presume she was a relative of yours?"

"Great Aunt."

"My condolences to you and your family."

"Thanks. So should we expect every tenant of hers to come waltzing through the doors of the church?" Considering the Queens-sized grudge my mother holds against her aunt, I imagine a standing-room-only capacity congregation hurling rotten tomatoes at their reviled landlord's casket. Maybe my mother's contempt is well founded.

"I expect a few will come to mourn her. She was a special woman. I'm honored to have been her friend."

I'm growing angry with him for saying such lovely things about Aunt Donna. Wait. I have a better reason to be mad at him. Before I can lecture him, he adds, "Oh, I have to apologize to you again. I'm mortified by what little Stella did to you. At the very least, can I compensate you for the damage she did to your shoes?"

Hmpf. I can't even harangue him for the pee incident in the park last weekend because he apologized first. What a tool. A tool who's rocking his navy suit. His pants fit him in a manner that makes me contemplate decidedly unfunereal notions about how he'd look without them. I pinch the base of my thumb to banish the thought. *Ow!*

"I threw out the shoes. They were old, anyhow. No matter." My answer does not resemble the invectives I had wished to hurl at him moments ago.

Compared with the lack of bereavement either my mother or her siblings have shown, Johnny appears to be the rare individual here today who cared for my aunt. If I ignore my well-developed hostilities for a second, I don't hate him. I might even want to…

Oh, Lauren. No. You don't want to have anything to do with Johnny freakin' Skeegs. Step away from this man before he confuses you any more.

"Thank you for paying your respects to Aunt Donna. Enjoy the funeral."

I take my leave, mumbling to myself, "Enjoy the funeral? What's gotten into you?"

Emma, Brandon, and Troi are parallel to me in the center aisle. I turn, nod ever so slightly at Johnny, and return to the front row. They slip into the row behind me.

"Who is that delicious creature you were talking to?" Troi circles his head and eyes in a dramatic sweep toward Johnny.

"*That* is the man with the pissing poodle. And the bane of my existence in high school. Now he's some poor schmo my aunt took pity on and rented an apartment to."

"I wouldn't mind renting him a place in my—" Troi remembers Brandon is mere feet away. "In a spare room in the home Brandon and Emma are gracious enough to have invited me to share."

"Honey, the way he's staring at our lovely Lauren, I wouldn't expect him to sign any lease you offered." Emma clutches Troi's hand sympathetically.

"I will not turn around, but I promise you he is not staring at me." I sniff with disgust. Maybe it's not the most *authentic* display of disgust. But seriously. Why would he stare at me? I rub the back of my hair, searching for a wad of gum or bird poo stuck in it.

Troi braces his hands on the back of my pew and swivels his neck to the right. "Who's the woman in the widow's weeds coming down the aisle? Did Aunt Donna have a secret wife?"

Of course. Not regarding my aunt being a lesbian. I mean, of course, Great Aunt Shirley is taking things to the limit. Wearing a rumpled, moth-eaten and ill-fitting suit that she may well have dug out of the local cemetery, Aunt Shirley holds her head stock-still as she marches to the front of the church. Her gnarled hands grip Gerald's arm. She peers through the veil of her black velvet pillbox hat at the crucifix on the wall. Letting go of her son's arm, she genuflects and crosses herself from shoulder to shoulder, forehead to knee. If I'm not mistaken, Aunt Shirley never stopped attending services at her local Methodist Church after she married Uncle Albert.

Reaching the front row, she jerks her head to her right, where Aunt Simone and her brood have artfully arranged themselves for a last set of portraits. She turns to her left and shoos my mother from her spot on the aisle. My mother heaves a sigh and complies. The Piccolo family is present and accounted for. No, wait. Where's my brother?

The organ springs to life, and the cantor leads us in the opening hymn while the priest processes, followed by the pallbearers wheeling the casket. Aunt Shirley caterwauls, "Oh!" People turn to stare at her. "Hah!" she coughs into her fist. She fumbles for the lace-edged handkerchief Gerald offers her with a showy flick of his wrist. They must have practiced their routine for hours.

The priest calls Emma Davis to the altar for the first reading. For a moment, I ponder the coincidence of Aunt Donna knowing two people with the same name. Emma rises. Oh. Of course, the priest meant my cousin. I tamp down the shred of jealousy building inside me for not being invited to speak today.

While she reads a passage from the Old Testament at the podium, the clattering of shoe leather against the marble floor distracts half the congregation from Emma's heartfelt recitation.

I give in to my curiosity and turn toward the commotion. My brother Daniel is tiptoeing along the side aisle. I bet my mother will admonish me for arriving at the church earlier than my brother.

I swing my legs into the aisle to let him enter our pew. My mother plants a kiss on his waiting cheek. "Where's Genevieve?" she whispers loud enough for all to hear.

"She sends her regrets. We had a major presentation scheduled for today. It's bad enough I had to miss it. There's no reason for both of us to ditch work for this thing."

Emma's reading is lost on my family. Isaiah wasn't kidding when he said, "The righteous perish, and no one takes it to heart." If my family can't treat Aunt Donna's

28

funeral with dignity, I hate to imagine what will happen at the reading of the will.

The burial didn't elicit better behavior from my relatives than they had shown at the service. At least Cousin Gerald didn't fall into the grave after losing his footing near its edge. True, he shouldn't have chased the quarter he had dropped in the first place. The clatter of the errant coin spinning atop Aunt Donna's coffin perfectly synchronized with his wobbling effort to regain his balance, though.

Daniel and Stew missed the performance. When they realized that legends of the New York mafia lay buried nearby, they embarked on a mob boss headstone treasure hunt. Daniel won by default. Stew had used his knowledge of the whereabouts of the mobsters interred in the cemetery as a ploy to go smoke a joint.

My mother paid closer attention to her phone than to the burial rites while Uncle Curtis studied his watch, calculating the precise moment to return to Vegas and Ms. Ross. Aunt Shirley continued her Oscar-worthy display of histrionics. And poor Aunt Simone had to come to terms with the irreconcilable differences between evening wear and clothing suitable for standing in a somewhat damp patch of grass. Thankfully, the photographer wasn't on hand to capture the crust of mud forming on the hem of her dress.

After the priest dismisses us, I stand with Emma, Brandon, and Troi, unsure if I'm ready to abandon my great-aunt and return to normal life.

"Hey, sweetie. You OK?" Emma strokes my back.

"I'm sort of in a daze. I had hoped the funeral would have been more cathartic, but the constant stream of distractions lodged itself between me and some serious mourning."

"You'll grieve for Aunt Donna when you're ready. Don't let anyone prevent you from missing her."

Brandon checks his watch. "I need to head back to work. Lauren, we have room for a fourth in the limo since my father-in-law has arranged his own transportation to JFK. My driver can drop the three of you at our place before taking me downtown to my office."

"That's awfully kind of you, but—"

"Emma mentioned your aunt was a bourbon drinker. I had my driver stock the bar in the Bentley with a nice bottle with which to toast Aunt Donna." Brandon, Emma, and Troi cock their heads at the same angle, pummeling me with their puppy dog eyes.

Troi breaks his pose first. "What if I threw a hunky mourner into the mix?"

"I beg your pardon?"

Pointing over his shoulder, he says, "Him. Your friend from the funeral. His posse is leaving, but he's not moving. He's staring straight at you like he's expecting something from you. Invite him to join us for a tipple."

When I glance at Johnny, he takes it as his cue to approach me. I search for a mausoleum to hide in, but we're in the wrong section of the cemetery.

He takes my hand in his. A delicious shudder slithers into bits of my body neglected as of late by such shudders. I'm not OK with my reaction to him.

"Lauren, I want to offer my condolences to you and your family. Donna was like a grandmother to me. What an incredibly special woman she was! I'd love to trade stories with you sometime. Here's my card. Get in touch if you want." Studying my stony expression, he adds, "Or not. In any event, I hope to see you again under less sad circumstances."

If I possessed the magical powers to transform Johnny into a man whom I had never met, I would pee my pants with excitement. Not because I had magical powers, although being a witch would be pretty cool. But because of the impact Johnny has on me.

The surface of my hand retains an imprint of his

delineated by tingles. His eyes mesmerize me. They brighten with the heat of campfire embers. He has cast a spell on me, turning me to stone. I can't move. My heart is a mess of goo because of how much he cared for my aunt. This is a man worth knowing. But Johnny Skeegs, the boy I remember from school, decidedly is not. I'd give anything to forget the old Johnny and embrace the new version, but I'm not a fool.

I slip his card into the pocket filled with forgotten cough drop wrappers and emergency tampons within my pocketbook. It will give me a start when I find it while fishing around for a lost item five months from now. I'll deal with that later. At the moment, my primary goal is to remove him from my sight. I can't allow him to continue to make my heart sing and my skin beg for another round of contact.

My body doesn't know what it's asking for. He's the human equivalent of a zit appearing the morning of prom. Disgusting and capable of ruining one's day. "Yeah, thanks, Johnny. Well, we need to head home now. Thanks for coming today." I pivot away from him and march toward the Bentley.

Emma, Brandon, and Troi run after me. The driver opens the door for us, and we pile in. After Brandon hands me a glass, a chill spreads across my palm, mirroring the inch of icy bourbon in the Baccarat crystal glass I clutch. I press my face against the window. With a painful swallow, I watch the grounds crew dump dirt on top of Aunt Donna's coffin.

Truthfully, it doesn't matter whether Johnny is Johnny or a magnificent stranger. I have enough on my plate. No need to complicate things with a man, no matter how good I believe he can make me feel.

CHAPTER FIVE
THAT'S ONE NAKED COWBOY

Two days after the funeral, throngs of tourists and the ratty cartoon characters who manhandle them surround me in Times Square. I studiously avoid this part of the City even in the dead of winter when the crowds are at their thinnest. Desperate to hide in a cave while I mourn Aunt Donna, I instead prove what I already know: tourist traps are my personal hell. But since my parents have trained me to cater to my clients' whims and with my client's whim being that she wants to meet up with me while experiencing Times Square for the umpteenth time, I have to suffer for my job.

Becca, my client, arrived in the City by way of Nebraska a month ago with dreams far larger than any apartment she can afford to rent. Her demands for her future home have the makings of a stand-up comedy routine.

After three prior unsuccessful tours of apartments, I have found the perfect one to show her. It ticks most of her boxes. Hardwood floors, stainless steel appliances, no roommates. Plus, the apartment is in Manhattan near public transit. Best of all, it's one-hundred-fifty dollars below her budget. She has to like it because it is literally the *only* apartment for rent in Manhattan in her price range today. It's either this apartment or something in Bayonne, New Jersey. And no one wants to live in Bayonne.

If it weren't for finding rental apartments for clients like Becca, I wouldn't have any income. As monumental as choosing a home can be, finding a rental property is easier than choosing a home to buy. I love the instant gratification of unearthing a place capable of bringing the type of smile to someone's face where their shoulders rise and they hug themselves with excitement. The City and its architecture sparkle anew when viewed through a fresh pair of eyes.

I come upon Becca taking a selfie with the Naked Cowboy. I bet the real cowboys in Nebraska wouldn't dare to mount a horse while wearing only a pair of tighty-whities. "Becca! Hey! Want me to take one for you?" I yell at her.

"Oh, would you? That would be so awesome!"

I've never been within an arm's reach of the Naked Cowboy before. Yup, he's a real-live man wearing not very much besides his underwear, boots, hat, guitar, and billions of muscles. I have the urge to stare a little longer. It has been ages since I've taken in an eyeful of man flesh.

Before I can stop it, my brain switches over to an image of Johnny. Gah! I make a note to schedule a lobotomy to prevent myself from ever transitioning from musing about naked men in general to Johnny in particular.

I flash Naked Cowboy a shy grin before snapping a couple of shots with Becca's phone. She giggles as she pulls some bills from her wallet to give to him. He tips his hat at her.

Becca talks nonstop about New York on the subway ride up to Washington Heights. She has entered the transition period between being a tourist and becoming a

New Yorker. Well, more accurately, she's in the earliest stages. Her eyes bulge when she notices we've pulled into the station at 137th Street. She takes a break from her seemingly endless chatter about how much she loves Times Square and asks, "Where are you taking me? My mother instructed me never to go higher than 96th Street and only on weekdays while it's light outside."

"I grew up twelve blocks north of your mother's border. You're missing so many wonderful parts of the City if you stay in the tourist areas. We're getting off at 181st Street. The apartment I'm showing you is a short walk from Fort Tyrone Park, which is beautiful. And oh! The Cloisters museum is in the park. You'll love the neighborhood. Trust me."

She shadows me at an uncomfortably close range when we land on the sidewalk outside the subway station. Her head swivels to offer her worried eyes a three-sixty view of a part of New York not on the route of the double-decker tourist buses.

We enter a pale brick building and cram into its elevator. I tug the accordion door closed. "I told you this apartment comes in well below your budget, right? What's even more amazing is it's the nicest one by far I've found for you. Here we are."

I open the apartment door and usher Becca inside. She takes tentative steps across the hardwood floor. "It's nice," she says with quiet disbelief.

"Look at this kitchen! Brand-new appliances."

"Oh, my gosh!" Her enthusiasm ramps up to a near-Naked Cowboy-selfie level. "I'm so glad it has white counters. I don't like dark, gloomy kitchens."

She enters the main space, scanning it with a robotic sweep of her head. "This is the living room?"

"Yes, and it's also the dining room and bedroom. It's a studio."

"It's small, but that makes it cozy. I'm glad there isn't any furniture in here. I can dress this space up however I want. I see lots of pink." She giggles, tugging at her pink T-shirt, which she wears over a pink and white polka-dotted skirt. "It's my favorite color."

You don't say?

"Uh, huh. Oh, great news: the landlord will allow you to paint the walls. You'll have to get his approval on the color, but I'm sure whatever you pick will be, um, tasteful."

"Lauren, this apartment is almost good enough for me to consider even though it's *way* above my preferred neighborhood." She opens a pair of closet doors. Turning toward me with a look of consternation, she asks, "Did I miss the bathroom?"

I bite my lip. "Um, follow me." We walk out of the apartment and down the hall. I shuffle the keys on the ring. Selecting the key with a green sticker on it, I unlock the door.

Becca walks into the bathroom. She turns toward me. "It's weird that it's not in my apartment, but at least I can keep it locked."

"Let me tell you the coolest part: a member of the building staff cleans it three times a week."

"Wow. That's an amazing perk."

"But here's the thing. It's a shared bathroom."

"Whom would I be sharing it with? You said I get to live alone."

"Right. You'd have to share the bathroom with the other tenants on this floor."

Judging from her expression, Becca would have a hard time choosing the grosser of the options of either sharing the bathroom with strangers or cleaning it with her toothbrush twice daily. "No way. I can't even. You have to find something else. Something with its own bathroom."

I don't blame her for balking. But she doesn't know how few decent, affordable apartments there are on the market. I lock the door behind us, wishing I could find a suitable apartment for her.

I peer into Mrs. Ramos's apartment, bracing for another attack of the clutter that ate Manhattan. A week after she agreed to let me list her apartment, I'm not ready to handle any more stress. Much to my surprise, nothing scary jumps out at me. I swing my tote bag through the door, hoping to avoid clobbering the homeowner with the cookie sheet plotting its escape from my bag.

I dump the bag on the kitchen counter and sling my bulging pocketbook next to it. "Oh, your home will make a great impression on buyers during today's open house. Aren't you glad you took my advice and tidied up?"

Mrs. Ramos quirks the corner of her mouth and shrugs. "You ask me, if someone can't see that this is a good apartment whether it's fixed up nice or not, they're not the right buyers."

I want to argue. But the fantasy realtor I strive to become is too elegant to give in to childish impulses. I paste on my most beatific smile and say, "True. A serious buyer needs to use their imagination to erase the personal touches of the current owner and place themselves in the space."

"I don't care for you talking about erasing me. I still live here, you know." Mrs. Ramos throws me a scowl far more biting than any I've ever received from Troi.

"Please forgive me, Mrs. Ramos. I didn't mean for it to sound like I wanted to erase you. You're right. An apartment reflects the sense of home its current owner has found in it, and that quality also makes a positive impression on buyers."

It's funny how my well-heeled imaginary clients never treat me as poorly as my actual clients. I remind myself for the gazillionth time that I am lucky to have a listing at all. It's ridiculous to imagine I'll ever land my dream multi-million-dollar listing if I can't even sell a home like Mrs. Ramos'.

"Do you have everything you'll need for the next five hours, Mrs. Ramos? The open house begins in forty-five minutes. I want to be ready to welcome any early birds, and as I told you, homeowners shouldn't attend their open house."

"It's not fair being kicked out of my house. But I'll leave. Don't go around moving my things, you hear? I've got everything where I want it." She eyes me sternly, and I remove my hand from the cat/clock tchotchke I had hoped to hide behind a picture frame. It beams a victorious, somewhat constipated grin at me.

Not so fast, little cat. While your momma's away, the real estate lady will play interior decorator.

I reach out to pat my client's shoulder to reassure her. She takes a step backward, leaving my hand dangling in mid-air like the Road Runner as he continues running off a cliff. Ignoring her slight, I say, "Selling a home is stressful. I want to do everything in my power to turn anxiety into excitement. Who knows? Maybe someone will make a cash offer today, and in a few weeks, you'll be living in your dream home."

"I'm only interested in offers above list. And if you think I'm eager to go live with my sister and her snobby daughter-in-law in Elmhurst, you don't know a thing about dream homes."

Her negativity is killing me. But I need to make this sale. Through gritted teeth, I say, "I hear you, Mrs. Ramos. You're the boss. But you have to leave now. Have a great afternoon." I hold the door handle with both hands so as not to give her a helpful push through the doorway.

Alone at last, I attack my prep list. I preheat the oven first. The scent of freshly baked cookies has magical powers on prospective buyers, or so my mother has told me repeatedly.

I had the highest hopes I would have prepared a batch of cookie dough this morning to bake once I arrived at Mrs. Ramos's apartment. It wasn't to be, alas. Emma, Troi, and I tucked into another round of margaritas last night. With my head pounding out a speed metal rendition of *La*

Cucaracha and my stomach giving me the finger, wrangling with food wasn't in the cards. Plus, I had overslept. I barely had time to buy a tube of dough at the local bodega on my way here.

I deposit pieces of dough onto my cookie sheet in neat rows. While the oven continues to preheat, I place buyer information sheets and a stack of my cards on the coffee table. I relocate a few of the "decorative" items while I'm at it, hiding them behind larger objects. Mrs. Ramos should be none the wiser.

Holding the cat/clock with his wry smile and one closed eye, I take a sniff of the air. That can't be good. A sharp aroma redolent of melting plastic wafts toward me. And in case I missed the billows of smoke pouring from the oven, the alarm above me screeches, "Fire! Fire! Fire!" in between irritatingly loud — especially for people who are nursing hangovers — beeps.

I run to turn off the oven. Upon opening the oven door, I release an eye-watering cloud of smoke. The alarm keeps stating the obvious at an unreasonable volume. I drag a chair beneath the alarm and stab at the buttons on the device. My ears, now located inches from its speaker, fill with spiky shards of sound. I alternate which hand covers an ear and which pushes the buttons. Neither hand succeeds. Before I lose my hearing, I wrest the blasted thing from the ceiling and disconnect the battery.

Ah, silence! How I've missed you.

If only I could disable the battery responsible for keeping the smoke in the apartment. I dash to the far side of the apartment to open the window that overlooks the narrow, dark space between this building and its neighbor. I'm not sure fresh air would ever venture into such a dank alley, but I have to try.

Sprinting into the kitchen, I turn on the exhaust fan. It whines at me in disgust for being roused before giving up entirely. I make a mental note to stand with my hand over the switch later in the event any curious buyer deems it necessary to test the working order of the apartment's appliances.

With my hands swaddled in potholders, I venture into the oven to uncover the source of my woes. The charred remains of a stack of books crackle next to what I can only guess was a Lucite cookbook holder in its former life. At least Mrs. Ramos had stored a metal serving tray on the lower rack. It catches the drips from the melted cookbook holder, sparing the oven itself from the indignity of the last few minutes.

After shuttling the destroyed items to the sink and emptying my bottle of Febreze onto every inch of carpet and upholstery, it dawns on me that Mrs. Ramos's version of tidying her house might yield a few more surprises. I open each built-in cabinet, revealing jam-packed spaces. I fear they may be black holes leading to the underworld. A client who stares too long runs the risk of one sucking them into it.

I have a mere four hundred-fifty-square feet to work with and seventeen minutes. What magic can I conjure to make her home smell fresh and her cabinets appear capacious?

The doorbell rings. Perfect.

Please. Come on in and admire this tiny apartment with its bad decor and inadequate storage. That smell? Why, yes. It does come with the apartment.

I truly deserve the Realtor of the Year award.

I open the door for a man who enters the apartment teeth first. Oversized, over-bleached teeth too large for the mouth of a man with a weak chin. Bearing skin overworked by plastic surgeons and spray tan salons alike, he grins at me like a hungry shark.

"Hello, dear," he croons in a voice more oily than a bad slice of pizza. "Are you by chance Richard and Zara's daughter?"

"I am." I leave enough space between the words to drive an armored truck through. How could he know who my parents are before I've introduced myself?

He answers my wary expression with a handshake. "I'm a good pal of theirs. Leon Zelinsky."

Oh. I've heard about Leon. I wipe my hand on my pant leg. My parents have never described him as a pal. He has a reputation for stealing listings and clients. I hear he prefers to work in the million-and-above price range, so this listing should be safe from his claws.

He guides his nose on a tour of the apartment with an arc of his head and a grimace. "What do I smell?"

I give him a quizzical look. "I don't know. What do you smell?"

"Something horrid. Young lady, it simply won't do to invite buyers into an apartment burdened by such a stench. Take my card. Once the apartment has had a proper cleaning, then I will determine its worthiness for two of my clients. Good day!"

I gladly shut the door behind him. And breathe a sigh of relief for my mishap with the oven. It turns out my brother isn't the only scientist in our family. I believe I have just invented Leon repellant.

CHAPTER SIX
JUST LIKE MRS. MAISEL

Before I can kick off my shoes, my mother's voice cuts through the silence of my apartment like an over-enthusiastic fire alarm. "Is that you, Lauren? How many offers did you get?"

OK. I know some people would think, "What? Not only do you work with your mom, but you also gave her your key? And you don't mind if she lets herself in when you're not home? No way I would give my mother my key."

Well, my mom isn't just my boss, she's my— I'm not going to say best friend. Yes, I sometimes consider her to be my friend, but I wouldn't go so far as to call her my best friend. No, what I'm saying is she's my landlord. Yup. I live with my parents.

My home life isn't so different from Mrs. Maisel's. I didn't return to the roost following a divorce; I moved back home after college. But our apartment is kind of like the Weissman's. If you squint.

Was I to withhold a portion of the truth, I'd mention our house is a Classic 7 Pre-War four-bedroom/three-bath apartment on the Upper West Side and leave it at that. Fancy, huh? Location is everything, and our block of West 108th Street, down the street from a school and next door to a locksmith, isn't exactly the most glamorous piece of Manhattan real estate.

Compared to Mrs. Ramos's studio, though, our home is a mansion. You can't sneeze at having more bedrooms than occupants. Unless you're accustomed to Emma's sprawling abode.

Our apartment is lived in. The toilet in the powder room has been broken since I was in high school. The kitchen, outdated when my parents purchased the apartment in 1988, would only be familiar with the word *renovation* were it to have read the dictionary. And while a buyer's information sheet would boast of loads of original woodwork, it would not dwell on the abundance of nicks and scratches in said woodwork. None of this matters, provided we're not trying to sell the place. Our apartment is my home and always has been. And that counts for a lot.

I shuffle into the living room where my parents are celebrating cocktail hour. "I didn't receive any offers, but traffic wasn't bad. Two or three couples and a handful of brokers stopped in to see the studio. Oh. And your friend Leon mentioned he has two clients who might be interested."

Placing her wineglass on the coffee table, my mother says, "Don't believe a single word to come from Leon's mouth. He always has 'two clients.' I've yet to meet any of them. He attends open houses only to suss out the competition or to see if the listing is worth stealing."

My father nods. "Did the apartment show well?"

I roll my lips and hum to myself. Should I tell them how no one stayed in the apartment for over five minutes because of the stench of commingled plastic and air freshener? I'm so not in the mood for them to scold me over an accident that was barely my fault. Baking cookies had been my mother's idea, after all.

But if I don't tell them, I would be lying. With closed eyes, I exhale tensely. "I experienced an inconsequential mishap before anyone arrived. I did as you told me and brought cookie dough to bake." With an artful pause, I search for the most expedient, Lauren-is-not-to-blame way to explain the situation. "How was I supposed to know she used her oven for storage?"

My mother throws her hands into the air, and her lips, though pursed, clearly are dying to say, *Duh!* Taking a moment to self-edit, she tells me, "Everyone in New York uses their oven as an extra cabinet."

"We don't."

"We are blessed with ample storage. Oh, no. Did you turn the oven on without looking inside first?"

I hang my head.

"Oh, Lauren! You should have known better."

"And now I do."

"So you set fire to the apartment?"

"No flames, no hunky firemen taking an axe to the door to rescue me. Just a lot of foul smoke."

"I hope it cleared before Leon arrived. We don't need him telling our colleagues we can't be trusted to care for our properties."

"He may have arrived shortly before one o'clock."

"And when did your little escapade happen?"

"About twelve forty-five."

"Oh, Lauren!" My mother can express a multitude of emotions by inserting *Oh* before a name.

My father shakes his glass of Scotch, the ice in it tinkling its own version of my mother's favorite phrase. "You can never show weakness to another broker. I've wanted to protect you, but you need to learn that you cannot trust anyone in this business." He coughs into his napkin. "Except for us, of course. You can always trust family."

My mother sniffs. "*Some* families can't be trusted." She rolls her eyes for the benefit of an imaginary friend who is in on her joke. I'm sure she's referring to her beef with my Great Aunt Donna. Two days after the funeral, and she still can't bury her grudge.

I could use a little more support from my parents this evening. Perhaps I'm being overly sensitive, but I've detected a slight imbalance in the amount of love they show me versus the amount they've showered on my brother over the years. It's most noticeable whenever I'm having a tough day.

Daniel is not exactly a dutiful son. While he pursued his Ph.D. at Columbia University, which is half a mile away, he rented a crappy apartment much farther uptown rather than live with his family. He regards our home the way the members of our family who live in Manhattan regard their former stomping grounds in Rego Park, Queens. Which is to say an area ripe for a stringent quarantine.

My straight A's somehow never were on par with his. We each made it into elite schools in the New York City public school system, but his was better if for no other reason than he had been a student in their hallowed halls.

Fast forward to his brag-worthy career — and boy do my parents get a lot of mileage out of it — working for a biotech company in Manhattan. He leads a team developing the next miracle diet pill. Thanks to the company's patent on America's favorite pain medicine, they can afford to pay him an obscenely large salary.

He's successful in love, too. The first time he brought his fiancée Genevieve home, my mother doted on her with the fervor of someone whose wish to have a daughter had finally come true.

Daniel and I aren't close. Go figure. I suppose no seventeen-year-old boy who is hanging with his friends wants his twelve-year-old sister to burst into his room every half hour shouting nonsense words while wearing his underwear as a hat. I only did that once, by the way.

He gives me better reasons to annoy — and be annoyed with — him as an adult. Like turning down a research position devoted to eradicating waterborne illnesses in developing nations in favor of inventing a diet pill for the evilest of evil pharmaceutical companies. I love inserting snide remarks about his gifts to humanity into random conversations.

I'm not bitter about my parents fawning over his success. One day, I'll give my parents reason to believe in me. So long as I remember to look inside ovens before turning them on.

My father's eyebrows dance aggressively while he continues to work through his issues with his nemesis. "Leon is one of the more untrustworthy realtors. Make things right with Mrs. Ramos before Leon swoops in and steals her, too. Replace whatever you destroyed. Consider sending her flowers."

My mother asks, "Did you at least remember to bring a bottle of Febreze with you?"

"Yes, Mom. I spritzed the heck out of every surface. The place smelled better when I left than it did before I melted her belongings." Provided you consider *better* to mean different. And more asthma-inducing.

"Well, at least there's that. You still may run into problems with him, though."

I stare at my mother, my eyes opened to max capacity. "Should I be worried about losing my listing?"

I've been counting on the commission from selling Mrs. Ramos's apartment since my parents matched me with her for my first solo listing. I dream of the independence it could buy me. And maybe a few splurge purchases, too. It was a milestone for me when they trusted me to handle it alone. And nothing would boost my spirits more than to show them they were right to trust me.

With a dramatic swish, my father pulls his glass off the table for another sip. "Bolster whatever sense of loyalty you've earned from her and hustle. You have it in you to close on the apartment. Tomorrow, contact every single lead you gained today and then dig up a thousand more. Get a contract for the apartment before Leon can pop in a breath mint and introduce himself to your seller."

My mother rises to refill her wineglass. "Lauren, aren't you having a cocktail with us?"

"Emma, Troi, and I may have enjoyed more than our share of margaritas last night."

My mother's lips press into a judgmental smirk. "That explains why you resembled a zombie when you woke up at eleven this morning. You plus Emma and Troi always equals the consumption of a bathtub's worth of gin."

"Not always. In fact, hardly ever. And we were drinking a rare tequila last night, not gin." I slip into a memory of Emma's father, a retired cop, discovering the two of us deep into a twelve-pack of his beer when we were teenagers. "Best you don't mention anything on the topic next time you speak to Uncle Curtis."

"Why worry? She's of legal drinking age. What can her father say? I presume Brandon was away on business?"

"Yup. But he came home today."

"Now, if she isn't the luckiest woman, I don't know who is. To marry someone as handsome as him—"

"And as rich," I add on her behalf.

"I wasn't referring to his net worth, but since you've brought it up, having billions at one's fingertips isn't the worst thing in the world. And since he travels for work so often, they can't get sick of each other."

"Are you saying you're sick of me?" My father's eyebrows spike upward in mock indignation.

"Oh, Richard. Even if I were sick of you, I could live with it."

Who says romance is dead?

My father chuckles. "Which means I'll never know whether I've overstayed my welcome."

"Oh, you'll know, Richard. You'll know." My mother studies me. "Lauren, honey, doesn't Brandon have a friend for you? Or are you going to tell me you wouldn't be interested in dating a man who is—"

"—as rich as him?" I interrupt.

"Again with the money talk. Money isn't everything. I was going to say you should find yourself a man who loves you as much Brandon loves Mavis."

My mom may very well be the only person who still calls Emma by her odious given name. As a student, my cousin signed homework with only her first initial to avoid having to confront the offensive moniker. *M* morphed into Emma. Perplexingly enough, despite having married Brandon Davis, Emma hasn't legally changed her first name. Those of us who don't want to piss her off know better than to call her Mavis, or worse, Mavis Davis.

My mother continues, "Should you find a good man who is passionate about his job and who wants nothing more than to take care of you or perhaps to become a father — not that I'm pressuring you to make me a grandmother, mind you — you'll be a very content woman. Just like Genevieve. She must be the happiest woman on earth being engaged to your brother."

My contented state of being single is another way they consider me unequal to my brother. I reflect on the one man I've met recently: Johnny. Ugh. I'd rather remain single. Could he even make a woman happy? Using my mother's formula, I can't say whether he loves being a dog walker. He lacks the skills to deal with the Stella of it all, that's for sure. But his eyes. A woman could lose herself in them, especially when they melt into limpid pools of compassionate—

I yank myself from my unwelcome fantasy with a shudder and issue an admonition to myself to avoid entertaining any such thoughts about Johnny ever again.

My mother turns toward me. "Too bad Becca didn't like the apartment you showed her yesterday. She won't find anything that shows as well. I hope she'll change her mind."

"I checked the listing this afternoon. Someone else

snapped it up. I wish she would reconsider sharing an apartment, but a month of couch surfing has convinced her she wants to live alone. We'll keep trying."

"I don't know where these kids get the idea they can find their dream home at such a young age. They want what we have, but that's simply unrealistic," my mother says with a sigh.

"How old were you when you moved into our apartment?" It's a rhetorical question — she was twenty-eight, and I expect my mother to perform serious acts of contortions to exempt herself from her own judgment.

Great Aunt Donna purchased our apartment building a little over thirty years ago. My parents began renting their apartment right after she closed on the building. My aunt spent about half of the list price (the sum of which today wouldn't buy more than a half-dozen of the fifty total units in the building) on the down payment and on refurbishing the public spaces and the apartments without tenants. When she began the co-op conversion process, my parents used my mother's inheritance to purchase our apartment for a song.

"I bet the rent you paid in the eighties wasn't much more than what Becca's budget is at today's dollar." In other words, the rent my parents paid for their four-bedroom apartment then is about equal to the rent on a crappy studio today. Becca isn't unrealistic in what she wants; it's the market that is unrealistic.

"Oh, Lauren. Those were different times. You can't compare apples to oranges." Exactly. My mother sips her wine, avoiding my eyes.

"Zara, I think Lauren has a point." I turn toward my father, surprised to hear him contradict my mother.

My mother studies him. "The point being?"

"The point being that rents and listing prices have risen faster than inflation and salaries. And we were the beneficiaries of a rare stroke of luck. I still can't believe Simone and Curtis turned down Aunt Donna's offer to buy apartments in this building way back when."

My mother purses her lips in thought. "I do see your point, Richard. We were lucky indeed. Lauren, tomorrow I'll give you a hand and see if we can find a gem of an apartment for your client. You're going to make her dream come true. I can just feel it."

OK. I'll admit I may have the tendency to underestimate my parents' love for me.

CHAPTER SEVEN
BEIGE IS NOT YOUR FRIEND

"Only you, Lauren. Only you." Troi is savoring each bit of my story about my oven mishap way more than he should when I describe it to him and Emma two days later.

"All I did was forget to check the oven before turning it on. One tiny detail—"

"Details always matter, honey. Haven't you learned this lesson yet?" He scowls at me, shaking his head. "I've answered my question. Beige is not your friend. Did you even look in the mirror when you tried on your suit in the store?" He grabs the hem of my jacket between his thumb and middle finger, wincing.

I pull away from him to remove my clothing from his judgy mitts. "It was on sale. I don't exactly have the budget to buy gorgeous clothes."

"There are workarounds. Shop with me. I'll help you find fabulous bargains. Or better yet, shop with Emma. You can buy clothes at full price. She'll pay."

I smile at Emma, shaking my head sympathetically before responding to Troi. "Unlike you, I don't have time to shop. Some of us work for a living."

He rolls his head, holding his hands to his chest in a dramatic expression of deep pain. "I work for a living."

"Uh, huh. Doing what?"

"Business things."

"That's not an answer. One day, I will find out what you actually do."

"Better you use your sleuthing skills to uncover a decent outfit than to spy on me."

Emma steps between us. "I rarely take sides, but Troi, come on. Not everyone is as obsessed with clothes as you. Say you're sorry to my cousin." She shoves him toward me.

"Lauren knows I love her. I was having a bit of fun. I didn't mean anything. But I'm sorry; it was unkind of me. Let me make it up to you by having Emma fund a little shopping spree." He engulfs me in a soul-warming hug.

I kiss his cheek. "All is forgiven. But I am putting you in a two-week timeout from having a dig at my wardrobe."

"Do I have to agree?"

Emma gives him a playful slap. "You are incorrigible."

"And that's why you both love me. Shopping now?" Troi is practically panting at his own suggestion.

I say, "No thanks. I'll wait until I have a little money of my own. Perhaps after I earn the commission on the sale of my client's studio."

"Or perhaps when you inherit a little something something from Aunt Donna?" Emma holds her phone toward me. "Check your email."

"Who sends emails anymore?" Troi asks, peering over Emma's shoulder.

I pull out my phone. "Rankin, Rankin, and Gould, apparently. Sounds lawyer-y. Is that the email I'm supposed to read?" I ask.

"Yup."

I open the email and scan its contents. Half the words and all the sentence constructions appear to exist only to confuse me. Definitely from a lawyer. "They've summoned me to a meeting at Aunt Donna's apartment next Monday to discuss her estate. Did you receive the same letter?"

"Yup," Emma says again. She arches her eyebrows, glancing at me with her head at an angle.

Rolling my lips, I mimic her pose. This is an unexpected — and most welcome — surprise. "I assume she'll divide her estate between the elder generation. They'll probably inherit the big shares, but you and I and the boys could walk away with a shiny, four-digit check. How sweet of her!"

Truthfully, I have imagined scenarios in which I inherit well over a thousand dollars. Inheriting Aunt Donna's apartment for starters. If I could live in a luxury apartment with to-die-for views rent-free for the rest of my life, I'd be one happy lady. But I'd also love to be the listing agent for it. It would be my first listing above a million dollars. It's such a fabulous home, even I couldn't screw up the sale. Of course, the biggest fantasy I've conjured would be to step into my great-aunt's shoes and preside over her entire real estate portfolio. I see myself in a well-appointed office, meeting client after client, matching each with—

Emma interrupts my fantasy. "Do you know her net worth?" She shuffles the already neat stack of magazines on the coffee table, feigning disinterest in my answer to her question.

"Not a clue. There's her apartment, of course."

"Put on your realtor hat for a second. What's it worth?"

Troi giggles. "I'd hate to see what such a hat looks like. Besides, isn't Lauren's suit enough to remind us she is a real estate lady, not a realtor?" Emma's glare is harsh enough to make him run his fingers across his lips in a zipping motion.

I feign an exasperated sigh. I come by my real estate lady genes honestly. And I'm proud of the moniker. "A two-bedroom penthouse on West 69th Street near the park? I'm not sure what the exact square footage is, but I'd spitball it to be maybe twelve hundred not counting the outdoor space. On the conservative side, I'd say it's worth around two mil." Troi whistles. "Plus, she owns our building. She sold most of the units, but she still draws an income from a handful of rentals. Oh, and the rent we pay for the commercial space at street level. I believe she also owns at least one other building."

Johnny materializes in my mind. Not the nearly naked version— Oh, crap. Yeah, the nearly naked version as inspired by the Naked Cowboy.

Shoo! Begone! I have no need for Naked Johnny!

My brain once again free from debauched thoughts, I remember he told me Aunt Donna was his landlord. I dig through the junk pocket in my purse and pull out his card, which is creased and stained with lipstick. As my fingers now are. The cap must have come off a tube of lipstick. I wipe a streak of hot pink from my fingers onto the back of his card. Holding it by a tiny, unbesmirched corner, I turn it to face me. I learn nothing more about him than his address, phone number, and email address. I mean, who'd want to brag about being a dog walker on a business card?

"The guy I knew at the funeral rents an apartment from her on West 97th Street. I suppose she converted it into a co-op, renting the unsold units."

Emma says, "None of this means her estate is liquid. She might have other assets, but hearing myself say it aloud, I realize it's tacky to size her up by her net worth. I'd still rather have more time with her than her money."

"Even in my financial straits, I agree with you." I can't allow myself to think of her death as an opportunity for me to rise out of my current situation.

I can picture my entire family camped out in Aunt Donna's living room, fighting with each other to inherit more than their fair share of her estate, though. While I'm experiencing an invigorating rush by learning that I might inherit a pile of cash, imagining the worst from my family makes me dread next Monday's meeting. "You know there's bound to be drama over the will. Let's pledge that no matter what anyone else does, we will be gracious with whatever — if anything — we receive and stay out of the fray." I extend my pinky to Emma.

She hooks hers in mine. "Agreed."

I hope I've underestimated my family. And myself. Aunt Donna deserves better.

CHAPTER EIGHT
DO-IT-YOURSELF ESTATE SALE

"Oh, Richard! Is five minutes before we need to leave really the time to reorganize your tie collection?" Judging from mother's pinched expression, I'm guessing there is but one right answer.

"After spending three minutes searching for the tie I want to wear today, it struck me that the next time we were in a rush, the process would go much quicker were my ties organized. Before I forget, I've decided to take care of the problem today." My father beams with pride. He shouldn't. He chose the wrong answer to my mother's question. What dooms him further is that he inserted the word *struck* into his answer, giving my mother an idea of how to deal with the situation. Her hand twitches, debating whether to swat him upside the head or punch him in the nose.

The tension is moot. If we dawdle, we can make it to Aunt Donna's apartment in twenty minutes. It's nine-o-seven. The meeting about her estate is at ten. For someone who has shown zero interest in anything to do with her aunt, my mother is two-for-two in arriving well ahead of the appointed time.

I overheard her debating modes of transportation with my father last night. She mulled over the choices of walking, taking the subway, or springing for a cab. In the event anyone spotted us mid-transport, she wanted to send the right message. My father suggested we hitch a ride on a drone. The conversation ended abruptly with an "Oh, Richard."

Subway it is. We take the train to Lincoln Center and walk up Columbus Avenue in the flirtatious warmth of a spring morning. When we turn onto 69th Street, the bustle of Columbus Avenue fading away, I slide into a dream of inheriting my aunt's apartment.

With restaurants, entertainment, and shopping opportunities half a block to the west and the Central Park half a block to the east, its location is worlds better than ours. I shake my head to purge it of apartment lust. I can't indulge in fantasies about inheriting Aunt Donna's estate. Who am I to believe I deserve it? And as Emma and I agreed last week, I'd rather have my aunt in my life than her money.

After an absence of four years, I step into the lobby of her building. Guilt oozes through me when I measure the time since my last visit.

The elevator operator greets me with a handshake. "Lauren! Good to see you."

"Good to see you, too, Elias! It's been a while."

My mother scrutinizes me as if I had exchanged greetings with a drug dealer we passed on the street. I had always assumed she knew I snuck over here for the occasional visit. I guess she didn't.

"We're going to the penthouse," she tells Elias.

"Right away, ma'am."

We ride in silence. My mother fidgets with the knot of my father's tie. He holds his breath, not daring to upset her again. The elevator dings when we reach the eighth floor.

Aunt Donna's apartment is one of two on the top floor of the building. Her door is ajar. My mother pushes ahead of me and walks into the apartment chin first.

"Mrs. Bent, I presume?" asks a man in a navy suit at the door.

She doesn't look at him, instead peering into the apartment through narrowed eyes. "Yes. And you are?"

"Alexander Rankin. I'm your aunt's lawyer. If you'll—"

My mother doesn't wait for him to finish. She marches into the living room. Her sister and Aunt Shirley are casing the joint, lifting various figurines and lamps, perhaps in search of price tags.

Aunt Simone returns the large Steuben swan to his home with the rest of the glass aquatic creatures on the sideboard when her sister enters the room. "Zara."

"Simone."

Heartfelt greetings with her sister shared, my mother turns her attention to Aunt Shirley, who continues to assess the net worth of the apartment's contents. An enormous leather bag hangs from the crook of her arm. She eyes the bag and then my mother before returning the first edition of *The Jungle* by Upton Sinclair to its display rack.

My cousins Stew and Marc sit like stiff bookends on either side of Uncle Brock on the white sectional. Perhaps Aunt Simone told them naughty boys need to sit still and wait for her to decide their fate. At least they're not wearing matching outfits today.

Gerald emerges from my aunt's bedroom, wiping his hands on his pants. On his better days, he resembles the farmer from *American Gothic*, minus the overalls and the pitchfork. But when he's in a good mood and attempts to smile, like he's trying to do now, he leans more toward Riff Raff from the *Rocky Horror Picture Show* impersonating the farmer from *American Gothic*. His sunken eyes widen, and he bares his teeth threateningly. "Isn't this just so exciting?"

"Um, I suppose? We'll catch up later. I want to check on the plants on the balcony. They may need to be watered." I make my escape to the terrace before he can ensnare me into a conversation.

Spectacular as Emma's apartment is, hers doesn't have a balcony. Aunt Donna's more than delivers the outdoors with its wraparound terrace offering both northern and eastern exposures. The northern view is of little beyond the next building and its water tower. But to the east lies an unobstructed view of Central Park.

Emma and I never spent the night at Aunt Donna's apartment. But we used to beg her to let us sleep under the stars. "One day, girls. One day." I should ask Emma if today's the day for us to sleep on the balcony. Who will stop us?

My mother waves to me. Catching my eye, she points to the space on the sectional next to her. I give her a nod and go back inside.

My father engages in an elaborate process of selecting a chocolate mint from the bowl on the coffee table (they're all the same, by the way) and then removing its wrapper.

"For heaven's sake, Richard. Haven't you ever unwrapped a piece of candy? Must we listen to the unceasing sound of you wrinkling the paper?"

With a twinkle in his eye, my father pops the chocolate into his mouth.

I entice my mother with another distraction, pointing to the door. "Daniel's here. Hmm. No Genevieve, though. Well, Emma and Uncle Curtis are right behind my brother. I suppose we're good to go."

"Daniel, sweetie. Over here. Where's Genevieve?" She gives me a shove. Rather than slide over, I vacate the couch.

Daniel helps himself to a candy. With a mouthful of chocolate, he says, "Work."

I claim a barrel chair in front of the TV after I hug Emma. "We've been having tons of fun since we got here.

Everyone is relaxed and in generous spirits. Not."

"I'm not late, am I?" She drops into the chair next to me.

"Nope. No Troi or Brandon?"

"I made Troi stay home. Brandon's traveling again."

We stop chatting when the lawyer addresses us. "Thank you for taking time out of your busy schedules to meet with me today. We'll start by watching a video your aunt recorded. Can everybody see the TV?"

"Why do they get to sit in front?" Aunt Shirley shakes her oversized bag at Emma and me. I can't say for sure, but I think I detect a clinking sound coming from within it.

Emma and I scoot our chairs to the side of the sectional. Mr. Rankin clicks the remote.

Aunt Donna smiles at us on the screen. Tears puddle in my eyes. Her white hair pulled tight into her signature low ponytail, she has a bemused expression. She sparkles with vitality. It makes it harder for me to imagine her gone. Her blue eyes delight in speaking to her relatives from the grave.

"Well, hello Piccolo clan. You can't get rid of me so fast. For the record, today is Tuesday, January 2nd, two thousand and eighteen. Seeing how I find myself to possess a sound mind and what passes for a sound body, I'm starting the new year by recording this video to discuss what my wishes are for my estate after I die."

All of my relatives, except for Emma, scoot forward in their seats and murmur to themselves. I contract with embarrassment.

"If I should be so lucky, I will have many years to change my mind from where it stands today. And you'll have many opportunities to change your minds about me. Suffice it to say, until change comes, this could be my final word on the subject."

My mother whispers in my brother's ear and gives him a jab with her elbow. "Excuse me," Daniel says to the lawyer. "The recording is over two years old. Can you prove it's the most current copy of her will?"

The image on the TV freezes. "She left this DVD in her safe deposit box. It was the only DVD. The man who helped her to record it says she never requested him to film a newer version. Based on this and other evidence, we are confident the recording we are watching best represents her views at the time of her death, may she rest in peace." The lawyer bobs his head, awaiting further questions. None come, and he resumes the video.

The words Aunt Donna speaks mean less to me than the opportunity to once again listen to her gravelly voice, rich with a classic Queens accent. Like Uncle Curtis — and occasionally, my mother, at least when proving she's a native can help with a sale — she never abandoned her roots. My aunt's accent is both audible and visible. She drops her jaw and makes the corners of her lips do most of the labor. When she speaks, she appears to be blowing us kisses. "Shirley, let's start with you. My brother Albert named you the sole beneficiary of his estate. I have more than a passing knowledge of his estate since I contributed a sizable amount of money to it over the years and helped him to manage it while he was alive. Despite having enough assets to make his golden years more golden, he chose not to dip into his funds. And you have continued to live parsimoniously.

"I respect that you treasure the simple things in life, and I wouldn't dream of forcing you to take something you don't want. Therefore, I leave you fifty thousand dollars as a small token."

"Small indeed. What kind of sister would spite her brother's poor widow? I will be contesting the will." Shirley attacks the bowl of candy with her fist. She shoves the three mints she fished from it into her mouth.

The video continues to play. "Gerald, I had looked forward to welcoming you into my family, but alas, you kept your distance. I doubt you said more than a dozen words to me since your mother and my brother married.

While it's none of my business why a man spends over sixty years living with his mother, I hope one day you'll exert your independence. To help coax you into the big, wonderful world, I leave to you one-hundred-thousand dollars."

Gerald's face contorts in all its cadaveric glory. He bumps his knees together in a rapid tattoo, unable to contain his glee. His mother pierces his bubble with a pointed stare.

Aunt Donna continues, "Shirley and Gerald, my lawyers will provide you with the paperwork to claim your inheritance once the probate court has approved the will. I ask that you leave the meeting now, for what I have left to say is between my blood relatives and me. So long!"

Mr. Rankin offers Aunt Shirley a hand. She bats it away, grabs the crystal bowl of chocolates from the coffee table, and shoves the bowl, candies included, into her bag. It resonates with a muted *ding* when it lands.

Scanning the living room, I search for gaping holes where once stood a cherished collectible or knickknack. I detect a few possibilities but can't say what's missing.

Butterflies tango in my belly. Since Aunt Shirley and Gerald received such generous inheritances, what could be in store for me?

CHAPTER NINE
THAT WILL KEEP THE BOOKIES BUSY

After escorting Shirley and Gerald from the apartment, Mr. Rankin hits the play button, summoning Aunt Donna again.

"Now that it's just the nine of us — not taking into account your spouses/significant others and my lawyers, by the way — let's talk business. Having never married or had children of my own, I cherished my brother Joe's children like my own. Curtis, Zara, and Simone, you were rays of sunshine in my life for many years. I fancied myself the fun aunt, the person you came to when you needed to be with an adult who let you be you.

"I taught you how to drive; I bought you your first legal drink. We have secrets we swore we would never tell your parents. I won't embarrass you now by sharing your personal stories, but I hope you take a moment to reflect on how much we loved each other once upon a time."

My mother's smile is downright beatific. She sinks into the couch, relaxing her posture for the first time today. Is a dormant love for her aunt re-materializing, or does she presume the words her aunt has spoken improve her chances for being named a major benefactor of the estate?

"Upon the birth of your children, well, my happiness increased beyond measure. Daniel, Stewart, Emma, Lauren, and my youngest little dumpling, Marc—"

Marc's cheeks turn ruddy. Aunt Simone narrows her eyes at Aunt Donna, who bears a Mona Lisa-worthy smirk. Marc lost his baby fat years ago. In fact, he has skewed on the scrawny side since he entered school.

"—I joyfully looked forward to being a part of your lives as you grew. Emma and Lauren followed in their parents' footsteps, forging bonds with me that warmed my aging heart. Perhaps I didn't know the boys as well, but I loved each and every one of you dearly."

Daniel shuffles his butt around on the couch, searching for a comfortable spot.

"Here's where the story grows complicated. Simone, you were the first to sever ties with me. You had turned twenty-one a month before your parents met their untimely end.

"Perhaps determined to relive your rebellious teenaged years, you rebuffed every effort I made to step into the role of guardian. Like your brother, you refused my generous offer of a rental unit in the building I bought on West 108th Street. Simone, you made it clear you wanted money, not guidance or cheap rent from me. And even the generous gifts I gave you and your children years ago were never enough. When you asked for ever-increasing loans and handouts, I reassessed my generosity toward you. From then on, you kept your distance. I'm sorry to say I did the same."

Aunt Simone presses her lips into a tight line. The sizzle of air pushed through her nose warns her husband to remove his hand from her shoulder.

"Curtis, you were neither as cold to me as Simone nor as warm as Zara. I admired your devotion to your career in law enforcement. You told me you wanted to support your family solely on your salary, and I interpreted your intentions to be a mark of your character. I am also grateful that, while you took little interest in being with me, you raised your beautiful daughter to regard her great-aunt as a surrogate grandparent."

Curtis nods to Emma with a smile. She grins and bows toward him, pressing her palms together, the sides of her pointers resting against her lips.

"Since you didn't want my cash, I established a trust fund for Emma with money equal to what I gave to your siblings. I designated you to be its guardian until she turned twenty-five."

Aunt Donna pauses and lifts her eyebrows, expecting a reaction.

"Dad?" Emma's eyes burn with hurt and confusion.

Uncle Curtis clenches his jaw, furiously rubbing the back of one thumb with the other. "We'll talk about it later. You don't know how things were for me after your mother left. She took everything, cleaned out our accounts. I also want you to take into consideration what your financial situation was when you turned twenty-five."

"I had been married for three months. Brandon made me sign a prenup. Maybe I didn't need the money on my twenty-fifth birthday, but who knows if I will one day?"

It's my turn to bore Emma with a concerned stare. She shakes her head and mouths *later*.

Bracing her hands on the arms of her chair, she leans toward her father. "What's the balance of my trust fund?"

Uncle Curtis holds a pointer to his lips and turns to face the TV.

Aunt Donna begins speaking again, saving him. "I'm so sorry to spring this on you today — and in this way — Emma. I could not have been more disappointed in you, Curtis, after I discovered your activities with Emma's account. For you to have betrayed your child was unforgivable. You are the only person I've voluntarily cut from my life."

Emma propels herself from her chair in a burst of fury.

She heads to the kitchen for a glass of water. I begin to rise to offer her comfort, but upon hearing Aunt Donna say my mother's name, I stay seated, transfixed.

"Which brings me to Zara. You were my little clone. We both had such a passion for real estate. I saw firsthand your savvy when you jumped at the chance to purchase your apartment. I don't need to tell you that as of today, the market value of your unit is worth six times what you paid for it."

Aunt Simone launches an expression of disgust at my mother, who subconsciously pats the handbag she clutches in her lap.

"Except for your single investment, professionally you preferred to sell real estate; I loved buying it. Our differences did not make us natural partners per se. I hoped to lure you to my side of the business. But we had a heart-to-heart a little over a dozen years ago. The gulf between us following our discussion proved to be impossibly wide, and it grew wider over the years.

"It would have been one thing had you declined my offer to become my partner while still maintaining our familial relationship. Instead, you let our differences destroy our loving bond. You showed such contempt for the manner in which I invested my money, you forced me to re-examine my real estate philosophies. I concluded then, as now, that I wanted to maintain my commitment to doing things my way, even if it meant I would be on the receiving end of your hostility."

My mother whispers across my brother's chest to me. "Don't believe a word she says."

I shrug my shoulders, my eyebrows folded in confusion, and continue to listen to my aunt. "Your hatred of me poisoned your son against me. Daniel, I regret not being on hand to cheer each of your academic and professional successes. The brains on you! While I haven't said this to you face-to-face in years, I want you to know I am proud of all you have accomplished."

His head bowed, Daniel bites his bottom lip. Rocks pummel my heart as I hear my beloved aunt hurt the people I love and admire. I have to remember that we each spurned or at least ignored her, leaving her alone in her later years. I can't blame her for hating us a little. A mournful hollowness draws my attention away from the TV until I hear my name.

"Lauren, my sweet girl, you were so brave to defy your mother and continue to love me. I had such high hopes you would come to work with me, and I did my best to entice you. I can't blame you for choosing to remain loyal to your mother, but once you made your choice, you faded from my life. I've missed you and can only hope your absence will be short-lived."

Tears prick my eyes. I hate myself for disappointing my aunt. Existing between two warring parties always confused me. I never told my mother about Aunt Donna's offer.

My mother turns toward me, her eyes expressing sorrow. I don't know if it's because she gets that her feud put me in a difficult position or if she's upset with me for even thinking there was a choice. I hope it's the former.

"Stewart, I don't remember the last time I enjoyed a visit with you. Unless your mother brought you to a family function — and big family gatherings seem to be a thing of the past — you and I never had our own visits. I never truly knew you.

"And Marc, I met you but once — at your Uncle Albert's wedding — when you were a chubby, sweet little toddler. We never knew each other, and I'm sorry this has to be your introduction to your great-aunt."

Marc is the lone innocent among us. Truthfully, he appears to be bored rather than savaged by the day's revelations.

"Finally, there's my lovely Emma. You paid me a visit only a week ago. Were it not for your calls and our occasional lunch dates, I would not even remember I have a family."

Emma stands apart from us, taking hamster-sized sips from her water and ignoring the mass of relatives staring at her with various levels of contempt. It hits me: Emma, whose husband's net worth far eclipses Aunt Donna's, may very well be the lucky benefactor. Which is fine with me. I care for her far too much to let another family feud break us apart.

"You were a loving companion, but you also hinted that we were meant to remain tied together as relatives, not business partners. You paid little to no attention to me when I discussed my business philosophies with you. As much as I'm tempted to reward you for your devotion, what I offer may not be the right fit for you."

Hmm. I'm not the only one present to weigh the significance of her last statement. Family members who a minute ago had primed for a fight lower their shoulders and appear to be calculating their odds at this juncture. I picture frantic bookies tearing strips of paper from adding machines at a busy sports desk in Vegas.

"I haven't painted the prettiest picture of my potential heirs, have I? What is an old woman in my situation to do? A few of you probably regard me as someone who built a fortune, and my wealth appeals to you, doesn't it? My relationship with real estate evolved. Zara knows this better than any of you. And she rejected my new point of view.

"I do not leave behind an empire designed for you to fiddle away the rest of your lives while frolicking in pools of gold and gemstones. I leave behind a mission in need of a guardian.

"I genuinely wished some — or all — of you had already proven yourselves willing and able to step into my now-empty shoes. But to date none of you has. It's a huge leap of faith for me to believe at least one of you will prove me wrong, but I have to hope.

"I have allowed for my indecision to remain in my will, much to the consternation of my lawyers. There are a maximum of seven potential heirs: Curtis, Zara, Simone, Daniel, Stewart, Emma, and Lauren." We squirm in our seats upon realizing we still stand a chance of inheriting part of her fortune.

Aunt Donna leans toward us from the screen. "Marc, honey, you are still a minor, and given the problem I had with establishing a trust fund for your cousin, I have named you a contingent beneficiary should your mother earn her place as my primary beneficiary.

"Each of you must show your worthiness to be my heir through a series of tasks, participating individually. Your spouses may join your team, as it were, and Marc, you'll also team with your mother. Overseeing your progress in gaining yourself a place in my will is the man holding the camera for me while I record my message to you." We search the room, forgetting the video isn't live. The only non-family member is Mr. Rankin. That must be whom she meant.

"He and I met when he was twenty. His genius ability to fix a problem pipe at one of my properties landed him the job of super. I can't tell you how many conversations he and I have held over countless cups of coffee. But what I can tell you is he and I are like-minded when it comes to my mission. Three years ago, I made him my right-hand man.

"I'm not Miss Moneybags to him; he insisted I leave my estate to a relative. But he knows me as well as anyone does, which makes him the ideal person to judge whether any of you deserves to inherit my estate. John, please introduce yourself."

Like Willy Wonka's Square Sweets That Look Round, we turn toward the entrance in unison.

Oh, hell no.

Johnny effin' Skeegs strides toward the living room, rubbing his hands together.

Shit just got real.

CHAPTER TEN
BRUTALLY APPROACHABLE

I struggle to draw a breath. The rest of my family fails to take note of my imminent death. They are engrossed in arranging themselves into a tableau pretty enough to persuade Johnny that my great-aunt had gotten it wrong about them. My synapses crackle and pop, informing me they are abandoning their posts in protest against processing my aunt's information dump and the arrival of my nemesis.

Air. I need air. Unlatching the door to the balcony, I escape the nightmare playing out in the living room.

Emma follows me. "That's the dude from the funeral, isn't it?"

I nod, swishing my mouth to rid it of a bitter taste.

"You'd totally have this thing in the bag if the two of you hooked up."

More like I'd have a case of crabs. Ew, no.

"It's bad enough we have to compete against each other, but can you imagine Johnny and me becoming a thing? What would the rest of the family say?" I shudder. Well, the part of my brain devoted to holding onto my ten-plus years of contempt for him rids itself of the thought with more gusto than had I touched a poisonous frog. The parts of my body free from such prejudice shudder for completely different reasons.

He's not dressed in his stressed-out dog walker outfit today nor is he wearing the funeral suit whose pants hugged his rear like... *Oh, Lauren!* He's wearing an outfit brutally designed to make himself appear approachable.

There's no way he could have thrown on a pair of jeans tight enough to elicit fantasies without taking their appearance into consideration. His chambray shirt, its sleeves rolled up to display his sinewy forearms and unbuttoned over a snug white T-shirt, is studiously casual. Embarrassingly so. Perhaps he expects me to throw myself at him in an orgasmic fit.

Fat chance, Buster. I'm onto you.

Emma says, "You should grab any advantage you can. You're the most deserving person here. I'm half-tempted to remove myself from consideration, to be honest. Aunt Donna pissed me off. What right did she have to air her grievances in front of everyone?"

While I continue to glower at Johnny over her shoulder, I say, "She did drop a lot of bombs only to run away before they exploded. We still don't know all the details. Consider the story she told us about your dad. I bet it's not as bad as she made it sound."

Emma turns her head, scanning the corner of the living room where our fathers are engaged in a conversation. "Maybe, but I still bet it's worse than whatever version of it he'll tell. I'm not ready to listen to it."

"Of course." Johnny keeps glancing at me, making me squirm. I lean toward Emma. "I want to tell you something. Promise me you won't breathe a word of it to anyone."

She jerks her head forward and widens her eyes, prepared for gossip. "I promise. Do you know anything about the quests?"

"Not exactly. I went to school with Johnny."

"You mentioned something at the funeral about him being the bane of your existence in high school."

"Right. I couldn't stand him then, and I hate him even more now. But there's more: I ran into him right before Aunt Donna died."

"Oh, my God! In the park, right? Was he the guy with the poodle named Stella?"

"Oh, yeah. Huh." My synapses have the right idea for wanting to abandon ship. Was Johnny walking Aunt Donna's dog? If he was her dog walker, that means he was with her when she died. How come he didn't tell me he knew her after I mentioned her or confess his true relationship with her at the funeral? My fury toward him multiplies. I hope Stella pees in his bed. She owes me.

My brain creaks into action, connecting pieces of information. I shake my head in disbelief. "I bet Stella is Aunt Donna's dog. Johnny and I have run into each other twice, and on at least one occasion, he knew his boss was my aunt. He should have said something."

"His silence might be a wise move. It shows he takes remaining impartial seriously."

"Trust me, if he's anything like he was in high school, he takes nothing seriously. And, as he did then, I expect him to take an awful situation and make it worse."

My mother has her hand raised in the air à la the Statue of Liberty. Instead of bearing a torch, she's snapping her fingers at me. Emma grabs my hand and drags me into the living room.

We keep our distance from the greedy scrum rearranging themselves in front of Johnny. His head bounces as he counts us.

"Welcome back. I had a chance to express my sympathies to most of you at the funeral. Once again, I am truly sorry for your loss. Losing her has left a void in my heart. I was with her when she died." Aha! I was right! "If she had a heart condition, she never let on, and it's the strong and vibrant Donna I will always remember. Over the next few months, we'll get to know each other better and perhaps share happy memories."

The next few *months*?

My mother stands. "Cut the crap. You know my aunt's opinions of us, which means happy memories have nothing to do with the mess we're in now. You probably hate us because she did. Just tell us how we can sort out the will without turning it into a popularity contest."

"Zara—"

"Mrs. Bent." My mother is not having it. Good for her.

Johnny crosses his arms over his chest. "Mrs. Bent. My apologies. Let's not begin our relationship as antagonists. Your aunt left me with explicit instructions to help us through the process of determining who amongst you is best suited to continue her legacy. Her grievances died with her. You and I begin with a clean slate. Who you show yourself to be from this point forward is the only person I will judge. Nothing from the past will in any way influence my decision. Have I made myself clear?"

Aunt Simone presses out the folds of her slacks with her palms. Planting a grin on her face sweet enough to give Johnny diabetes, she says, "Please excuse my sister. Unlike her, I'm fully committed to doing everything you say. I can't stand not having patched things up with my dear aunt. Honoring her wishes is the best way for me to express the overwhelming love I had for her."

My mother's eyes roll heavenward. My father reaches for a candy, forgetting they left the building with Aunt Shirley.

Johnny chokes on the treacle. We wait for him to finish coughing. "For the record, your quests have not begun. Let me explain your first task. And remember: you are each acting as individuals. Don't shout out answers or inadvertently share clues with your relatives. OK?"

We nod.

"At four o'clock today, visit a spot in Manhattan that

was dear to your Aunt and you. She designated three specific locations that meant a great deal to her because she shared them with you. I, or one of my associates, will meet you at the correct locations. Take my card on your way out. Should you find yourself where we are not, call me."

Curtis holds up his pointer. Johnny spreads his hands toward him, inviting my uncle to talk. "That's it?"

"That's it. Like I said before, we all have happy memories of your aunt. What better way to begin our journey than to go back to before you drifted apart?"

My mother wraps herself in an impenetrable layer of smugness on the subway ride home. While I am certain about the spot I picked, it's not a place I ever visited with my mother. Where is she going? Is hers the right spot? I can't doubt myself. I refuse to give Johnny the satisfaction of me failing.

My mother and I brush past each other in silence and limit our interactions during the few hours we spend at our office. I wish Johnny hadn't pitted us against each other. Given the amount of information Aunt Donna revealed today, I would love to dissect what I learned with my mother.

Perhaps we'll both win this afternoon's quest. Provided Johnny doesn't give us instructions for a second quest today, I hope we can relax together this evening over a cocktail. I'd love to hear her take on what Uncle Curtis did to Emma. And I should pump her for a little more info on her fight with Aunt Donna.

Wait a second. She knows what Aunt Donna's mission was. Doesn't it give her a *huge* advantage over the rest of us? And Emma, disinterested as she might be, listened to Aunt Donna discuss her business philosophy. This is so unfair!

No. I can't let Johnny mess with my head. I love my mother. And Emma is more than my cousin; she's my best friend.

I challenge myself to a second quest. I pledge to envy no one for their inside information or grow distant from the people I love as I try to prove myself worthy of being named an heir. Family means more to me than money ever could. The only person I need to resent is Johnny.

CHAPTER ELEVEN
MEET MY FATHER, A HORSEMAN
OF THE APOCALYPSE

My mother talks to me over her shoulder as I hold her jacket for her. "Your father and I are leaving. You'll lock up?"

"Sure thing."

I glance at my phone. It's two-thirty. I try to deduce where they are heading based on the time she has allowed for the journey. For a subway trip, she doubles the estimate provided by the MTA and adds fifteen minutes. Were she traveling to Rego Park in Queens, a trip that takes the rest of the population of New York an hour to make from our subway stop, she would have left at one forty-five. To get somewhere on foot, she estimates it will take ten minutes per block instead of the normal one to two minutes. Hmm... What landmark could she be visiting within ten blocks of home? The Cathedral of St. John the Divine is two blocks away. Too close, and I don't associate it with my aunt.

"Shouldn't you be leaving now, too?" my mother singsongs.

My stomach believes her and searches for its jacket in a nervous frenzy. I exhale and circle my shoulders back into their sockets. No need to stress. My trip will take half an hour by subway plus a short walk.

"I have a couple of minutes to spare. Good luck to you. Bye, Daddy!"

My father emerges from the kitchenette with a fresh mug of coffee. "You're leaving, Lauren?"

Gasping in horror, my mother interprets what my father has said to mean he is one of the Horsemen of the Apocalypse. "Oh, Richard. I told you we were ready to go. Why have you made yourself a coffee? You can order a cup when we get to—" My mother's eyes bug when she realizes her error. "—When we get home. That's what I meant."

Aha! She's going to a restaurant. My brain whirs through my memory banks. My aunt and I didn't have a favorite restaurant. While I suppose either of my favorite Aunt Donna locations is coffee-adjacent, neither is a site you'd go to specifically for a pick-me-up. My stomach quakes again.

"Well, good luck, Mom. I'll see you later."

"Not if we see you first," my dad says with a chuckle. My mother grabs his elbow, dragging him out of the office in a huff.

The silence they leave behind unnerves me. In need of a distraction, I troll real estate sites in search of a fresh listing ideal for my would-be rental client, Becca. Nothing materializes.

The rental market is unfriendly to people with normal-sized incomes. I wish I owned a building where I could maintain a stock of affordable rentals. That would be a noble goal for spending an inherited windfall, focusing on affordable housing. I switch my search criteria, looking for a hypothetical building to buy. Within seconds, I'm salivating over a gorgeous apartment I wouldn't mind calling home.

I shut my browser a minute later. Obsessing over how to spend a mythical inheritance, whether for noble or greedy purposes, is not much better than turning my family members into adversaries. I need to manage my expectations, including how I would conduct myself should I be named the sole benefactor. Just as Aunt Donna spent years handing money to everyone in her family, so will I. Similarly, if I lose, I will not expect anyone to give me anything.

I leave the office a few minutes earlier than planned. I don't rush. Was it only a couple of weeks ago that I made this same trip? The air is warmer, delivering on the spring it promised me earlier. My heart is far less hopeful than it had been, though, before I set fire to Mrs. Ramos's apartment or attended my aunt's funeral. Or ran into Johnny.

Today, I enter Central Park at the Museum of Natural History. I soak in the park's lushness, savoring what a gem it is. I plot my route to cross all the bridges in this section of the park. Aunt Donna taught me the names of each crossing. Triplets Bridge with its adorable, rustic sides; Oak Bridge, which overlooks a particularly scummy portion of The Lake; and my favorite, Bow Bridge. I love the fairytale circles and swirls of its white stone railings, and the weathered planks beneath my feet always remind me of a beachy boardwalk.

The decorative urns marking the end of the bridge overflow with recently planted flowering foliage. I caress a trailing stem as I pass. The tree cover above me has filled in since my previous visit. Right around the corner is the spot where Aunt Donna loved to sit, but the tree blocks my view of it.

I meander on the last stretch of path. I'm fifteen minutes early. Even left to my own devices, I can't escape my mother's habit.

I lift my gaze, scanning from the body of water on my right to the benches on the other side of the path. A man naps on one of them. Underneath the bench lies a blue backpack. The man's elbows rest on the back of the bench. His head dangles over the top of the bench, out of view. His legs stretch onto the path, thrusting his back forward to create a miniature poodle-sized gap behind him.

Specifically, a space big enough to house a strawberry-blond miniature poodle. The dog slithers from her hiding spot onto her person's lap. He rises and waves at me. My head fills with conflicting emotions.

Yay, I picked the right spot, the competitive center of my brain cries.

Ugh. Why didn't Johnny assign one of his 'associates' to wait at this spot? groans the sensible part of my brain.

"I knew you wouldn't disappoint your aunt. Come. Take a seat." Johnny pats the forest green planks beside him.

I harrumph. "My aunt preferred this bench." I claim a seat on a bench two away from his.

He points to the small metal dedication plaque behind him. "I wouldn't be so sure."

I return to his bench, my brow furrowed in doubt. He slides over, revealing an inscription etched on the brass plate bolted to the back of the bench.

> *"It is prodigious the quantity of*
> *good that may be done by one man,*
> *if he will make a business of it."*
> Benjamin Franklin

I want to protest. How could he know which is her favorite bench? She's my aunt. This is our spot, and I have memories collected throughout my childhood to prove it. Besides, Aunt Donna's name isn't on the plaque. The helpful librarian in my memory bank plays an audio clip of my aunt reciting the same quote to Emma and me many years ago. Damn it!

You can pack your things, librarian. And no, I will not give you a letter of recommendation.

Stella jumps into my lap when I sit next to Johnny. Instinctively, I massage her ears. "Fine. You win. Does this mean I didn't pick her favorite spot?"

"Nah. You were close enough for jazz. I wonder who else may show up here."

"Emma, perhaps. Aunt Donna and I never came here with anyone else." Stella takes advantage of my open mouth to insert her tongue in it. "Ew!" I deposit her onto Johnny's lap in disgust.

He chuckles. "Sorry. I should have warned you she's a kisser."

"And a pisser. Two strikes against her. She's Aunt Donna's dog, right?"

"Yup." Johnny wraps Stella in a hug to prevent her from reclaiming my lap — and mouth — as hers.

"Stella is everything Aunt Donna dreamed of in a dog. Except for the behavioral issues. When did she adopt her?"

"About a year ago. Your aunt loved Stella something fierce. The dog went everywhere with her. And rarely on foot. I've done my best to remind her she's a dog by taking her on the occasional walk with my pack. Like we were doing when I ran into you a few weeks ago."

"You've known all along that Aunt Donna was my great-aunt. Yet, even after I told you I was thinking about her, you didn't say a word. Why didn't you at least tell me Stella was hers?"

"I couldn't because I swore to your aunt I would remain neutral in the event I ever met any of her relatives. She never learned that we knew each other. I made the executive decision to keep my secret from her so she wouldn't have to rethink her plan by bringing in another person to preside over naming her heirs. But only because I understood her, perhaps better than anyone else."

His minor brag aside, I admit to myself that Johnny is conducting himself with unimpeachable character. While I remember him being lazy, entitled, and a litany of additional sins in high school, dishonest was not on the list.

Except for the whole American history test debacle our sophomore year. On the day of a big test, I caught him standing at his locker, staring at the answer key. I ripped it from his hands.

"Cheater!" I had yelled at him.

"I'm not looking at the answers. I'm trying to figure out what to do with it."

"Yeah, like I'd believe you. I'm taking it straight to our teacher and telling her you stole the answer key."

"I didn't steal it; I found it. I swear." This was probably the first time I experienced the power of his eyes. They widened and softened, imploring me not to accuse him of a high crime. I believed him a tiny bit.

When I turned the answers in to the teacher, telling her Johnny had found them, she banished us from the class during the test. Since we had seen the answers, we weren't permitted to take the test, and both of us received F's. It was my first and only failing grade, and I could never forgive Johnny for torpedoing my average.

He refused to tell the teacher or me who had taken the answers from her. The part of me seething over failing the test was quick to accuse him of stealing them. But the rest of me, swept into the gentleness of his soul visible through his eyes, determined he was honorable, a guy who wouldn't rat out the true thief.

OK. So this nearly upstanding human whose hair I want to sweep away from his heart-breakingly gorgeous brown eyes and whose ease with himself and the world has a gravitational pull on me isn't the worst person to sit alongside while admiring my favorite view in New York City.

His phone dings twice. It's ten past four. Time to learn who knew my aunt as well as I did.

He reads from a text. "Your mother made it to Bemelmans Bar at the Carlyle. That's where your aunt took your mother and her siblings for their first legal drinks. Emma, too."

"I remember Aunt Donna telling me we would have a belated birthday drink at the Carlyle. I was away at school on my twenty-first birthday. We never made it. Speaking of which, have you heard from Emma?"

"Yeah. She chose the fountain at Lincoln Center. Also a correct location."

"That was my second choice."

Without turning toward me, he says, "I'm glad you chose Central Park."

I study his expression. He gives nothing away with his face, but a quality in his tone makes me suspect his words carry a personal message.

I don't bother to analyze it. "I guess we need to hear which locations Aunt Simone, Uncle Curtis, Stew, and my brother chose."

On cue, his phone rings. "Hi, Simone. Arriving late isn't the issue. Someone would have waited for you had you gone to the right place. It wasn't the King Cole Bar at the St. Regis. It was Bemelmans at— No, we can't make an exception just because of how divine the Bloody Marys are at the St. Regis. I'll be in touch with the next phase."

He snickers. "Your cousin Marc has to sit outside the bar with his father because minors aren't allowed inside. That fact, plus picking the wrong location didn't stop your aunt from ordering a second drink."

"Classic Aunt Simone." Stella makes a play for my lap while Johnny's hands are busy with his phone. I wipe my finger across my sealed lips, warning her not to help herself to a second kiss. She gives the dog equivalent of a shrug and curls into a ball.

Johnny slides his forearms onto the top rail of the bench. I have a front-row view of the position I found him in when I arrived. I can't help but zoom in on the hem of his T-shirt, which lifts a bit as he stretches his legs forward. And my common sense must be on vacation because I can't resist taking a peek at the exposed triangle of flesh at the top of his waistband. My urge is to hook a finger under his shirt and lift it a little higher. I pet Stella furiously, refocusing my attention away from Johnny.

He raises his head when his phone dings. Reading his texts, he says, "Quest number one is in the books. Your brother returned to Donna's apartment, but the doorman wouldn't let him upstairs. Curtis went back to her church in Queens. I haven't heard from Stew. I've texted him, though."

"He probably got stoned after the meeting and forgot about his assignment. Which means my mother, Emma, and I won. Is there a prize?"

"No prize. Nor am I saying anyone won or lost. These are the results I expected. The three of you had forged deeper bonds with your aunt. Curtis, Simone, and Daniel weren't wrong with their choices. They selected locations they identified with your aunt."

"And Stew?"

"Is a blank slate. He had the most limited relationship with her. No quarrels or exceptional moments between them. We're not aware of his ambitions. Who knows? He may surprise us later in the challenges and reveal characteristics ideally suited to carry on her mission."

"Don't count on any revelations from him being intentional on his part."

He sits up. "Hey, wait a sec. I was wrong: you did win a prize."

I straighten my back with a jolt. I love being rewarded for my efforts. "I did?" I ask with as much humility as I can muster. "What?"

He points to the sleeping dog sprawled across my lap. Her paw, dangling over my knee, twitches. My knees twitch, too, and my eyes dart around in their sockets.

"I tried with her. I really did. But Stella is wreaking havoc on my pack. She terrorizes the other dogs. I have to feed her in a separate room. Otherwise, she hogs their food and growls at them if they dare approach their bowls. She has claimed every piece of furniture. I haven't sat in my easy chair since she moved in. With her as the new pack leader, my dogs now ignore the house rules. Plus, she refuses to walk more than ten blocks. When she's done, she's done. She lies flat as a dead leaf on the sidewalk and whines."

And he expects I'll take her home with me based on his glowing sales pitch? *Not so fast, Johnny!*

He bends over his knees to pull the bulging backpack from under the bench. "You'll need this." Unzipping the backpack, he removes a baby carrier. "Hand her to me and put this on. The pouch goes in the front."

"Is she at least housebroken?"

"Yes. But just in case, I've stuck a couple of wee-wee pads in the backpack. I'm also sending you home with her bed, her favorite toy, and a bag of food — by the way, if she doesn't eat by five o'clock, she may well explode."

"She sounds awful. Does she have any qualities to recommend herself?"

His eyes plead with me. They're even more persuasive than Stella's, which she is manipulating with puppy dog precision. "How did it feel to hold her in your lap?"

The velvety, caring tone of his voice, coupled with the irksome fact that I'm enjoying his company makes me want to invite him into my lap for a round of cuddling. But we are talking about Stella, not Johnny.

Massaging the curls on her back is hypnotic. And knowing I am responsible for the level of contentment she projects encourages me to continue to drag my fingers through her hair. A smile spreads across my face. "Like there was nothing I'd rather be doing besides petting her."

"Exactly. She's a championship-level lap dog. Your aunt adored her beyond measure. I bet you'll love her just as much."

Stella's head pops out of the top of the carrier after Johnny plunks her into it. She licks my chin and peers at me with a level of adoration I've never experienced. Wait a second. They tricked me. I don't remember agreeing to adopt a dog.

CHAPTER TWELVE
FAILING THE RORSCHACH TEST

"My teeth are aching from how sweet she is." Stella jumped into Emma's lap within seconds of our arrival, and Emma hasn't let go ever since.

I stare longingly at my wooly little hot water bottle, but I brought her to visit her aunt, intending to share the love. "I want to resent Johnny for forcing me to adopt a miscreant, orphaned dog, but I can't entirely. For every pain in the ass thing she does, she more than balances her sins by loving on us so hard."

"Emma, it's my turn. I need to plan a wardrobe for her." Troi snatches Stella and deposits her into his lap. He sighs with happiness. "I want a dog. Can I have one? Pretty please?"

Emma grins at him. "Taking care of you is enough trouble. You're lucky my husband let me bring home a friend to keep me company when he travels."

"Oh, honey. You know I'm his insurance plan. If you're with me, how can you run off with another man? Besides, he counts on me squealing like a squirrel in a trap if I ever suspect you to be up to no good."

Emma's forehead crumples, and she swishes her mouth to rid it of an unpleasant taste.

"Speaking of doing the wrong thing, did your father come clean to you about the trust fund?" I ask.

Still not recovered from Troi's comments, Emma screws her face in hurt and anger. "I should hire a lawyer. Aunt Donna certainly should have when she learned what he had done. No matter his reason for making 'loans' to himself with the money left to me, he committed a crime."

"But…" I contemplate her posture. She appears resigned to doing nothing.

"But he says my mother cleaned him out. He spent the money to provide for me. Can I blame him for that? He did a good job of raising me, up to a point. I turned twenty-two the same year he retired from the force. He and the rest of the trust fund went to Vegas, leaving me to fend for myself. Aunt Donna discovered his crime after he moved. And now I have to decide whether to forgive my father."

"We're not letting him set foot in our home ever again." The intensity of Troi's declaration uproots Stella from her napping place. She sits on the floor in front of me, drags her butt on the carpet, and whines.

"Stella has to use the facilities, and she means NOW!" I hustle to grab her leash. If she lets loose on the silk rug, I may join my uncle on the list of unwelcome visitors.

Stella and I pace the sidewalk along Fifth Avenue until she deems a patch of concrete worthy of her waste. While I wait, I replay Troi's comment about Brandon keeping tabs on Emma's fidelity in my head. It reminds me of the cryptic comment she made during the video screening regarding her marriage. I have to ask her what she meant.

Eager to dig for news upstairs, I pressure my dog into action. "Stella, quit being picky and get on with it. Mommy wants to be inside."

She turns toward me, her huge eyes limpid pools of obeisance. "Good girl, Stella!" I bag what she produces and fling it into the trashcan on the corner. "Come on, girl. Back to the castle in the sky."

Emma and Troi are poring over photos of artwork on her iPad. Upon laying eyes on one another, Troi and Stella reenact the 'lovers running toward each other in a meadow/airport' trope. I take his place on the couch next to Emma.

"Whatcha looking at?" I rest my chin on her shoulder.

She enlarges a photo of a sculpture constructed from twigs. It looks like a depiction of an elephant and a hunchback wrestling over a can of tuna.

Emma answers, "My friend Marci has an art exhibit coming up. She asked me to help her choose which pieces to display and to suggest some pairings."

I swipe through a few of the photos and try to derive meaning from them. One painting depicts what may be a key stuck into the hollow of a bent lamppost. Or maybe it's a pe— I quickly hand the tablet to Emma. If this a Rorschach Test, I'd rather not find out I have male anatomy on my brain. Because I definitely haven't been thinking about Johnny lately. Nope. Not even that delicious bit of flesh poking out above his waistband.

Quick. Find a neutral topic, Lauren.

"Do your friends pay you for your curating services?" I ask.

She shrugs. "Every once in a while."

"You should be paid all the time. You have a talent. Other people get paid to do what you do."

"I don't need the money."

"But will you ever need money of your own?"

"To the best of my knowledge, Brandon's business is strong."

Subtle hints aren't teasing out the information I seek. I don't know whether Emma is purposely avoiding my questions or if I'm being too subtle. "That's not what I mean. What were you saying at the meeting at Aunt Donna's? You know, when you told your dad that you might need the money she left for you. After I gave you a questioning look, you mouthed, 'Later.' I thought you were referring to trouble in your marriage."

Emma stiffens her back. "You read something into the conversation. I meant we'd discuss my father's actions another time."

Her eyes flicker away from me. Her body language leads me to believe she's not being forthright. I don't want to push her, so I make a slight detour in the conversation.

"I'm sorry I misunderstood you. Let's return to our previous discussion. Needing to work to support yourself is only one reason to draw an income. For me, it also provides a sense of self-worth. Receiving payment proves that I fulfilled my goals. And income equals independence. Money earned is yours alone. I don't know what the future holds, but having money of my own and a means of earning more is my dream. I'm not there yet, obviously, but my dream is what gets me out of bed each day."

She relaxes. "I remember believing the same thing when I began working, but my gig as a receptionist at an art gallery became more like a prison to me. Helping friends curate exhibits or their shop inventories on my schedule represents freedom to me. I do it with love. It's sort of a mission of mine. I can bring beauty and order to a space and then move on to help someone else."

"Aunt Donna used the word 'mission' in her video. And Johnny also mentioned it last week. The estate is more than its monetary value; it's a mission for us to inherit."

Emma nods. "She taught me to pursue a mission rather than to gain wealth for the sake of wealth."

"So you know what her mission is?"

Emma coils like a threatened snake. "I didn't say I do."

"But she said she told you."

"I swear I don't remember."

"Uh, huh."

"You don't believe me."

Troi strokes Stella with one hand and pretends to eat popcorn with the other as he watches the tension rise between us.

"Quit it, Troi. Your mommies aren't having a fight." I throw him a lethal glare.

"That's right. We aren't. Troi, go fetch me a refill." Emma hands her water glass to him. Disappointment clouding his face, he leaves the room. Stella hops on the couch between us, ready to soothe our frayed nerves.

I hope to have a similar impact on Emma. The last thing I want is to upset her. Or make her mad at me "I believe you. Right now, it might not be in your active memory, but her words lie buried somewhere in your brain. One of the quests might jog your memory."

"Are you assessing me as your competitor?"

I take a breath. This isn't going the way I had planned. "No. The opposite. I'm already living through the ugly side of the competitive spirit of the quests. My mother barely said a word to me before the first quest. And when she did speak, she clothed herself in smugness. Our relationship changed, and it's all because Aunt Donna turned us into adversaries. Your prediction was right.

"And she spilled the beans about what your father did, making him your sworn enemy. Just because we failed Aunt Donna doesn't mean we've all neglected each other. But by the time they settle her will, I'm scared we will hate each other."

Emma pushes her defensiveness aside and strokes my hand. "We may not be the closest family, but we do OK. Look at the two of us. We're best friends. And you and your mom will be fine. We're not competing against each other; we're competing as individuals. More than one of us may prove themselves worthy."

"Exactly. You and I could form an alliance like they do on *Survivor*. You told me I should embrace any advantage I can. We spent more time with Aunt Donna over the last ten years than anyone else. We knew her best. I understand real estate; you understand her mission. And we're not greedy and bitter like my mom, your dad, and Aunt Simone. We deserve to win. If Johnny names me the benefactor, I'd make you my partner. What do you say?"

She pulls her hand into her lap. "I've reconsidered what I said about grabbing advantages."

"I beg your pardon?"

"The concept of using advantages against each other doesn't mesh with who Aunt Donna was. We should follow her plan and do the quests independently."

"But you said you weren't interested in inheriting her business, and you thought I was the most deserving. We wouldn't be preventing anyone from succeeding on their own, but come on. You have a husband, and so do my mother and Aunt Simone. Daniel has Genevieve. Everyone else but me has someone to help them. Please?"

"I believe helping you would be highly deceitful and unfair, Lauren. It goes against the very core of what Aunt Donna asked of us. And considering what my father did to me, I'm a little touchy on the subject of deceit. We shouldn't even be discussing her will. Let's promise from now on, we'll never mention inheriting her estate to each other. OK?"

I stand, tucking Stella under my arm. "That will be easy for me. Stella, we're going home now."

Panic in her eyes, Emma reaches for my arm. "Wait. I didn't mean for you to leave. I'm just putting any discussion about the quests off-limits."

I wriggle my arm out of her grip. "You accused me of being deceitful and unfair. Which means you think I'm a cheater. How dare you accuse me of cheating!"

CHAPTER THIRTEEN
SNOOKUMS POOCHIE-POO HAS A SET
OF TEETH ON HER

Two days later, I'm still fuming mad at Emma. The fight came out of nowhere. How did we get from me revisiting points she made during the meeting at Aunt Donna's to her denouncing her positions and calling me a cheater? For someone who thrives on restoring order and beauty, she sure has made a mess of things.

What made her change her point of view? Every answer I try on for size doesn't fit. Is it because she's mad at her father? Her mother? Perhaps I'm right to assume all is not perfect between Brandon and Emma. Changing her mind and fighting with me are so unlike her. She owes me an explanation, but I'm not ready to listen to it.

I thump my fist on my desk. Pens tremble in their cup. Stella wags her tail at me in her best imitation of a rattlesnake. I hoist her onto my lap and try to subdue my mood with a dose of rubbing her belly. She squirms for a moment but submits when I refuse to release her.

I didn't say anything mean to Emma. Whenever her body clenched or retracted, I changed the course of the conversation to protect her. I wanted to support her. Yet, when I also needed her to support me, she rejected me.

I bash away on my laptop in our office. Stella is not having it. She seeks harbor in the tranquil waters of my father's lap.

"Look at this puss. Who's a little snookums poochie-poo?" he coos to her. She consumes his baby talk like she does everything else in her universe.

Until she can open the fridge herself or propel herself onto the counters, we have the upper hand in managing her insatiable appetite. But once a morsel of food drops to the floor, woe be unto the person who tries to snatch it from her. My father's little snookums poochie-poo has a set of teeth on her.

And a pair of lungs. You should hear her caterwaul when we try to leave her in the crate. However, a week after moving into our home, she's in no danger of receiving an eviction notice. Not even from my mother. Despite — or maybe because of — being my Aunt Donna's dog, she has the magical ability to wipe away the stress and drama that have begun to erode our family's peace.

Stella sleeps with me each night. Or on me. Or pressed up against my face, forcing me to inhale poodle curls with each breath. Regardless, having a warm being who is eager to kiss me whenever I open my eyes isn't the worst thing for a single woman to endure. True, her kisses have sparked a bit of daydreaming in which Stella morphs into a man who may or may not have an unnerving resemblance to Johnny. But I'll forgive her.

I guess there's a lesson here. A dog who annoys me in so many ways more than makes up for it by delivering the love. Like Johnny. Great. I add *thinking of Johnny* to the 'con' column of Stella's pro/con chart.

Like Stella, he has an overwhelming list of flaws. But every once in a while, he temporarily erases my disdain for him. He has called twice to check on her. You can't hate a man who loves dogs, can you? It didn't suck to hang out with him last week in the park, either. We should make a doggy playdate. I kind of owe it to him to regard him as the adult my aunt knew rather than hold him in contempt for the boy he used to be.

Except he's the guy overseeing the whole Aunt Donna inheritance quandary. Which makes him indirectly responsible for my fight with Emma.

My father clears his throat, interrupting my maelstrom of annoying musings. "Lauren, honey. What's the situation with Mrs. Ramos?"

I wrinkle my nose. "None of the leads from the open house panned out. We're holding the next one on Sunday."

"Good job. You're doing exactly what I would do. I suppose Leon never contacted you?" My father scathingly enunciates each syllable of his nemesis's name.

"Not a peep from him."

"That's in your favor. It's been what — a month? — since the first open house?"

"It will be four weeks on Sunday."

"Have you considered lowering the asking price?"

"Mrs. Ramos won't go lower."

"Another month on the market, and we may have to persuade her, but for now, keep it where it is. I'll triple check my leads for potential buyers. I have a good feeling about this listing, honey. I have faith you will close on it real soon."

"Thanks, Dad. That means a lot."

His words wrap me in warmth. Between my mother and Emma, it seems like no one is in my corner. I desperately want to convince both of them I mean no harm.

A breather between quests would help. Tensions would diminish. And everything would be normal again.

Dashing my hopes for having enough time to encourage a détente to develop, my mother and I receive envelopes from Rankin, Rankin, and Gould on Thursday. At least they contain something helpful: a one-thousand-dollar check.

"Is the check because we proved we knew Aunt Donna best in the first challenge?" my mother asks me. "How could my brother and sister have forgotten about Bemelmans? I guess sharing a first drink with a favorite relative just didn't matter as much to them as it did to me."

If I'm not mistaken, my mother has let her hatred for my aunt slip her mind.

"No, Mom. Read the letter. They're compensating each of us for our time."

"Oh, I bet your uncle complained. He's the one who ran off to Vegas with Emma's inheritance. So what if he has to buy a plane ticket whenever Johnny or the lawyers summon us? He can stay home for all I care."

My mother's implied message jangles my nerves. She seems determined to eliminate her competition — me included — and pocket the whole estate. I wonder if I actually even know my own mother.

Not a hint of the scent of melted plastic or charred cookbooks sully Mrs. Ramos's apartment. The air is a little stale, but nothing a spritz of air freshener can't handle.

I deposit a box of cookies onto the counter. "Are you going somewhere?" I ask Mrs. Ramos, pointing to the collection of suitcases by the door.

"Eh, my sister is getting a new hip tomorrow. I'm moving in with her for a couple of months because that daughter-in-law of hers won't lift a finger to help her while she recuperates. And my nephew. He's a no-goodnik, too."

"I'm sorry to hear your news. And isn't it terrible when family members don't take care of each other? Your sister is lucky to have you. Now, my family—"

"I didn't hire you to listen to your problems. You deal with them on your own time. Tell me, you going to find me a buyer today?"

"I'll do my darnedest, Mrs. Ramos. Beautiful spring days like today always bring in a lot of potential buyers."

"I hope a parade of curiosity seekers or people looking for free cookies don't traipse through my home today. Get me a good offer, and I'll be happy. I'm not crazy about having to pay the mortgage, tax, and fees on this apartment for the next two months while I'm living in Queens."

A light bulb illuminates in my head. No. Not just a single light bulb but an incandescent wonderland deserving of a Tony Award for lighting design.

"Mrs. Ramos, I have the best idea. If we don't receive a suitable offer today, would you consider renting your apartment to someone either until you return from helping your sister or until it sells? I have the most trust-worthy client who is in the market for a rental. While she's hunting for a permanent place, her days of sleeping on her friend's couch are numbered. Well, more like a negative number. She needs a place ASAP."

"What would she pay me?"

"Her budget is eleven hundred dollars firm."

"Hmm, it's not enough to cover the bills…"

I prevent myself from blurting out how it beats receiving nothing. I hold my breath while I watch her eyes flicker and calculate the offer.

"She can't use my sheets or towels. And when I come home, I want every trace of a stranger living here to disappear."

"Oh, you won't regret it! I'll text her the news right now."

Becca's family in Nebraska must hear her whoop with excitement when I break the news. She makes herself at home once the steady stream of visitors who poked and prodded each corner of the apartment during the open house leave. Solving one client's problem while doing my best to bring in an offer for the other is the perfect antidote to the Aunt Donna drama. I'm a real estate lady, damn it! This is what I'm supposed to be doing.

CHAPTER FOURTEEN
HITTING THE RESET BUTTON

It finally dawned on me what I found to be so unforgivable in Emma's words: she accused me of cheating. People have falsely denounced me when I've been equally innocent. Whether the punishment for my honesty was failing a history test or losing Emma, my best friend, it's not fair that I'm the one who suffers when I've done nothing wrong.

In the six weeks since our last quest, she and I have had the briefest of text exchanges, but I haven't forgiven her yet. For some reason, I never was free to get together the days she suggested. Oh, darn.

I'll have to confront her face to face in a few days, though. Rankin, et al., have demanded my presence on the Northwest corner of Broadway and 34th Street this coming Saturday for quest number two.

"We're going to Macy's!" my mother trills when she reads her letter. "I could use a visit to the store to replenish my summer wardrobe. Perhaps Aunt Donna had store credit."

"I doubt we're going shopping, Mom. Read the letter.

It says to wear comfortable clothing suitable for outdoor activities."

"I'd better call your brother to make sure he received his invitation. Unless you think they invited only the winners of the first quest?"

"The letter says family members and significant others can join us. I'm sure Daniel received his invite. Besides, Johnny told me they weren't eliminating anyone who missed the mark on the first challenge."

"So he's letting you in on his little secrets, is he now?" My mother's nose and lips bunch petulantly.

"I've disclosed everything I've learned. He told me no secrets whatsoever. How many times do I have to explain it to you?"

"You're being too sensitive, dear. It's only a fun game."

If you call being the target of your mother's cutthroat tactics fun, sure.

On Saturday, my parents and I head to Midtown. My mother's eyebrows pantomime the clipped *Mmm* she utters when she judges my outfit. She's dressed to show a million-dollar property to a new client. I'm wearing shorts, a sleeveless blouse, and a pair of white sneakers, complying with the dress code mentioned in our brief. One of us is more likely to wilt in the early June sun than the other. Just sayin'.

We are the first to arrive. Go figure. My mother doesn't let the twenty-three minutes remaining before the meet-up time spoil the fun of condemning the rest of her relatives for not taking the quests more seriously. Of course, she spares Daniel from her critique, instead worrying that a dreadful fate must have befallen him and his fiancée Genevieve to prevent them from arriving early.

Getting here early enough to head home and back before anyone would know we were missing isn't enough to calm her nerves. "Lauren, where did your father go this time?"

"I wouldn't worry about him." I halfheartedly scan the area, hoping not to spot Emma instead of my father.

"I swear he does this to me on purpose. He'll say he's spontaneous, but I don't believe it's a coincidence that he chooses the exact moments when I'm most concerned about being punctual to wander off. It's quite the calculated behavior if you ask me."

"Look, Mom. He's across the street, carrying three cups of coffee. Wasn't that nice of him to make a coffee run?"

My mother is plenty wired already, and now he's bringing her caffeine?

"Well, he should have told me where he was going. I would have asked him to bring coffees for Daniel and Genevieve. They can share yours, I suppose."

I count on my father dosing mine but good with whole milk. Because that's the way I like it. Definitely not because my brother is lactose intolerant or anything.

Several members of my family swarm on us at ten o'clock. Troi, dapper in a seersucker suit and straw hat, air kisses me. Emma's eyes plead with me to forgive her, but I offer her a tight-lipped nod. She is equally cold to her father, whom only my father cares to talk to. Aunt Simone, Uncle Brock, and Marc arrive by cab and stand apart from us.

Johnny emerges from the subway station. He plants himself in the middle of us. "Piccolo family, thanks so much for coming. I see we're still waiting for Daniel and Stew. No worries. Our schedule is flexible."

Like me, he's wearing shorts. I appraise his pale, somewhat scrawny legs with relief. Lusting after a pair of muscular legs attached to *him* would fry my brain, given the hostilities between my clan I'm enduring.

His bony knees point themselves toward me. "Hey,

Lauren. How's the little princess?"

"You can't be referring to me." I take a step back, narrowing my eyes.

He holds up his hands in surrender. "Not hardly. I meant Stella."

Phew. "She was not at all pleased with the arrangements for today. I spent fifteen minutes luring her into the crate. It was killing her: the smell of bologna, peanut butter, and last night's steak was impossible for her to resist, but the proximity of the food to the crate would send her hiding under the couch. My father and I finally trapped her and threw her in with a toy and a slice of bologna. She uttered a few choice words for us after we locked the door. I pity our poor neighbor who volunteered to take her on pee breaks throughout the day."

"I told you to be consistent with crating her. Teach her that her crate is a good place. She's a smart girl, and so eager to please." Is he describing Stella or me?

Johnny glances away from me. "Ah, here we go. Daniel and Stew have arrived. Wait, what are they doing here?"

Gerald and Aunt Shirley stand behind Stew. Gerald is wearing a short-sleeved white button-down shirt and baggy gray slacks. Aunt Shirley's ready for another funeral in her dowdy black shift and black hat.

I sip my coffee while Johnny makes his way through the crowd toward the interlopers. My mother fusses over Daniel. I wonder why Genevieve didn't join him? Whatever Johnny has planned for us today, I dread the impending awkwardness between our fractured family unit.

Johnny's hands dance with guarded acceptance of whatever Stew has said to him. "OK. We're ready to make our move. Here's something you may not have known about Donna: she rode the subway to Brooklyn two or three days a week for the last three years of her life. I'll leave where she went for another day, but as a Brooklyn boy myself, I thought it would be fun to take you someplace she and I visited each of the last two summers. I have a MetroCard for each of you. Follow me to the downtown Q platform. In case we lose each other, we're getting off at the West 8th Street stop in Brooklyn. The ride is an hour long. Everybody ready?"

Resembling the least prepared/most grumpy day campers ever, we follow our counselor below ground. Aunt Shirley and Gerald wrestle with his card at the turnstile. With each swipe, he pushes forward only for the turnstile to deny him access. Aunt Shirley threatens to sue the MTA. Johnny takes the card, flips it, rotates it ninety degrees, and gives it a final swipe. I imagine a fireworks display marking Gerald's admittance to the wonderful subterranean world of New York City for what may be the first time in his life.

My mother and I, both possessing the eager-to-please gene, stick to Johnny like a wad of poorly disposed of gum. Emma and Troi inch further down the platform, choosing to ride in a different car than me. Marc wanders up the platform to listen to the blues singer performing near the benches in the middle. Aunt Simone and Uncle Brock shadow him, nervously creating a barrier between their golden boy and the scary world of the subway platform.

As our train clatters into the station, my father walks away from our group, followed by Uncle Curtis.

"Richard!" my mother screams. She leaves us in a huff. I step into the car and lean my head through the door. My mother has my father's cuff pinched between her fingers. They, my brother, and Uncle Curtis enter the next car, joining Aunt Simone and her family.

If I were Johnny, I'd be having my third heart attack of the day. Our haphazard approach to traveling together doesn't raise even a bead of sweat on his face. I kind of hate him for remaining calm. He gestures to the seat beside him. I stand instead, holding the pole in front of Aunt Shirley. She and Stew bookend Gerald.

"Don't think about cozying up to me, young lady," Aunt Shirley spits at me.

Her statement leaves me speechless. Cozying up to her isn't high on my list of favorite activities.

"I see what you're doing, standing close to me. Well, you're not getting any of the cash your aunt gave me. There's not enough for me let alone you."

"I wouldn't dream of denying you the obvious pleasure of enjoying every bit of your inheritance, Aunt Shirley."

Her knuckles whiten as she clasps her handbag. She's either trying to prevent me from dipping my hand into it or she's securing a better grip on it to bash me in the head. I switch to the pole closer to my cousin.

"Hey, Stew. How's it going?" I ask.

"Quite well now that I have a partner in crime." He jabs Gerald playfully with his elbow. Gerald shies away at first, protecting himself from bodily harm. Deducing the intent of Stew's gesture, he relaxes his pose and swats Stew's shoulder with the heel of his hand. Stew's head careens into the pole I'm holding, smashing my fingers with his skull.

"We're partners now," Gerald explains to me while I rub my fingers.

"Are you now?" I ask Stew.

He waves me off. "It's not going against the rules. I know Aunt Donna didn't want him to take part in the quests. He's not helping me in that way. You see, I have this amazing startup idea, but I needed an investor. When Gerald comes into his inheritance after the court approves it, he's going to invest in my company. If I inherit Aunt Donna's estate, I'll shoot a little cash his way. If I don't inherit her fortune, I bet I'll be swimming in profits from my venture. He wins, either way."

"And what is this idea of yours?"

"A dating app."

If Stew is knowledgeable about dating — or creating apps — it will be a surprise to me. And what of Gerald having any familiarity with dating apps? I pity the women who helped him gain his experience.

"Uh, huh." My eyelids flicker with disinterest.

"But it's different from the other apps. Mine will be a virtual reality app. Not only do you meet your potential partner through the app, but you can go on dates in it, too."

"Sounds great. Very original." The seat next to Johnny looks more interesting with every second.

"Do you want to invest in it?"

"I'm good. But best of luck to you two."

I take my leave, detouring toward the subway map.

"Oh, no you don't," Johnny scolds me.

I lower myself onto the pale blue plastic seat one space away from him. "I bet everyone else has already read the map and determined where we're headed."

"Don't you want to be surprised?"

"I prefer knowing what lies ahead so I can prepare for it."

"Not being a fan of surprises is one way you're *not* like your aunt."

Hope stirs in my chest. "You think I'm like her in other ways?"

"Yeah, I do."

"Give me an example."

"Some of the ways might prove to be to your advantage."

"You're not going to tell me, are you?"

"Nope. Wouldn't be fair." He appears to be contemplating a riddle when his eyes meet mine. "Why are you and Emma fighting?"

"She decided that sharing notes on the quests is unfair. I swear I wasn't being unethical by mentioning them. I've since decided it's best to keep to ourselves."

He deflates and stares at me with sad, puppy dog eyes, which makes my heart skip a beat. "It would upset your aunt to learn the two of you were not getting along."

I refuse to give in to him. "Well, Aunt Donna's the one who split our family. Think of the terrible things she revealed about each of us. And then she's making us compete against each other to be her heir."

"You have the wrong idea. Family meant everything to her. While you may have neglected her in recent years, if she can somehow bring you back together, it would be a significant legacy to leave behind."

"But she says we're competing individually. Doesn't that mean we're competing against each other?"

"No. One person's success doesn't undermine another's. Or, put another way, I'm not ranking you. And this is not a competition. It was her wish for all of you to prove worthy of carrying out her mission. Do you understand now?"

"Uh, huh. But I still believe the quests bring out the worst in some of us." My mother, Emma, to name two.

"And that's what today's challenge should address. She designed it as a reset button, as a chance to bring you together to have a fun family day. Trust me."

His velvety brown eyes implore me once again, and I want to believe him. But more than believe him, I'm beginning to want to do things to him that are definitely not appropriate for a family outing. I can't help but wonder if I hadn't put all my energy into despising him for making me fail the history test in high school, would I have succumbed to the power his eyes had on me when I was younger?

CHAPTER FIFTEEN
CONFESSIONS ABOARD THE
LOG FLUME

Like a schizophrenic amoeba having a bad day, we reassemble on the subway platform at our stop, moving in opposite directions from each other without actually separating.

"Oh, we're going to the aquarium," my mother says, reading a sign rather than taking in the view from the elevated platform.

Beyond the steel structure of the elevated subway platform lays Coney Island. A mishmash of colorful rides, new and old, separate a busy road from the beach.

Aunt Simone susses out what lies beyond the signs. "We're not amusement park people," she explains to Johnny.

Aunt Shirley, no surprise, informs us she doesn't do amusement. Period. My mother continues to extol the virtues of visiting the aquarium. Emma appears unmoved by Troi's burst of excitement to ride the Cyclone. And my stomach hasn't decided whether it fears a day with my family or the rides themselves more.

Johnny stands in the center of our group. "My family couldn't spare money for vacations. Trips to the local beaches were all we could afford for our getaways in the summer. My favorite day each year was when my parents splurged on tickets for the rides at Astroland here in Coney Island.

"The best summer job I ever had was working in the park when I was fifteen. Despite reeking of deep fryer grease even on my days off, I loved being in the thick of the action of the park and enjoying the rides more than once during the summer. But Astroland closed, ending my short-lived career in amusement park concessions.

"No one else in my family has a sense of nostalgia for visiting the amusement park at Coney Island. Desperate to share it with someone, I brought Aunt Donna here to what is now known as Luna Park two years ago. Turned out she loved roller coasters even more than I do. The woman was a maniac on the rides." He drifts away in thought, a grin spreading across his cheeks.

He returns to the conversation. "Family meant everything to her, and—"

My mother erupts into a coughing fit. She's faking it at first, but something goes awry, and soon her face is as red as the letters for the sign on the Cyclone. Serves her right.

"You OK, Mrs. Bent?" Johnny bends, peering up at my mother who has doubled over.

"I'm fine. Ignore me." She clears her throat before whispering loud enough in my father's ear for all of us to hear, "Family meant everything to her? Hah!"

Johnny pretends he didn't hear her. "I understand the burden she placed on you to prove your worth as potential benefactors. Today isn't about who deserves to inherit her estate. I hope you'll embrace the opportunity to have fun and reconnect as a family. Everybody ready?"

An unenthusiastic murmur rises through the crowd. We descend the stairs and cross Surf Avenue. After Johnny collects our wristbands from the ticket booth, we make our way to the Cyclone.

"To me, this roller coaster defines the park. Even though it's nearly one hundred years old, it still delivers the quintessential roller coaster experience. Don't you agree, Lauren?"

"I've never been to Coney Island," I say with a shrug.

"Whaaat?" he shrieks.

"You can't be surprised."

"True. The conversation on the subway platform kind of gave it away. We're definitely going to ride the Cyclone first."

I guess Saturday mornings in early June aren't peak season in Luna Park. We wend through the crowd-free maze to enter the ride. The fourteen of us form pairs, some more naturally than others. Aunt Shirley sits next to Uncle Curtis, wearing an expression more appropriate for waiting for her hairdresser to finish drying her hair after she realized he got the color wrong. Gerald whoops with excitement in the seat next to Stew. I wind up in a car with Uncle Brock.

The first drop launches my stomach into a state of suspended animation. When we barrel around the curves, I'm thrown into the padding on the side of the car or into Uncle Brock's shoulder. I wish perhaps I had a different man into whom I could collide. No one in particular, I should add. Johnny and my brother are having fun together, though.

Back on the sidewalk, Aunt Shirley adjusts her hat and the hem of her dress, demonstrating how unmoved she is by the experience. My heart bleeds for Gerald when he tumbles out of his car. Having begun the journey with such a sense of optimism, it must crush him to discover he and roller coasters get along even less famously than he and subway station turnstiles. His face is the color of pond scum. Stew steers him toward a garbage can to slog through his discomfort.

"This, Gerald, is why I told you that you could not go on any rides," Aunt Shirley screeches at him.

My mother wobbles a bit upon exiting the car. Aunt Simone reaches into her bag for a facial towelette, which she hands to her sister. My mother takes it without even a sliver of hostility. Look at that: two family members have bonded over their dislike of roller coasters.

Emma and Troi abandon our group after the ride. My parents and Aunt Simone's family also go their separate ways. Uncle Curtis runs after them, but they ignore him.

Aunt Shirley hitches her purse strap onto her shoulder. "Gerald, we're leaving."

He braces his hands on the rim of the garbage can. "But Mother, we've only just gotten here. Please, can I stay a little longer?" A lost little boy peeks through the eyes of a sixty-year-old man when he asks for her permission.

"Is this how you want to spend your day, leaning over a trash bin?"

He wipes his mouth and sets his eyes, growing into a man. "I'm having fun. I am staying."

Aunt Shirley nearly topples from the shock of Gerald's disobedience. Her lips flap against each other like a fish until she finds her words. "Suit yourself. But when you come home with an upset stomach from too much excitement, I will not be nursing you through it."

"I understand. I hope you have a safe journey home." Gerald straightens the collar of his shirt and holds his head high.

Aunt Shirley digs in her purse for her MetroCard. She crosses Surf Avenue, leaving us without another word.

Stew wraps his arm around Gerald's shoulders. Gerald beams. "Mother always tells me I'm built for a quieter life. Maybe I am, but I'd still enjoy seeing you kids have fun today. Give me another minute, and then we can go explore the park."

I need to build new synapses in my brain for dealing with my step-uncle. His mother may have messed him up, but underneath Gerald's mortician-confused-by-the-world persona lies a very dear man.

I hand him a bottle of water. "I'll probably nix half of the rides the guys want to try. We can keep each other company while they try to die."

He trusts the wall behind him to hold him upright until his legs are ready for the task. "That's nice of you, Lauren. But don't stay behind on my account."

"So where to next?" Johnny asks.

Stew scratches his head and searches the map for the most barf-inducing rides. "Dude, I gotta try the Soaring Eagle. You're suspended below the track on your belly. Oh. And the Thunderbolt looks cool, too."

"Totally. You guys ready?" Daniel asks, offering Gerald a hand.

They and Stew lead the way. Johnny falls into pace next to me on our way to the next section of the park.

"I never knew you were from Brooklyn," I say. It hadn't occurred to me in high school that students at my school on the Upper East Side lived in boroughs other than Manhattan. "How come you applied to Roosevelt?"

"It was my eighth-grade girlfriend's top choice. I wanted to go to one of the technical schools, someplace I could learn to work with my hands, but my parents pushed me to apply to academic-heavy schools like Roosevelt. I figured it wouldn't suck to go to the same school as my girlfriend, so I applied."

"Who was she? Was she in any of our classes?"

"Nah. She didn't get in."

"But you did." It startles me to hear my tone express surprise.

He laughs. "They knew the deal with me. A guy every teacher swore was smarter than his grades implied. They saw such *promise* in me, convinced they alone could turn me into a scholar. Guess I showed 'em."

Daniel catches up to us and commandeers Johnny's attention. I fall silent, lost in my mind. It's funny how insulated people are as teenagers. At an age when we think we are fearless, we stick with the familiar.

My friends and I earned similar grades, came from similar families, and had the same interests. I missed the chance to discover a world beyond the one in which my parents had raised me. Even had the whole history test incident never happened, I instinctively had written off a boy because on the surface, he was nothing like me.

I realize I haven't grown more adventurous in adulthood. And it's not simply because I live and work with my parents.

Aunt Donna's apartments — both the one near Lincoln Center and before that, in a building she converted in Tribeca — offered me my first taste of luxury real estate. Since my parents were realtors, I must have combined my desire to live in a fancy apartment with following in their footsteps professionally, which then morphed into my dream of selling fancy apartments. It's one thing to dream. But it's another to make the dream a reality. And, despite trying, I have nothing to show for my efforts.

I could have accepted Aunt Donna's offer to join her business. Or chosen a different broker as my employer. Instead, I've chosen the path of least resistance by working with my parents. And not done very well. I'm not unhappy with my life. But talking to Gerald — the king of keeping things safe — and learning a little more about Johnny has sparked something in me. I'm ready to take a more active role in realizing my dream.

"Earth to Lauren." Daniel pokes the top of my head.

"What? Were you saying something?"

"You want to try the new flume ride?"

"Oh, totally. That's way more my speed."

"Let's go together."

My brother wants to go on a ride with me? Alert the media. But wait. He's my brother. He has to have an ulterior motive. "Promise me there'll be no splashing."

He holds his fingers halo-like over his head. I'm not buying it.

"So, how's the diet pill business going?" I ask.

"I'll tell you something, but you can't say a thing to Mom."

"I won't, so long as you don't splash me."

"Hmm. Splash my sister or confide in her?" He pretends to deliberate on his choice. I elbow him. "Ouch. OK. I'll confess. So things went really badly during our first round of testing on humans. We didn't collect enough data to determine whether the diet pills worked. The subjects suffered from tons of side effects. No one died or anything, though."

"Well, at least there's that."

He continues without acknowledging my sarcasm. "What with the lawsuits the company is dealing with because of the pain meds/addiction issues and fears our experiment could bring on more, they made staffing cuts. I lost my job in March."

The conveyer belt deposits our boat at the top of an incline, and we plummet into a splash pool. I'm too busy screaming to say anything comforting to him.

When we jerk into motion, ascending the next belt, I say, "What a bummer. Did Genevieve also lose her job?"

"They moved her to a different department."

"Well, at least you still have her income. You looking for a new job?"

"Yeah, and a new place to live. We split. I guess I'm too much of a loser for her or something."

"Daniel, I'm—" We descend again. A huge wave engulfs our boat. It could be my imagination, but my mouth burns when it fills with water. I lean over the side of the log to spit it out. Ew, Brooklyn!

I turn toward Daniel. "I was saying I'm sorry before the tsunami hit us."

"You and me both."

"Why don't you move home? At least you'd be able to save money while you're on the job hunt."

"No way. I have enough to deal with. Being under Mom's watch would not be good for me. Inheriting Aunt Donna's money would."

"It sure could make a lot of dreams come true."

"Yup. Look, I'm not off to a good start with this competition. I was hoping to get to know Johnny, see if I could weasel a hint or two from him. You guys are all chummy. You planning the same thing, using him to your advantage?"

I bolt upright in anger. "I'm so totally not. Come on!"

"But you two are hitting it off. You were the first of us to spend one-on-one time with him when you met him in the park for the first challenge."

It hits me: no one knows Johnny and I went to school together. Anyone could have heard us discussing high school earlier, but they didn't. He and I should discuss what to do if anyone discovers our history. Regardless, I'm certainly not going to use him to my advantage. That would be unfair.

I shake my head. "Johnny swore his role is to remain neutral."

"OK. So maybe my plan's DOA. But you were closer to Aunt Donna than anyone else except for Emma. You know stuff about her that could help me win. Do you want to work together secretly? I'd share some of the

113

inheritance with you if I won. And you, of course, would do the same for me."

I gag from the metallic taste Daniel's suggestion leaves in my mouth. My stomach lurches. I think of Emma. No wonder I made her mad.

I suggested forming an alliance with her because she might remember an important fact Aunt Donna had revealed to her. Daniel asked for my help because I'm in a better position than him. What did he offer to do to help me win? Nothing.

We both did something far worse than cheat. We sucked up to a relative, motivated to use them for our own gain without reciprocating.

I hate myself as much as I hate him, but I can't push him away. It sucks to be him right now. "Thanks for the offer. I'm not into the whole idea of competing against each other, but Johnny explained how we aren't really doing that. We each have to prove we're worthy heirs. It doesn't feel right for me to make a secret pact with you. But I hope you win. And if you don't but I do, I promise to take care of you. OK?"

"I suppose. But let me know if you change your mind."

"You got it, bro."

I shouldn't tell him I have my fingers crossed behind my back.

CHAPTER SIXTEEN
STEALING VICTORY FROM CHILDREN

The *Rocky Horror/American Gothic* version of Gerald went back to Queens with his mother, leaving behind a man I've never taken the time to get to know. Also missing in action is my urge to ditch him like a plate of Alfredo sauce and olive brine-drenched wedding cocktail hour sushi scraps. While Johnny, Daniel, and Stew risk life and limb on the rides, Gerald and I lean against one wall and then another, talking with each other. True, my eyes glaze over from his unending detail-filled description of his job as manager of a GameStop in Queens. And while purging my Gerald-related prejudices improves the experience of hanging with him, I'd still prefer not to make a habit of it. Especially when I glance above me, searching for Johnny's sneakers amongst the circle of screaming people riding the Luna 360 and imagining what I'm missing.

The daredevils finally disembark the ride, but being back on the ground doesn't mean Johnny is ready to stand still. He runs toward a game kiosk with a shriek.

"Water Racer! I love this game!"

Three young kids sit in front of targets, swiveling the inactive water guns in front of them. Another two hand their tickets to the attendant and claim seats. Johnny grabs my hand.

"Water Racer will be more to your liking. All you have to do is squirt water at the target. Whichever player lights their pole first, wins."

I'm not loving him thinking I'll only have fun doing baby things. I grudgingly take the seat on the end. The attendant stands next to me and tells us to begin. I try to swivel my gun toward the target. It has a mind of its own, veering hard left and targeting the attendant.

He stamps his way toward me. "Young lady, game's over. Rule number one is no squirting me."

"But the gun—"

"No buts." He points behind me with his thumb, evicting me from the game.

A bell rings. Johnny springs from his seat and runs back and forth behind the other players. "Water Racer! I am the champeeeeen!"

He taps the shoulder of a young girl who sits dejected following the trouncing she suffered at his hands. "Which prize do you want?" he asks her.

"The blue guy," she says, reaching for the stuffed animal when the attendant hands it to her. Her grin glows brighter than the lighted column in front of her.

Johnny zooms back to our group, bursting with pride for having vanquished five young children and a woman with a broken water gun. "What next?"

"Can we go on the Wonder Wheel?" I ask.

"Ferris wheels are for wusses," Daniel teases me.

"I have no problem being labeled a wuss."

Stew fiddles with his wristband. "Another company owns the Wonder Wheel. You need to pay for it separately."

"Again, not a problem."

"I'd go with you." Johnny's eyebrows lift when he makes eye contact with me.

Daniel rolls his eyes. "Stew, let's take another run on Screaming Eagle."

Stew turns toward Gerald. "What do you want to do?"

"I think I'll find a bench and enjoy a little rest."

I clap my hands. "Sounds like a plan. Let's meet back here in half an hour, OK?"

My brother and cousin race toward their ride. Because the sun has sapped my energy, I move in slow motion next to Johnny. I'm relieved to take a break from my brother and my cousins. Johnny's relaxed vibe suits my mood, encouraging me to broach a sore subject.

"I never got over failing a test because of you, you know."

He chuckles. "Oh, don't I know it. Little Miss Straight A's took a walk on the dark side, and she didn't like it."

"It was so unfair. I didn't look at the answers. I thought I was doing the right thing by turning the answer key in to Mrs. Larch."

"Was assuming I had stolen it the right thing to do?"

"When I gave Mrs. Larch the sheet, I told her you had found it."

"And I thank you for putting it that way. But did you really believe my story?"

He has a point. I didn't have proof he had stolen it, but secretly, I never fully believed him.

"You never told me where you found it. I couldn't help but suspect you weren't telling the whole story."

He leans against a light pole. "Can I tell you my side of the story?"

"Of course."

"I ran into Jake Lipschitz, Donny Bellingham, and Carlos Villanueva on the subway to school that

117

morning."

"I would have died if I had been on the subway with you! They were like royalty at Roosevelt." I sigh for my teenage self having missed an opportunity to be with the objects of my crushes outside of school.

"Please. They weren't anything special. Would you have wanted to date a cheater?"

The word *cheater* makes my heart screech to a stop. "What do you mean?"

"I sat with them on the subway. They were poring over the sheet, writing the answers on their arms in marker. Donny confessed to having stolen it from Mrs. Larch the day before."

"No way!"

"Way. Since they had finished with it by the time we got to our stop, they handed it to me. I didn't want to tell on them, but I didn't want to get caught with it, either. You made the choice for me. I was sorry you got in trouble, but it was the right thing to do, giving it to Mrs. Larch. Keeping silent was no better than lying. I admired you for handling it with such a firm sense of right and wrong."

"You did?" I wish my younger self could have appreciated the decision Johnny faced. I assumed the worst about him. That's not who he was. Or is.

He brushes his hair out of his eyes. The gesture makes my heart race. He holds my stare until I have to turn away, scared he'll read my mind. And trust me: he'd be blushing as hard as me if he had any inkling about the scenes playing in my mind.

His eyebrows pulse again before he answers my question. "I did. And I admire you still. You cared deeply for your aunt and have a strong moral sense."

I lower my chin, feeling the blood rising in my cheeks. "So, am I winning yet?" I throw him a playful grin.

"Can't say."

We walk in silence. I take quick peeks at him along the way. How could I have had crushes on Jake, Donny, and Carlos when Johnny was clearly the better choice? I chalk it up to not being mature enough to appreciate him for who he was.

He buys credits for the ride from the clerk at the booth and ushers me toward the one-hundred-year-old iconic Ferris wheel. "Do you want to ride in a swinging car?"

I watch the red and blue cars scoot and swing within the wheel's structure. They induce my stomach to churn. "No thanks. The white cars go higher. We'll get a better view."

With so few people waiting in line for the stationary cars, the attendant gives us our own car. My stomach swings and soars. I've been alone with Johnny before. Why is this different?

I know why. This is the first time we've been alone since I've banished the mistaken prejudices I've carried with me for over a dozen years. Johnny is a decent man, one who puts me at ease, who has a strong moral center. But he is also a man who makes my palms sweat and my hormones sing. A man whose leg presses against mine, competing with the early June sun as a source of warmth.

Our car rises a few feet to bring the car behind us to the platform. Four more people wait for their turn to board. I can't wait to be airborne.

We jolt to a stop again. We're now high enough to see the ocean. Before I sync with the tranquility of the view, a blue Ferris wheel car careens toward us from behind. "It's going to hit us!" I cling to the cage in fear.

Johnny laughs at me. "Man, you would have been fun to watch on a swinging car."

"I thought stationary meant we would be safe. Where

are the seat belts in this thing?"

"I'll protect you." His eyes grow fiery with passion, and I need no convincing he's up for the job.

Finally, we reach the top. The entirety of New York City spreads below us. The waves etch pale, wiggly lines in the water. In the distance, the skyline of Manhattan appears in miniature. The sounds of the piped-in music of the amusement parks and the shrieks of the attendees below grow quieter.

Johnny's arm collides with my shoulder when he points to a cruise ship sailing beneath the Verrazano Bridge. I lean into his arm. The view becomes far less engaging as my skin prickles from touching him. He blinks in slow motion and rolls his lips to moisten them with a quick flick of his tongue. My back arches ever so slightly.

He lowers his hand into his lap and bends toward me. I hold my breath. His kiss is weightless. I can't determine whether the spinning of the wheel is making me dizzy or if it's the touch of his mouth on mine.

He pulls away, again licking his lips. His eyes form a question. I answer by grabbing his head and drawing him to me. His neck stiffens, and his eyes crinkle, testing my desire to return to kissing him. It's my turn to lift my eyebrows before I grin at him.

Our second kiss loses the tentative touch of our first. His hand slips between my back and the bench. His fingertips dig into my shoulder blade with a rhythmic pulse. He smells of the spicy warmth of the knish he ate before we rode the Ferris wheel, but I taste only the peppermint candy he popped in his mouth after his snack. I may forever grow horny whenever I eat at Nathan's or encounter a bowlful of white and red-striped candies.

His stubble grinds against my neck, but I don't mind. The thing he's doing with his tongue behind my ear is totally worth the stubbleburn. I roll toward him and straddle his lap. My hair cascades into his face. He spits a clump out of his mouth. We don't have a chance to laugh because he's pulling me in for another kiss. Boy, I'm glad this ride doesn't have safety belts.

His hands wrap around my butt, keeping me from sliding off his lap. I could kiss him all day long. It's impossible to resist taking a break to stare at him, though. His eyes are full of sparks now. They reflect my face. Not that I need a mirror to recognize how happy I am.

The wheel lurches to a standstill. We're one stop away from descending back to earth. I lunge for a last, sweet kiss. Our lips break apart with a pop when the attendant opens the door.

I want to grab his hand, to remain tethered to him. But my family is nearby, and Johnny is the last person I should be making out with.

He reads my mind and lets the distance expand between us while we walk to our meeting spot. Daniel, Stew, and Gerald are licking snow cones. I immediately conjure lascivious fantasies involving Johnny and frozen treats. Sigh.

Daniel rises from the bench to meet us. "I heard from Mom. They're ready to leave. We'll meet them at the subway station."

I nod. "Sounds good."

Johnny catches up with Stew and Gerald. I'm aching to be near him again, but separation is better for appearances.

Daniel furrows his brow. "Hey, why's your face red?"

"Maybe I have a sunburn?" I touch my cheeks gently, registering the puffiness and heat of the skin on my jaw. More like stubbleburn.

Please don't figure it out. Please don't figure it out, I plead with Daniel telepathically.

He stops, disappointment oozing across his face. "Shit, Lauren. Tell me you didn't."

"Didn't what?"

"Don't play this game. I don't believe your innocent act for a second. I made you a decent offer to split the estate fifty-fifty. But you were all holier-than-thou, telling me we shouldn't gain any advantages over our relatives. Meanwhile, you were plotting to make Johnny your bitch. You kissed him, didn't you? Unbelievable!"

He quickens his pace to catch up to Johnny and my cousins.

"Wait, Daniel. If you say anything to anyone about Johnny and me, I'm telling Mom your news."

My threat stops him. But when I reach him, he starts walking again.

I raise my voice. "You have the wrong idea. I don't know what I was thinking. It was a mistake to kiss him. Just a stupid thing that means nothing to me whatsoever."

Johnny's head whips around. He tames the burning flames in his eyes into focused lasers upon meeting mine. We stare at each other for a moment before he turns away. I drag my feet, falling farther behind the group.

What will my mother do if she finds out? Will one kiss doom my chance of becoming Aunt Donna's heir? And Johnny. How can I make him stop hating me? Regardless of which aspect of my life I question, each answer I stumble on pricks me like a poisoned thorn.

CHAPTER SEVENTEEN
MAKE WAY FOR THE REAL
ESTATE LADY

My heart swoops and plunges in a ride more terrifying than any at Luna Park. It's not like I want to pay attention to the cacophony in my head that drives my emotions. But sitting alone at the far end of the subway car on the journey home, it's impossible to ignore a certain recent event.

Hands down, kissing Johnny is now one of my absolute favorite activities. The memory of every tingle, every halted breath, every moment he gripped me as if I alone suspended him in midair above New York City cuts through the searing pain he inflicted on my heart with his parting glance.

The kiss tells only part of the story. His moral compass is true. I may have hated him in high school, but he also fascinated me. He doesn't lose himself by trying to please people. Nor does he force his personal agenda on the world. In his company, my mind doesn't race toward a hypothetical future or a mythologized past. The world slows enough for me to see the present. And with him, the present is good.

I didn't say what he thinks I said. How obtuse is he? Surely our kiss made his toes curl and electricity course along his spine. You can't fake chemistry. My words shouldn't matter to him. His body knows I meant everything I did to him while we were on the Wonder Wheel.

But right now, I can't explain to him why I said what I said. Not with my entire family coalesced into a mob around him on the other end of the car. Even Emma and Troi deigned to rejoin the Piccolo clan on the ride home.

This is all Daniel's fault. It's not enough for him to crash and burn; he has to take me down with him, too. He's a grown-ass man, yet he can't be honest with his mother. Johnny may not have marched straight to our teacher when he held the answer key in his hands, but he didn't deny that he had been in possession of it, either. A fifteen-year-old had a better sense of right and wrong than my thirty-four-year-old brother. The only thing keeping Daniel from spilling the beans about Johnny and me is his fear of admitting to our mother that his life isn't the model of perfection she imagines it to be. Real mature.

I don't want Johnny to be mad at me. And, oh, my goodness, I want to turn kissing him into a career.

Dang it. Even if he forgives me, we can't start a relationship now. Uncovering Aunt Donna's mission without destroying my family in the process should be my priority. What I need is a plan. Making plans is my jam. I feel better just thinking about plans.

Best I start with the least scary part of the plan, which would be patching things up with Emma. After she and I make up, I have to persuade Johnny that what I intended to accomplish with my comment was to defuse the bomb Daniel was about to lob. He has to believe my explanation.

Once I'm back in his good graces, I can determine how to have my Johnny cake and eat it too. Does he like me enough to wait until we complete the will-related nonsense? I hope so because I have a serious crush on the man.

I swoon over the memory of our kiss yet again.

Quit it, Lauren. You were formulating a logical plan to get you out of this mess, remember?

Without question, it's time for me to start killing it as a realtor. Enough with subsisting on the dregs and scraps my parents toss me. They're content to peddle lower-priced properties. With their top listings rarely soaring into seven-digit territory, mine never will unless I find my own leads.

Finally, I have to figure out whether my relatives really are as shallow and greedy as they've led me to believe. Even if they are, can I find a way for us to be kind to each other?

Ta-da! I have a plan. Good planning always yields good results, right?

My mother swings chimpanzee-style from pole to pole toward me. "I don't know why you chose to sit by yourself." She hovers over me rather than take the empty seat next to me.

"All the noise and action in the park was exhausting. I wanted to chill by myself for a bit," I lie to her.

"I monitored you the whole ride. Pickpockets target young women who sit by themselves. And you know how Brooklyn is."

I opt out of picking apart her prejudices. "Thanks, Mom."

"Everyone except for us is getting off at Herald Square. Emma will pay for someone to drive Gerald to Queens. None of us has faith he can make it home on his own."

"How sweet of her," I say in a monotone.

"Oh, of course Johnny isn't getting off with them. I guess he'll stay on the D train up to that *building* of Donna's."

Which reminds me my mother has a story to tell about why she and Aunt Donna had a falling out. I have to wonder what role the building on 97th Street plays in the story.

No. I'm not interested. I say to myself. *Focus on you. Letting everyone's drama during the quests suck me in spells doom.*

My mother adjusts her feet to counter the grinding turn the subway makes. "We'll switch to the 1 at Columbus Circle. I came here to tell you in case it confuses you when everyone else leaves the train."

Again, I keep my opinions to myself. No need to remind my mother I have memorized most of the New York City subway map, or at least the stations in Manhattan.

"Thanks."

"Why don't you come sit with us?"

"I think I'll stay here until Columbus Circle."

"Suit yourself."

I watch her repeat her pole dance the length of the car, feeling more conspicuous than before.

The day after mapping out a new plan for myself, I give myself permission to color outside the lines. While exploring real estate opportunities beyond those my parents pursue, I land on a listing no client of ours wants. Embracing freedom leaves me dizzy. I can't explain the jitters turning my innards into a power plant. I need a serious pep talk to push myself into the apartment when I attend the open house.

A realtor who is one part human, one part elf bounds in front of me. "Welcome! If your dream is to own a pristine, two-bedroom home in a full-service, prewar building on Central Park West, you've come to the right place. If you want a dingy hole-in-the-wall with no amenities, well, you'll be disappointed," he says with a forced laugh.

This is the banter of a realtor who sells properties in a higher price range? Clearly, I've been doing it wrong.

"I'm looking on behalf of my clients. They couldn't make it today. I'm sure they'll be sorry they missed the open house." I wonder what my fake clients are doing today? Entertaining the Queen at their home in the Hamptons, perhaps?

"They will love it. I'm Gus. Here. Take a sheet. It has all the facty-wacties on it. And here's my card."

The name of his company rings a bell, but I don't speak bell. I'll research it later. It's possible I've met other realtors from his office at one open house or another.

The apartment has been on the market for over a year. It's obvious the family no longer lives here by the staged furniture. Spare furnishings itching to be unobtrusively elegant imply people *could* live here.

I analyze the apartment from Emma's perspective. She and I have sort of made up, at least according to our texts. We're in the awkward I-was-a-complete-fool-and-don't-know-how-to-behave-around-you stage. Hallmark must have the perfect card to mark the occasion.

She once taught me to spot the difference between apartments furnished for living versus for showing. The choices here wouldn't impress her. They lack warmth and soul.

My fingers trail the edge of a heavy gray curtain framing the bay windows overlooking 64th Street. The park is tantalizingly close. Were this an end unit with east-facing windows, the price would soar well above its current one-point-seven million price tag.

A young couple takes tentative steps into the living room. The woman clutches the same paperwork I have already stashed in my pocketbook. The couple's eyes move quicker than their feet, darting from the fireplace to the bay windows.

Possessing no more courage than them, I force myself to adhere to my rules regarding step four of my plan: become the realtor I'm meant to be.

I point to the fireplace. "A little warm for a fire today, huh?" I smile, not trusting my words to be funny enough on their own.

"Oh, we're all for increasing the opportunities to sweat," the man says. "Or making the competition sweat. Are you planning to put in a bid today? 'Cause if you are, we will—" His companion makes a throat slash gesture at him. "Just kidding. We're not putting in a bid. This place is out of our price range."

"It's fun to look, though," I say. "Checking out listings above and below your range can help bring into focus what you want or need. I'm a realtor. I came to assess the apartment for some clients, but I don't think this is the home for them. They wanted a park view."

"The only park view we can afford will be a crayon rendition. Perhaps I'll commission my nephew to draw us one." His wan smile conveys his disappointment.

"Are you working with a realtor?"

The man screws his face and bobbles his head. "I wouldn't say we're *working* working with someone. He's shown us one listing so far and sent us here today. He's busy with another open house, which is why we're here on our own. Both listings are exclusive with his office, and both are not what we're looking for."

The woman chimes in, "We're motivated to buy. I'm not sure he's motivated to sell to us. Two listings in three weeks? Does that sound normal?"

I picture my parents' phones in front of their place

settings at the dinner table. If a client wanted to see listings at two in the morning, they would make it happen. An appointment ends when the client calls it a day, not when my parents run out of listings to show them. And under no circumstances would they only show a client listings well above their budget.

I tread with care. Instinctively, I know they are with the wrong realtor. But it would be unethical for me to offer my services or drop hints I am better than whatever realtor they've chosen. Were they to infer they need a new realtor on their own...

"You and your agent are still getting to know each other. If you want to step up the pace of visiting properties, mention it to him. And reiterate what your budget is. It's your money, not his. It could be he's taking your list of features literally and showing you apartments with everything you want. Discuss which features are negotiable."

"You've already listened to us more than he has. We're not bound to him, are we?"

"Buying a home is a monumental investment. You are in control, and the realtor you choose should enhance your sense of control, not diminish it."

The woman presses her fingertips to her lips. "Do you only show your own listings, or will you show anything?"

"Oh, I'll show you any units I think you'll like. I make it a point not to represent both the buyer and the seller."

The couple turns toward each other, speaking with their eyebrows.

"Could we have your card?"

Bubbles rise in my body. The elation would not be greater had I sold a multi-million dollar listing. I have never been so eager to hand someone my card before. But a molecule of sliminess oozes into my conscience, making me squirm. Is this how my parents' least favorite realtor, Leon, conducts his business?

I'm not like him. No harm will come from me offering them a card. "I would love to help you find your dream home. Before we discuss your needs, though, I hope you'll explain to your broker why you want to move on to someone else. Perhaps a little nudge is all he'll need to remember to give you the attention you deserve. In the event you still think he's the wrong realtor for you after you discuss your needs with him, tell him you're going to pursue other options and then call me to make an appointment."

For the first time since they walked into the apartment, the couple breaks into relaxed smiles. They assure me they'll be in touch soon. Without venturing beyond the living room, they make their departure.

Lauren Bent, real estate lady, is on the move!

CHAPTER EIGHTEEN
CREEPY, YET SWEET

E mma's eyes don't spark when she sees me from the entrance of the café. They dart around with distrust. My heart kathumps heavily while she makes her way to my table. Her hug doesn't bring its usual closeness. My stomach flops and twitters. I'm not sure lunch is on its menu.

I fumble for how to start our first real face-to-face conversation since our fight. It's day two of my New Lauren, New Life plan. Wasn't making up with Emma supposed to be the easiest step? "Thanks for schlepping to the Upper West Side. Work is busy, so my lunch break has to be short today." My words escape my mouth before my brain can catch them, tangling my tongue in curt phrases.

"Don't give it a second thought. I'm not doing anything today."

"But Troi is?" I had invited him to join us as a buffer.

"He's working."

I shimmy my head and hands in disbelief. "Stop the presses. He has a job?"

"Of course, he does. He may joke about maxing out my Black card, but he manages the bills for his ever-growing wardrobe on his own."

"Who knew?"

"Well, I did. You never asked." The tone in her voice doesn't encourage me to beg for her forgiveness.

The jangling bells on the door distract me. I peer at the guests who enter. Their features disappear in the shadows.

Emma's expression doesn't give away what's going on in her mind. I engage my defense mechanisms to minimize the searing pain of the distance between us. Turning into my teenage know-it-all self, I say, "I read somewhere that Europeans find Americans crass because we always ask people what they do right after we meet. I've decided to let people define themselves from the start rather than grill them about their jobs. If Troi doesn't want his job description to influence my perception of him, who am I to force the issue?"

She reaches for my hand and massages it. I will my skin to absorb any dregs of the quality moisturizer that have rendered Emma's skin smoother than Kenny G's music. "That's so you, Lauren. You're such a good person. I hate to have given you the impression I didn't believe otherwise. Can we move past our little tiff?"

My shoulders peel away from my earlobes. "I'm so glad you brought up the topic. I knew we had to talk about it, but I've been terrified about making things worse. I didn't know where to begin."

"All you had to do was invite me to lunch." She reaches for her menu with a laugh.

"I didn't mean anything dishonest by suggesting we form an alliance. After my brother made me a similar offer, albeit one with decidedly slimy motives, I heard my plan through your ears."

She fans her fingers in front of her. "I reacted too

harshly. But the way you reacted to me made me believe I had touched a nerve, which then made me doubt your motives. Which was wrong. I'm totally at fault here."

The wooden legs of my chair scrape against the tiled floor with a squeal when I scoot closer to the table. "No, I am. It was stupid of me to suggest partnering with you." I rest my elbows on the table. "And as for how I've acted ever since, it's only fair to tell you that being called a cheater is a trigger for me."

"We may have the same trigger, then. Troi had upset me earlier with his joke about keeping tabs on me in case I cheated on Brandon. I would never cheat on my husband. But for some irrational reason, I had been stewing over whether Brandon was cheating on me. I now realize my doubts are ridiculous. Between my cuckoo fit of jealousy and learning that my father had stolen my trust fund, I had my dishonesty filter set to high. I shouldn't have measured you with the same tools. Forgive me?" She cranes her neck forward, her face full of hope.

My worries float away. Crossing "fight with Emma" from my list of things that suck makes the rest of my problems appear smaller, more manageable. "Of course! And I'm sorry I held a meaningless grudge for way too long."

"Let's forget it even happened and talk about fun stuff. For instance, what's Daniel up to?" Her eyebrows pulse with her eagerness for family gossip.

I heave a sigh. "Tormenting me. He has his reasons for wanting to get his mitts on Aunt Donna's cash, but he asked me not to tell anyone."

"I'll pretend I heard you say he needs a cash infusion to pay for his wedding, which is shaping up to be a shindig worthy of a Saudi prince."

"Yeah, that'll do."

"Where does the tormenting his sister part come in?"

"He thinks he has dirt he can use to blackmail me."

"Does he?"

I am dying to talk to *anyone* about Johnny. Just over a week since the kiss, the sweetness of its memory has soured since he hasn't contacted me. Mind you, I haven't texted him to explain anything, either. I want to write the perfect text, one he will mean to ignore but can't once he reads the first few words. Needless to say, I haven't written it yet.

Emma's eyes widen as she anticipates my answer. I clear my throat. "No, he doesn't. My life is an open book. Tormenting was the wrong word. He's mad because I won't help him, so he's grasping for anything to force me to change my mind."

"He should ask your mom. You always say she'll do anything for him."

"Yeah, that's not going to happen. The 'him asking her' bit."

Our server interrupts us. "Can I take your order?"

I lean to the left to keep the lighting fixture behind his head from shining in my eyes. "I'll have the quiche." Rolling my butt against the chair's surface, I return to center.

I need to find my balance. Fighting — and making up — with my cousin doesn't send me off-kilter. But Johnny does. Interacting with him is worse than any gut-churning ride at Luna Park. I should ask Emma to help me sort through the flotsam. But I can't reveal everything.

While she places her order, I devise a plausible variation on the Johnny story to share with her.

I take a fortifying sip of my iced tea. When we're alone, I say, "So, I recently had a toe-curling, brain-altering kiss with a guy." I paste an enigmatic smile on my face, hoping to force Emma to beg for the story.

She falls for the bait. "Oh, my god! I need all the

details! Who is he? Any upcoming opportunities to kiss him again?"

"That's the thing. I need your advice about how to proceed. Here's what went down. I was out with a friend a week ago. We met a couple of guys at a bar. Anyhow, one of them and I hit it off. And we had this amazing kiss. I liked him a whole lot before it, but kissing him, man!" I don't need to rely on acting to sell the kiss to Emma via my expression. My lips buzz with the memory of Johnny's. I lean against the backrest of my chair and trace the patterns of ceiling tiles in my mind.

Emma interrupts my reveries. "He sounds perfect. Why do you need my advice?"

"The situation isn't as easy-peasy as it appears. First of all, he just ended a relationship, and the kiss took him by surprise. He said now might not be the right time for him to start something with me."

"I'm getting the impression the kiss didn't affect him the same way it did you."

I raise my voice in defense. "No. That's not it."

Idiot. You just made up with Emma, and now you're battling with her again?

Obviously, I missed a few holes in my re-engineered version of the story. Johnny had the same mind-bending experience during our kiss, right?

Dialing the tone knob down to friendly, I bolster my fake story. "He asked for my number after we kissed, and he gave me his. He seemed like he was interested in me and wanted to go out again in a month or so."

Her expression conveys doubt in my future with my hypothetical man. I have to remind myself not to take it personally, that I need a reason to explain why Johnny and I can't hook up right now.

Emma erases the silence with a snicker. "Uh, huh. And your question is?"

"I'm not done with the story. He and his friend left to

use the bathroom, and I began describing Gerald to my friend."

"A second after you kiss a guy, you decide what you really need to talk about with your friend is our cousin Gerald?"

"She was the one who wanted to find a date. It was awkward since she didn't hit it off with the other dude. I chose the least romantic topic I could conceive."

"That was nice of you."

"Thanks. So I'm saying to her how Gerald is really creepy, but I sort of think he's sweet, too. Anyhow, my would-be boyfriend overhears me and assumes I'm talking about him. I tried to explain, but before I could, he left the bar in a huff. My question is whether I should explain to him I was talking about someone else, or should I let it go? I mean, I like him. We connected in a way I haven't with anyone in ages."

A server passes our table, bearing a tray with ice cream sundaes on it. My eyes follow him to his table. A kid whose eyes reach an inch above the tabletop erupts with joy. He holds a long, slender spoon in his fist. His mother tucks a napkin into the collar of his shirt, laughing with him.

Emma drums her fingers on the tabletop. "Hmm. He has two strikes against him — he's not quite available, and he is a sensitive little bunny. I'd hate for you to build up your hopes he's ready for a real relationship if he's not. You wouldn't want to be his rebound, would you?"

"Honestly, that doesn't sound terrible to me. A second kiss would be great, but I haven't considered what I want beyond another kiss."

"It wouldn't hurt to text him, then. But make it a good text."

"I could use your help. All I've come up with is 'You're not creepy, but I am sweet on you.'"

"You've missed your calling. You should find a position in the greeting card industry."

"In my next life. But you think texting him is the way to go, right?"

"Since you want to kiss him again, yeah, reach out to him. His pride won't let him contact you."

"Men *are* sensitive little bunnies, aren't they?"

She does a slow shake of her head. "Way more than women. We had an exemplary role model in female toughness in Aunt Donna, didn't we?"

"Yeah, we did. Aunt Donna was the only unmarried woman I knew when I was a kid. I didn't understand it then, but later in, in college maybe, I understood how being single made her stronger and cooler. She did what she wanted; she was never lonely. She exalted in the freedom of being single."

"She erased the message behind the fairy tales for me. And then I found my Prince Charming and moved into a castle. I sometimes wonder if I disappointed her by marrying on the youngish side." Emma fiddles with her napkin, avoiding my eyes.

I reach for her hands, reciprocating the gesture that put me at ease earlier today. "She valued happiness above everything. And you've found happiness in your marriage."

She waits a beat before answering. "Of course. But look at how different my path is from hers. I wonder if it's pointless for me to try to win her challenge."

"Give me a break. My path differs from hers, too. She wanted someone to fill her shoes, but that doesn't mean we can't be ourselves while wearing them, does it?"

"That's a good way to look at it. And I suppose I'll have a better chance to judge my worthiness in next week's quest. You're going, right?"

"Yeah." I hope Johnny gets in touch with me before I

have to see him again. The last thing I need is to add more drama to my life. "My mother's surly because she has to take a few hours off during the middle of a workday."

"Tell me about it. My father texted me to say he can't fly in. I'm not exactly crying over having to miss a visit with dear Papa."

Despite making up with Emma, the remaining rifts in our family still cause my heart to ache. "I know we promised never to discuss the quests again, but I believe Aunt Donna bears at least some responsibility for splitting the family apart. Am I crazy?"

"Not at all. I've kind of wondered the same thing. But then there's Stew and Gerald becoming best buds."

"I know, right? They're adorable, the stoner and the loner."

"I'd go see that movie." The guests in the café swivel their heads toward us when we erupt in a fit of giggles.

She grows serious again. "You and I have made up, which is worth everything to me. And our parents spent an entire day together seeming no worse the wear for it."

"True. But now I'm fighting with my brother because of the quests."

She sniffs decisively. "Choose not to fight. We have no control over how anybody else acts. You do what is right for Lauren and don't worry about anyone else."

I envy her her conviction. "Everyone else is choosing to do what is right only for them."

"They'll either succeed or they won't. We don't know what Aunt Donna wants from us. Don't compromise your principals. And don't let anyone try to sink you. We may all lose, but you'll come out ahead provided you don't get sucked into the cesspool."

"Just in case, I'm going to wear a flotation device to next week's quest. A bright orange vest with a whistle and a light so you'll be able to find me."

CHAPTER NINETEEN
PLANNING IS OVERATED

J ohnny still hasn't replied to the texts I sent him last
night. While I shuffle behind my parents when we
exit the subway at Columbus Avenue, I reread the
thread for the fourteenth time, scanning it for any
unintentionally wayward and off-putting messages lying
below the surface.

Hey, Johnny- I'm still reeling from everything (good
& bad) that happened

Sorry it's taken me so long to reach out to you

My brother guessed what we had been doing
on the Wonder Wheel and accused me of
using you to get ahead

I swear I was just Lauren the woman, not Lauren the
potential heir when we were on the ride

I was scared Daniel would start spreading lies,

so I said things I expected would shut him up

Trust me, I don't think I made a mistake or did anything stupid

Totally the opposite

But we should talk

I don't want it to be super awkward for us to see each other tomorrow

Stella says hi, BTW

I shove my phone into my purse. Too many elements of my life are beyond my control. Can't we go back to April, before I ran into Johnny?

My brother wasn't being anything more than his regular douchey self. Emma hadn't learned what her father had done with her trust fund. And I wasn't riding the roller coaster of hating Johnny and not hating Johnny and then worrying that he hated me.

I could have visited Aunt Donna after meeting with Mrs. Ramos. I'm not saying I could have prevented my aunt from dying or anything. But I've never escaped the guilt of not telling her how much she meant to me one last time.

Most of all, that afternoon I had dreams and the motivation to pursue them. Desperation didn't drive me forward. I wasn't exactly sure of myself, but being unsure didn't leave me teetering on the ledge of an impossibly tall building, praying I didn't land splat on the sidewalk below.

I trip on the last step out of the subway station when I pick up my pace to catch up to my parents. My father grabs my arm to steady me. "Whoa, there. Don't want you to stumble. No need to run; we have plenty of time."

Of course, we do. We're forty-five minutes early. Mom never deviates from a schedule. Even now, while my father and I have dropped behind her, she keeps walking toward 60th Street.

"I've always meant to take a peek inside the Time Warner Center. Do you want to duck inside?" he asks.

He points to the curved building to my left. Its two glass towers, topped with serrated edges resembling eyelashes, slice through the bright blue sky. "It's just a shopping mall, but why not?"

My mother marches toward us with her features screwed up like a ticked off headmaster. My hands reflexively cover my butt in case she has a ruler she's ready to swing. "Richard, what are you doing?"

"Nothing, Zara. Lauren tripped, but I caught her. You should have slowed down when you noticed I wasn't with you."

"I didn't notice until I was a good hundred feet in front of you. You should have said something."

"Actions speak louder than words. Lauren may have fallen had I taken a second to inform you first."

It heartens me to see how my father's defense of me gives my mother a moment of pause.

He continues, "But I was thinking, since we're early, perhaps we could see what the Time Warner Center is all about."

"Oh, Richard. You and your spontaneous decisions. Just last weekend, you disappeared for two hours without a word."

"I didn't disappear without a word. Marc wanted to go on the rides. An aquarium can't compete with an amusement park, you know. Not for a twelve-year-old boy. Since Simone and Brock didn't want to take him, I volunteered. I assumed you heard the whole conversation."

"Clearly I didn't. But that's not the point. We had made plans to visit the aquarium, and you changed them on a whim."

"Um, Mom? We didn't make plans. Johnny did. And his plans were to go to the amusement park. So, technically, you were being spontaneous, not Dad."

My father's face radiates both victory and pride. My mother's, not so much.

She grunts and sniffs for a moment. "Why is it that people who make plans are always at the mercy of those who don't? Take these tourists. They're trudging along, not paying attention to where they're going or the fact that they're blocking the sidewalk. Some of us have planned our routes. Yet, because they're ahead of us, they're the ones who get to exert their influence over how and when we arrive at our destination."

"My apologies for suggesting we alter your plans. We don't need a detour." My father plants a kiss on the crown of her head.

My mother mutters under her breath, "Maybe we do need to detour. Would you believe the people in front of us? Five adults and two children spread across the width of the sidewalk like no one else is walking here."

She makes her move to bypass the blockage. When she veers around the little girl on the left flank, the girl points to the flags hanging at the entrance into the Mandarin Oriental Hotel. She pokes my mother in the gut and cries from the pain of stubbing her finger.

"Rude," says the woman holding the girl's hand to my mother. "Look where you're going before you end up hurting a little child."

My father wraps his arm around my mother's shoulder, preventing her from speaking her mind to the tourists. "Zara, you always assume a planned route takes you to the right destination. But sometimes life surprises us and takes us where we should be instead. Ooh!"

He drops into a squat. Rising, he presents my mother with a quarter. "If we had marched ahead as planned, I wouldn't have found this quarter. See?"

For the second time in less than two minutes, my father has stumped my mother. We may be looking at a personal record.

My mother remains silent while we wait on the steps of a church for the rest of my family. And Johnny. My churning gut won't let me forget about him. Nor will the parts of me that thrive on reliving the memory of our kiss. My body is way confused. You'd think I had tasked it with solving the problems in the Mideast.

My mother checks her watch with a harrumph. "They told us to be here at eleven-fifteen. Where is everyone?"

"Hey. Isn't that the lawyer we met at Aunt Donna's apartment?" I point to the one man wearing a suit amidst a sea of casually dressed tourists.

"Yoo-hoo! Mr. Rankin!" My mother waves her arms wildly. He responds with a gesture as conservative as his suit.

Emma emerges from a cab behind him, and I rush toward her. "You'd better hurry before my mother instructs the lawyer to hand out demerits to anyone who arrives late."

"Aunt Zara missed her calling. There's a position with her name on it in the German rail system."

A few minutes later, Alexander, the lawyer, counts heads. Our clan is smaller than last weekend. We number eight. Marc and Uncle Curtis aren't joining us, nor are Aunt Shirley and Gerald. And one other absence echoes dully.

Alexander says, "Right. We're set. Johnny sends his apologies; he has to manage a plumbing mishap at one of your aunt's buildings."

My heart flutters at the mention of Johnny's name. Did he stay home to avoid me? Isn't it better not to deal with him today, given my family's dynamic? I'd say I don't know what I want, but I'd be lying. I want things to be OK between us. And I want, well, him.

Alexander rubs his palms together. "Today you will take part in what was a weekly activity for Donna. Every Tuesday at eleven-thirty, she volunteered at the church's food pantry. I'm glad you're wearing comfortable clothes. Our task involves manual labor, but keep in mind it was work an eighty-nine-year-old woman could handle. You'll join two other volunteers to restock the shelves."

Simone quakes in her Tod's driving moccasins at the horror of manual labor. My mother examines her fingernails, perhaps to bid her manicure farewell.

"Nearly fifteen percent of the City's residents suffer from food insecurity. This shelter provides food for sixteen hundred of them. While donations ensure that the pantry has food to hand out, money alone doesn't get the job done. Your aunt was a devoted volunteer, and she hoped to awaken the volunteer spirit in all of you."

"I'd say leaving the house before noon proves I'm as awake as I've ever been." Only Stew chuckles at his joke. Aunt Simone steps closer to Emma and me, distancing herself from her offspring.

"Follow me." Alexander leads us into a garage repurposed as a grocery store-slash-warehouse. Stacks of wooden crates and cardboard boxes line one section. Wire racks with signs in English and Spanish form aisles on the other side.

We fall into a line that bridges the space between the crates and the shelves. I stand far from my brother. He avoids my mother. Pete, the head of the pantry, solves Daniel's problem by putting him and Stew at the start of the line where they have to hoist the boxes of food before moving them down the line.

Assembly line-style, we take a box from the person on our left and hand it to the person on our right without moving our feet. Half an hour later, we've moved everything from the warehouse section into the grocery.

People pay trainers a fortune to coach them through a similar waist-swivel maneuver using a weighted ball. If I'm able to bend over without excruciating pain tomorrow, I may have stumbled onto the most saintly way to workout. Thank you, Aunt Donna!

We kick the boxes to their designated shelves. Emma bursts with excitement when the boss instructs us on how to organize the shelves. Creating order is her drug of choice. She doesn't need to be told twice to put like with like and to make sure the labels face outward.

She places her pointer over her lips. "Are the sign locations set in stone? I'm visualizing a new pattern. Could we try it?"

Pete waves his hands frantically. "No. Please do not move any of the signs. It's essential we keep the food items where the clients know to find them."

Emma jumps away from the shelf as if she had been told it was a bloodthirsty sea creature.

Pete instructs Aunt Simone and me to remove the boxes and crates once they're empty. I grab four wooden crates and head toward the warehouse. Aunt Simone follows me with a cardboard box.

"Um, Lauren?" She studies the cuticle below her left thumbnail.

"Yeah?"

"You've been doing really well in the quests. You knew where to go for the first challenge, and you and Johnny seem to talk a lot to each other. Has he told you what any of this means?"

"I suspect Aunt Donna wanted to be appreciated. If we couldn't appreciate her while she was alive, perhaps we can by sharing her experiences."

"That's very deep, but what does it have to do with her money?"

I connect what I had said to Emma last week about defining people by their occupations and how my relatives are trying to define Aunt Donna by her estate. A jolt courses through me. My revelation brings me closer to my great-aunt. "That's the point. We don't know her worth in terms of dollars. And maybe she didn't tally her holdings in terms of dollars, either. Her wealth enabled her to be generous, like what we're doing today. That's who Aunt Donna was: she was rich for what she did rather than what she owned."

"So true," coos Aunt Simone. "I've always thought so, too."

Is that a fact, Aunt Simone?

The thwack of a wooden crate hitting the cement floor a few feet away distracts me. Out of the corner of my eye, I glimpse the charcoal gray of the lawyer's suit. Oh. Aunt Simone was performing for him. Without making eye contact with me, Alexander returns to the grocery area.

When he's gone, Aunt Simone closes her eyes and waves her hands, palms out, at me. "You make her out to be some sort of generous saint but in reality, she was a selfish, mean old woman. We're her family. She should have made sure we were taken care of when she died. I mean, you can't take it with you, right?"

I stare at her with hollow eyes. Aunt Simone interprets my silence as approval and continues, "You get it. Wouldn't you love to inherit fifty-thousand dollars? You could move out of your parents' home."

Pretty generous of her, bequeathing me the same paltry sum Aunt Shirley belittled, all for helping her win the whole enchilada. I bite my tongue, avoiding mention of my cousin Stew's living situation while I'm at it.

"What you don't understand, Lauren, is what it costs for Brock and me to maintain the lifestyle his job requires of us. It was fine for me to live in Rego Park when I was married to Stew's father. He was just a teacher, but Brock, well, as the finance manager of a boutique public relations firm, he has to keep up appearances. We're underwater on our mortgage, and I doubt we'll be able to continue to send Marc to private school."

I've heard my mother deliver the same speech. "How can Simone expect a man who earns in the low one-hundreds to afford a two-bedroom condo on East 98th Street?" My mother never seems worried about Aunt Simone, though. In fact, I suspect she delights in her sister's foolishness.

I want to advise my aunt to move into a more budget-appropriate home like I've recommended to my new clients, the Johnsons, whose previous realtor steered them toward unaffordable choices. Living in the City is challenging enough without going broke trying to put a roof over your head.

"I hear you, Aunt Simone. You're in a difficult position. And yes, it's a situation that money could improve. But I don't know how to help you inherit the estate."

"Could we secretly help each other? You can share the clues you unearth with me. Who knows? If I won, I'd be happy to throw you a few thousand dollars."

Emma may be the queen of recognizing patterns, but I might be gaining on her. Daniel, Aunt Simone. Who else will suggest forming an alliance with me before we finish? And will anyone offer to help me? No. They're each trying to become the sole beneficiary.

Between dealing with Johnny and my relatives, I'm ready to give up.

CHAPTER TWENTY
ON A BAD DAY YOU CAN SEE
NEW JERSEY

The second my butt touches the cushion of a chair in our living room, Stella springs onto my lap ready for a cuddle.

"No French kissing!" I cover my lips with my hand while I speak, laughing and whipping my head to wherever her amorous mouth is not. She wags, ever so pleased with herself.

"And chill, while you're at it." When the kissing game loses its thrills, she navigates the terrain of my lap, her little paws digging into my thighs and groin while she searches for the comfiest spot. Satisfied she has finally found it, she drops with happiness. Her head cascades over my knee, exposing her chin for a round of scratches from her human.

Having accomplished absolutely nothing at the office, and stinging from Johnny's radio silence, I relish the quiet of the apartment and cuddle time with my dog.

My phone disturbs the peace. I grumble as I reach for it.

My mood elevates in an instant. I spring from the chair, deposit a miffed Stella onto the floor, and bounce around the living room.

"Your Uncle Johnny finally texted!" The blooping sounds continue to pop like bubbles, filling my screen with a tower of messages. "Stella, guess what? He feels totally bad for assuming the wrong thing about what he heard me yell to my brother at Coney Island. And he wanted to say so in person yesterday, but he had to deal with an icky, smelly mess regarding a misbehaving toilet. But plumbing problems don't interest you, do they? You like Johnny, though. So do I. Do you want to see him and his pack? He invited us to meet him in Riverside Park in an hour. I know, your precious little paws aren't made for long walks. I'll carry you in your special snuggy-wuggy until you want to walk. Five more minutes of cuddles, and then we have to get ready for Johnny!"

My diminutive sidekick shadows me through my frenetic preparation efforts. Should I keep on my real estate lady uniform to make it appear that I went straight from work? I can't arrive date-ready. He made me wait over a week for him to apologize for snubbing me. Besides, it can't be a date with four pooches in the mix.

"Stella, do you remember what happened the last time the six of us were together? That's right. You peed on Mommy's foot. I've forgiven you, but we don't want the excitement of reuniting with your pals to lead to a repeat performance, do we? We do not."

I say this as much for my benefit as for hers. Not that I'm prone to peeing on anyone's shoes when I'm excited. But it wouldn't hurt to tone down my eagerness.

I leave the house earlier than a person who claims to be indifferent about seeing the man she kissed eleven days ago should, although it is half an hour later than my mother would have sanctioned. Stella peers out of her kangaroo pouch, pointing her little nose toward all the wonderful smells. I deposit her on the sidewalk. She adds her own scent to the overflowing garbage can on the corner.

We amble along Riverside Drive, discussing the virtues of the apartments on this street as opposed to, oh, say, ours. "If we lived here, you wouldn't need to ride in a carrier on your way to the park. We'd be ready to roll from the start. Look up. You see the top row of windows? The residents there have views of both the park and the Hudson River. And New Jersey, which may not be a selling point. Maybe one day Mommy will close on an apartment with a river view."

We continue our discussion on the merits of location while seated on a bench at 104th Street to wait for Johnny. His pack comes into view first. Three large mutts, two of the tan variety, one in black, pull him toward me. He's slightly more in control of his pack than he was two and a half months ago. The absence of Stella, all fifteen pounds of her, must be the difference. She wiggles up a storm at their approach.

"Robert, Jane, and Gizmo, sit." Two dogs obey him. The third, a wiry blonde graced with long legs sixty-nines with Stella. "Jane," Johnny growls her name with bemused menace. "Like her namesake, Jane Jacobs, she's not easily cowed when she's on a mission."

"Who is Jane Jacobs?"

Johnny weaves Jane's leash under Stella's, detangling the two dogs. "Short version is she opposed Robert Moses' plans to destroy Greenwich Village. This—" He tugs the leash of the largest dog. "—is Robert. He's the newest member of the pack. Jane did not take kindly to him at first. I didn't want to pay homage to Robert Moses, but realizing she would win each tussle with him, I had no choice but to name him after Jane's nemesis."

He scratches the ears of the black dog with white paws at his side. "This here's Gizmo. Came with the name, and it suits her. Those paws of hers are tools. She can break into anything. She opens doors, bags of food. You name it, nothing's safe around her."

I stoop to snout level. "Nice to meet you. Do you remember Stella? Rumor has it she was a giant pain in the ass when she lived with you. But she's a good girl. I promise she won't steal your dinners ever again."

But what if... No. I can't drift away, dreaming of living with Johnny and his pack. It doesn't matter that being next to him sets my heart's tail wagging with the same ferocity as Stella's.

He points toward the park. "There's a dog run just inside. My couch potatoes need their exercise. Stella had a blast whenever I took her. Want to check it out?"

What I want to do is to run my fingers through your hair, perhaps work up to some kissing.

"Sure." Stella can't sustain a game of "Chase me. I have the ball" for longer than fifteen minutes at home. I hope she'll give me longer than that to be alone with Johnny.

We claim a shaded bench in the dog run and unleash the hounds. I have to tear myself away from gazing into Johnny's enticingly deep brown eyes when Stella bounds toward the dogs already playing in the park. For someone who chafes at walking, she sure runs like she means it. I sit up in alarm, worried about whether she intends to harm the dog she has targeted.

Johnny places his hand on my knee. I wish I had worn shorts instead of keeping on my slacks. Then the warmth of his hand against my—

His voice interrupts my reveries. "Don't worry. She's a pro at the dog park."

Sure enough, she stops short of the first dog she encounters, slowly bridging the distance between them with her nose. They go through an elaborate ritual of sniffs and wags. Approval won, she runs away from her new friend, glancing over her shoulder. He chases her, and I watch Stella be a dog rather than a spoiled little princess.

"What did I tell you?"

Johnny keeps his hand on my knee even after I relax. My fingers inch their way toward his until they become entwined. I'm twitching like an addict, wanting more contact with him. He pulls our hands into the neutral space between our legs. My stirrings subside.

Speaking of plumbing… "All's quiet on the toilet front?" I ask.

"Yeah. Sorry I had to miss yesterday. The super at my building had a family emergency, so I had to oversee the repair for him. Alexander told me you did well at the food pantry."

"We unpacked everything and organized the shelves."

"I meant you personally. Alexander mentioned how you especially connected to the meaning of the activity."

The melty, contented sensation of being with Johnny gives way to a cold, uncomfortable feeling. I withdraw my hand from his. "I don't think we should talk about Aunt Donna or the quests. It's too weird. My family is too weird. And you being in charge of determining who deserves to inherit her estate makes it even weirder."

He scoots a few inches away from me on the bench. "You're right. I shouldn't have brought it up. We're in a bit of an awkward situation, aren't we?"

The way he peaks the inside corners of his eyebrows gives me the information I need, but I want to hear the words. "How so?"

"Well, for starters, I might have had something of a crush on you back in high school."

He couldn't have surprised me more had he

confessed to being one of the seven dwarves.

"I swear I had no idea!"

He laughs. "And I thought I had game as a teenager. The teasing, the incessant staring never tipped you off?"

Of course I had noticed how he acted around me. But once I had reason to hate him, I definitely wasn't interpreting his behavior as romantic.

He looks at me shyly. "Can I tell you that when I first found out you were Donna's great-niece, I dreamed up ways for us to meet?"

"Why didn't you contact me?"

"I figured you wouldn't be, oh, as receptive to a reunion."

Remembering our encounter in Central Park in April, I nod. "Yeah, you figured right."

"I had to shove aside thoughts about you once I helped Donna draft her will. But after seeing you again, well, it became a challenge. Everything I had liked about you in high school had grown into something more brilliant and magnetic."

My skin tingles with the heat creeping up my face. "To be honest, despite rekindling my decidedly harsher feelings for you when we met again, I might have noticed certain qualities about you that, well, I had failed to notice when I was younger. High school wasn't the right time for us. Not that it is the right time now, what with all the complications…"

I trail off, finding it difficult to believe my own advice to put aside the desire I have for him.

He grins at me. "I see what you mean about it being complicated since I'm Aunt Donna's right-hand man and you're so incredibly kissable."

Every molecule in my body lines up to do the conga. I cue the band to begin playing, hoping to drown out my sense of reason. "Exactly. Don't forget the situation where you, Aunt Donna's right-hand man, are also incredibly kissable."

His lips slide into a smile. "Sounds like a tricky pickle, but I assure you one has absolutely nothing to do with the other. May I show you my ability to put my focus on a single task?"

"Mhmm."

I shimmy on the bench until our thighs are touching. His left hand clasps my shoulder to bend me toward him. I want to throw myself on him. It takes my full supply of self-control to ease into the kiss. Oh, but it's worth it.

Our lips press together. We sync our breath. Rolling onto the side of the leg I've smashed against his, I'm able to wrap my arms around him. And then we fall into a full-on teenage make-out session. It's slurpy and our teeth bang together, but I don't care. I'm in kissing nirvana. Nothing could separate us.

Scratch that. One thing can separate us. The Queen of the French Kiss herself. Stella lands in our laps and sticks her nose into my chin. She whines until I break away from Johnny.

"Someone's jealous." He wipes his lips with the back of his hand.

"Unless Aunt Donna had a little something something going on with someone, Miss Stella may never have witnessed a proper kiss. My parents give each other quick pecks but nothing that merits a poodle intervention."

"Will she need to learn to accept us kissing?" Johnny snatches the hand I'm using to scratch Stella and plants a kiss on the back of it. His eyes rise like moons above my hand.

He renders me powerless. I lean over the dog to give him a better landing site for his lips. Stella is not having it.

"Hey, quit it, dog. Your toenails are weapons." I wipe at the stinging scratches she leaves on my neck.

A tiny voice cuts through the hormonally charged din in my head. I worry Stella may be channeling my aunt. Is she delivering a message to warn me to stay away from Johnny until they settle the will?

I wouldn't dream of using him to gain any kind of advantage, but it would be impossible to avoid it if we made a habit out of kissing. He'd lose his objectivity. With Daniel already suspecting we're a couple, and Aunt Simone not far behind him, who's to say I won't run into a problem with other members of my family? And then what happens if they discover we've known each other since long before Aunt Donna died?

I hate my inner voice of reason. It sucks. I like Johnny more than I've liked anyone in years. Of all the people in the world for Aunt Donna to hire, why did it have to be him?

"Lauren?" His eyebrows crunch toward his nose.

"Uh, sorry. I drifted away for a second. You were saying…?"

"The restaurant on the other side of the fence is dog friendly. You up for a drink?"

Am I really the sort of person who would walk away from an amazing guy just to appease a bunch of relatives? People who would jump at the chance to gain an advantage in the race to inherit a fortune?

I clutch his hand. "I'll take a rain check for after the whole Piccolo family inheritance issue ends."

"So no more of these?" He brushes his lips against mine.

The stirrings in my body beg me to give in and kiss him again. I pull away.

I hate myself; I hate myself; I hate myself.

With a shake of my head, I say, "You don't play fair. But I have to."

He drops my hand. The hurt in his eyes doesn't disappear when he laughs. "Well played, Lauren. You passed this test. See you at the next challenge."

His pack leads him out of the dog park, leaving me to ponder his parting words. He couldn't have meant the kisses were a ploy to derail me on the quests, right? His eyes conveyed an entirely different message. So did every square inch of his body each time we kissed. But I can't ignore the icy sludge seeping through me. I wonder whether he had been leading me on all along just to test me. Argh! Why'd I let myself fall for Johnny effing Skeegs?

CHAPTER TWENTY-ONE
WILL THE REAL ZARA BENT PLEASE STAND UP?

Johnny doesn't matter. He's nothing to me. So what if he's the world's best kisser? There's more to life than kissing. Putting family above my feelings for him is next to impossible when I crave another kiss, though. I need to concentrate on finding reasons I should resist the urge to forgive him for saying something I don't believe he meant.

Perhaps I was wrong to blame Aunt Donna for pitting my family members against each other. Johnny was in the room, filming the whole spiel about her estate. Who's to say it wasn't his idea to make us fight for it?

He's like the insurance commercials with the guy who introduces himself as Mayhem. Look at the carnage Johnny's left in his wake. But why sabotage the process? He has to have an ulterior motive. It would be so much easier for me if he did.

What could it be? I tease out each thread of the saga to try to solve the mystery.

Aunt Donna called him her right-hand man. He

started as a super at her building on 97th Street, but because he understood her mission, she promoted him. To what position, exactly?

He has never explained what his job is. Does he supervise the maintenance of all of her properties? I've never seen him at our building when the crew deals with a problem. He might manage her finances, which would mean he knows her net worth and more. Aunt Donna promised us he insisted she leave her estate to a relative, not him. But what happens to her estate if all of us fail her test?

The day I ran into him in Central Park right before Aunt Donna died, I mentioned to him I was thinking about visiting her. What if showing him how I still cared for her meant I started with an advantage? And then I won the first quest. Hmm. He also told me I had excelled in the last quest. Both of our kisses came *after* I had won a challenge.

My only two legitimate competitors are Emma and my mother. Everyone else failed the first quest. Curtis skipped the last challenge. He can't be in the running. Privy to Daniel and Aunt Simone's motives, I doubt they can pull off a victory, either. And Stew's hardly trying.

Does Johnny have a contingency plan for each of us, one he'd put into play based on whoever is in the lead? And why? What's in it for him?

Of course. Her estate. How friggin' devious of him! *Oh, I don't deserve to inherit your fortune, Donna. No, you should leave it to your family even though none of them deserves it. But wait. I have a plan to help you find the most worthy heir.*

Yeah, you have a plan, you assclown. Eliminate the competition. If none of us wins, you'll appoint yourself the sole beneficiary. Well, guess what? Your little plan won't work. I don't know what you have up your sleeve now. All I can say is, "Bring it!"

I grow dizzy from my abrupt about-face. A tiny blade of doubt pokes at my heart, but I have to ignore it for the sake of my family and my sanity. I mutter a few more choruses of *Johnny doesn't matter* to myself while I sit at my desk the day after our last kiss. I focus on formulating a plan for Mrs. Ramos's apartment.

It has been six weeks since I held the last open house. Not a single offer has come in, nor has anyone been to see the apartment in weeks. The price is a little high to be competitive. We need to lower it, but persuading Mrs. Ramos will be tough.

The Johnsons, my new clients, provide me with a different challenge. They have no interest in the three apartments I've shown them. No matter that all three meet their requirements. And that there are no other available units in their price range and neighborhood, according to my searches.

I would kill to be able to buy one of the homes I showed them, a completely renovated two-bedroom apartment on 101st, a half block from Central Park. It even has a doorman. I can't imagine a more perfect home for them, yet they turned it down because the bathroom needs a renovation. No point in asking them to submit a bid that allows room in the budget for a reno because the apartment went to contract the next day.

Times like these are made for leaning on colleagues. "Mom, I could use your help," I yell to her.

My mother shuffles out of the kitchenette in our office. "I'm brewing a fresh pot of coffee. What is it?"

"I'm searching for listings to show the Johnsons. Perhaps I should expand my search to a little above their seven hundred thousand dollar budget. Do you have any ideas?"

"Check my inbox for some paperwork. No promises, but I attended an open house a month ago. The list price is fifty above theirs. If it hasn't sold, it wouldn't hurt to put in a lower bid. Look for the specs for a two-bedroom on West 95th Street."

She ducks back into the kitchenette, leaving me to rifle through her papers. A double-spaced document in a large font catches my eye. The words *You became my mother when I lost mine* capture my attention before I flip to the next document.

I give a furtive glance toward the kitchenette. The smell of freshly brewed coffee doesn't yet waft into the office. The click-clack of my mother's heels on the linoleum tile doesn't grow louder. I have a few seconds to myself. I shuttle the four-paged document to my inbox, laying it facedown under the top document.

My mother comes up behind me once I've returned to her desk. "Did you find it yet?"

I startle like a guilty person. I don't want her to help me find the listing. If she notices that the document is missing from her inbox, I will give myself away. I lift a few more pages. "Oh, is this it?"

I hold a ripped listing sheet to her. She adjusts her glasses. "That's the one. Beautiful unit. Southern exposure. If you angle yourself just right at the living room window, you can catch a glimpse of the park."

"It sounds perfect. Who's the listing agent?"

"Leon." My mother spits out his name like a curse.

A spidery tingle crawls the length of my back when I recall the oily, orange-tinged realtor who came to my first open house.

My mother continues, "It surprises me that this is one of his listings. He prefers not to handle listings below a million dollars. I'm sure he'd love to unload this apartment to the first bidder. He never tries to make the sale on the lower-priced units. Try to search for the apartment online. I bet you won't find it."

"I'll take your word. His number isn't on the sheet. Do you have it?"

I take a seat at my desk, waiting for her to text me his number. With a sleight of hand, I extract the document I pilfered from my mother from my inbox and place it in front of the listing I'm holding. I read it. Tears prick my eyes with the first words.

My mother wrote a eulogy for Aunt Donna. A heart-wrenching, gorgeous tribute to a woman she clearly still loves. Nowhere in it did she vilify her aunt. Instead, she exposed the scars of painful lessons learned and regrets she couldn't undo.

My nose emulates my leaky tear ducts. I blow into a tissue with the trumpet of a goose in heat.

My mother leans away from me. "Don't tell me you're catching a cold."

"No. I have a confession to make. A few other pages came along with the listing when I slid it out of your inbox. I'm so sorry. I shouldn't have read them, but I did." I hold out the eulogy to her.

She snatches it from me, emphasizing her irritation with squinted eyes and a purse of her lips. "Oh, this."

"Um, yeah."

She shrugs, not fooling me into believing she doesn't care about what she wrote. "I figured I should be prepared in case someone asked me to read something at her funeral."

"It's not the eulogy I would have expected from you."

"Well, I had to keep up appearances while she was still alive. After nearly fourteen years spent avoiding Donna, I couldn't let on that I realized I had been wrong to hate my aunt, could I?"

I cock my head, stunned to hear my mother admit to being wrong. "Why didn't you make up with her?"

"The situation is complicated, Lauren. This *mission* of hers. I don't know where it came from. It went against everything she had accomplished. She had a knack for buying undervalued properties in neighborhoods two or three years before anyone else tried to gentrify the area. She made a killing on the Tribeca warehouse she bought in the late seventies. And then she did it again with a couple of other buildings before she bought ours. Our building was her biggest conversation project and her first for a building already zoned for residential use. It took two years to convert from a rental building into a co-op, but by the time she sold a quarter of the units, she had already made back her investment and more.

"Your father and I opened our little real estate office in one of the commercial spaces downstairs. I didn't pay attention to what she was doing at first. Your brother was a handful. And before long, you were on the way. We had enough on our plates initially.

"A few years later, I approached my aunt about working with her. She agreed to let us be the listing agents on units in our building. But tenants rarely moved out of them. I wanted to be more involved in her business.

"Fourteen years ago, I discovered she had bought a second apartment building — one with even more units — on 97th Street a year after she had bought ours. I asked to list those apartments, too. I swallowed the disappointment of her keeping the purchase a secret from me because I wanted to build on our professional relationship.

"Anyhow, that's when she told me she was no longer interested in co-op conversations. She explained how early on, she had converted commercial spaces into residential. Our building's conversion pushed out long-term renters who couldn't afford to buy their apartments. She didn't have the stomach for such enterprises. And thus she devoted the last years of her life to affordable housing, financing her whim with whatever funds she could still wring from her other properties."

The wisp of the pages of the eulogy sliding against each other in her hands fills the silence once she stops speaking. Learning additional information about my great aunt sparks my brain awake. And when I apply this information to the challenge we completed at the food pantry, it makes sense. More annoyingly, so do a few of the things Johnny has said. Things that make him sound like he's also an advocate for fair housing. His dog shares its name with a woman whose mission was to thwart gentrification, for instance. Would he have gone to such great lengths to hide his duplicitous nature just to inherit her estate? *Johnny doesn't matter*, I remind myself.

But my family does. What I don't hear from my mother is grounds for an epic, family-rending fight. "Did you stop talking to Aunt Donna because she kept her business a secret from you or because you seriously disapproved of her mission?"

"It's more complicated than it appears. Our disagreements evolved over a few months. Our divorce has more to do with pride than philosophy, I suppose. In recent years, I toyed with apologizing to her, but she was as stubborn as me. I didn't want her to reject me again simply to save face for her role in splitting us apart. So here we are."

She slumps and disappears in her thoughts, projecting a sense of isolation. Impulse propels me to hug her. Standing above her while she sits, the balance of power between us has shifted.

"Thanks for sharing your side of the story with me, Mom. Even though you didn't reconcile with her while she was alive, I bet a part of her secretly hoped you'd pull through and win the quests. I had pledged to myself I wouldn't discuss the quests with anyone because it makes everything unpleasant, but I want you to know I'm rooting for you."

She strokes my hand. "I suppose, if I were being true to her, I'd root for you. I believe she pinned her hopes on you. You have her sense of decency. Whether that's an asset for the real estate business, I cannot say."

Buried underneath the fishiness is a compliment. Desperate little suck-up that I am, I let it warm my soul.

"Despite all this, you still want to win, right, Mom?"

She straightens her collar and grins at me. "Oh, yes. I have such plans for the building on 97th Street and its fifty-four units. They're just begging to be converted into co-ops."

Ah! There's the Zara Bent I know so well!

CHAPTER TWENTY-TWO
ALL THE MAYHEM WAS FOR THIS?

My stomach squirms as I approach Mrs. Ramos's apartment. I spy a wreath on the door where once there was none. Baby's breath and green foliage form a heart through which a pink ribbon spins and twirls. A pink teddy bear reclines in the center. He's sporting a halo and wings.

To each their own. This apartment is also the home to a constipated cat clock/picture frame, after all. But the wreath, along with a welcome mat designed to resemble a watermelon, tells me Becca has made herself a little too welcome in someone else's home.

A blast of what smells like the entire stock of a candle store fells me when she opens the door. "Lauren!" Becca bounds into the hallway, hugging the living stuffing out of me.

"Hey, Becca. Thanks for being OK with me hosting an open house today. The place looks—" I swallow the first five adjectives to come to mind. "—nice and tidy."

And pink. As in Barbie's Dream House pink when Barbie is in her maximalist decorating phase.

Becca has erased every trace of Mrs. Ramos from the tiny studio. Inspirational quotes printed on pink backgrounds dotted with white kittens line the walls. Pink throws hide the mishmash of beat-up, earth-toned furniture. Fluffy, hot pink area rugs lie like stepping stones throughout the apartment. Were Mrs. Ramos to return today, the shock of what has become of her home surely would turn her an on-brand shade of rage-induced pink.

"Um, Mrs. Ramos forbade you from changing the decor. Remember?" I lift a pillar candle from a bookcase filled with books with pink covers, sneezing from the pinkness of its scent.

She crosses her arms, shoving her fingers under her armpits. "I've barely changed a thing. I can put her stuff back in no time flat. Besides, it was so depressing in here before. It's no wonder you couldn't sell the place. But now, everyone will perk up when they see it."

"Let's hope they do. I'd love to find a buyer today."

Father's Day is a crappy day to hold an open house. I'll add that to my "lessons learned" file. The experience of sitting alone for two hours inside the sensory equivalent of a jar of cinnamon stuffed into a bouquet of daylilies doused with pink whipped cream makes me question my sanity.

I run out of job-appropriate ways to entertain myself while I wait for buyers. To amuse myself, I stage a first date between a pink stuffed dog and a throw pillow embroidered with the slogan, "Girls rule!" They end their date with insincere promises to text each other later.

I check my phone for signs of life beyond this cutesy palace of pink. Rankin, Rankin, and Gould are happy to spend their client's money by working on a Sunday. An email arrives, stating that the pleasure of my company has been requested for next Saturday morning at a location in Brooklyn. They suggest that I wear clothing similar to what we wore for volunteering in the food pantry.

Damn. I have to see Johnny again. I definitely need a plan. The first order of business is to inform every corner of my body that we don't like him. I will not tolerate any swooning, tingling of the spine, curling of the toes, sighing, or racing of my heart. You guys hear me?

His glib parting words still echo in my mind. *Well played. You passed this test.* He thinks we're playing a game. Put me in, coach. Johnny is no one to me except the umpire. It will make my life a whole lot easier to stop taking him or anything he says personally, instead treating the quests like a game.

"Oh, Richard! Where have they sent us?" My mother descends the steps of the elevated subway platform with trepidation.

"Was our neighborhood any better when we moved into our apartment? I remember it had its share of graffiti and discount shops." He spins his head to take in the sights, clenching his jaw with reserved judgment.

"It was never anything like this. My word!" My mother presses the hem of her shirt to her hip, scared to let even a fleck of Brooklyn come into contact with her.

The claustrophobic framework of the subway tracks above us doesn't improve the ambiance. The cracked pavement of a crosswalk on a side street brings a welcome chance to escape the cage formed by the tracks. A rickety, graffiti-covered construction fence frames an open lot on the corner. Within it, a crew removes rubble from a demolished building.

My mother had mentioned Aunt Donna's uncanny ability to know when to buy properties in neighborhoods before they became gentrified. This section of Brooklyn is worlds away from the hipster havens of Williamsburg and Park Slope. I bet she imagined similar potential here.

We turn onto the designated street. Its jagged skyline alternates between single-story commercial buildings in various states of disrepair, sleek new apartment buildings rising above the rest, and row houses doing their best to hold the comfortable middle. We stop in front of the sketchiest structure we have yet encountered. Gang tags and *no parking* signs litter the faces of three metal garage doors linked by cinderblock walls and topped with razor wire.

"This can't be the correct address, can it? It doesn't have a number." My mother rereads her email. "Richard, check the next building. 885 is next door. We're looking for 875."

My father shuffles a little further down the road, peering at the number of the next building. "It says 869. The garages have to be number 875."

My mother places her hands on her hips. "They're trying to kill us. Why would they send us to this god-forsaken place? And then make us wait?"

I suppose now would not be the best moment to remind my mother it was her idea to arrive early.

"Zara, why don't you and Lauren go grab a cup of coffee at the fast food place we passed? I'll wait for everyone else."

"You'd have the two of us enter a building filled with junkies? It's safer here on the open street. Provided there isn't a drive-by shooting."

"The guy I owe money to hasn't located me yet, so I doubt he'll send someone after me today," my father says with a chuckle.

"Richard!"

You know it's bad when my mother omits the *Oh*

from an admonition. I dash across the street, pretending to admire the brand-spanking-new apartment building as cover from the maternal fallout. The building merits a closer inspection. Geometric shapes formed from terra-cotta bricks scatter across the facade of the narrow, gray tower. Windows shiny enough to fool even the most street-hardened New York pigeons into flying into them reflect the sky and the frightening mess in front of my parents.

My gut tells me Aunt Donna detected the beauty buried within this slice of Brooklyn. The property across the street, which I assume she owns, must be four times the width of the gray tower. The building in front of me is six stories high. Pairs of windows on each level have mismatched curtains, meaning there are probably two apartments per floor. A six-story apartment on the lot across the street could house perhaps forty families. And, based on the state of the neighborhood, the rents would have to be affordable.

A chill ascends my spine. Greedy developers would gamble on being able to raise the rents after the entire neighborhood underwent a massive gentrification process. Or they could convert the buildings to condos or co-ops, thus driving regular folks out of yet another affordable neighborhood. I hope what my mother said about Aunt Donna is true, that she devoted herself to creating affordable housing.

My parents are no longer fighting or alone. My heart stutters when I catch Johnny combing his fingers through the flop of brown hair slipping into his eyes.

Get a hold of yourself, Lauren!

A man with a black ponytail and a neck tattoo scratches the back of his head and approaches Johnny. He slaps him on the shoulder. They exchange a manly hug. My mother clutches her purse to her body.

I dawdle, not crossing the street until Simone, Stew,

and Marc emerge from the Bentley. Emma follows them, waving when she spots me.

Johnny and I exchange cursory greetings. His smile mimics what I hope mine conveys: uneasiness and no threat of friendliness. My shoulders slump from his rejection.

When Daniel and Curtis arrive, Johnny unlocks a garage door and flips on the light. The garage is empty except for a work sink, a few orange buckets, two cardboard boxes, a bulging shopping bag, and a collection of what look to be the world's worst bath brushes. If Johnny dares to trick me again, I'll flay his skin with a wire-bristled brush. I swear I will.

We step into the garage. The coolness inside brings relief from the sun.

"Thanks for coming today. I want to introduce you to a colleague of mine. Juan, meet the Piccolo family."

Juan waves at us. "Hiya, everybody!"

I narrow my eyes, focusing on his tattoo. Faded bluish-black ink forms a scorpion. I hate myself for shuddering.

Johnny clasps his hands together. "Before I tell you what we'll be doing today, I want you to hear Juan's story. You ready?"

Juan nods. "Yeah, man. So, really, I gauge my life by what happened before I met Donna and what happened after. I mean, everything changed. I didn't have a job or a home, my family wasn't talking to me, I drank a lot. I was up to no good." He draws his shoulders inward and rubs his hand furiously against his lower arm.

"Me and some other guys lived in a gutted out building around the corner. So anyway, I was having a smoke outside one day when this rich old lady gets out of a cab and marches right up to me. She asked me if I needed a job, a place to work or live. Just like that. She didn't know me. I thought she was from one of them shelters or something, so I told her I wasn't interested."

My parents orchestrate a stealth maneuver, surrounding me and pressing against my sides. If they believe they can protect me from Juan, hmm... Dad will wander off toward a distraction while Mom assesses Juan as a potential competitor for inheriting Aunt Donna's estate. In the event they are searching for new careers, I'd advise them against starting a security firm.

Juan continues, "But she kept going on, telling me this was her house now, and if we wanted to stay, we had to play by her rules. That was almost five years ago. No one else had ever given me a chance to make something of myself. She put us to work right away, cleaning out rat shit and trash and needles. And she paid us like she said she would.

"Me and another guy stuck it out. Not everyone squatting there could hack the work, so most of them left. But when the construction started, she got me and Manny jobs working on the new apartment building. When it was built, she hired us to keep it nice and let us live in it. She got us into the union. And now we're waiting to work on the next project."

He pauses and trains a finger pointed like a gun toward each of us. My parents press even harder against me. "You should know I thought your aunt was something special. I miss her every day."

Johnny massages Juan's shoulder, nodding his head in agreement. Why can't he act like the rat I'm sure he is? It makes things easier for me when he doesn't behave like a decent human being.

He scans the crowd, making eye contact with each of us. He holds my gaze for longer than is comfortable. I stare at him with the intensity of a tuna on the other end of a fishing line.

He says, "Up till now, we've flirted with whom your aunt was and whether you bore any similarities to her.

Today, I'll tell you what actually is at stake when we consider her estate. This." He spreads his hands to encompass the nearly empty garage. All of our family mayhem for a garage? I chuckle to myself, imagining Aunt Simone inheriting a garage and nothing else. It wouldn't be a total loss. She has complained about the lack of closet space in her apartment.

"Donna bought a similar site — the place Juan described to you — five years ago. It holds sixty rental units. We cap rent at twenty-five percent of a tenant's income. Each year, we re-evaluate the numbers. We have minimum and maximum income requirements for new tenants. And the system is a success."

"She, or rather her heirs, will go broke," Aunt Simone scoffs.

"Not with good management. Her two Manhattan buildings bring in income. And she put money aside to sustain her passion projects. Through her meticulous financial planning, she made sure construction on her last project could continue with or without her. Whoever inherits the estate will be in the business of providing decent, affordable housing for years to come. And now you all know what you're striving for during the quests."

"So what are we doing today? Testing the limits of our immunizations?" Uncle Curtis bounces his head at us, collecting laughs for his joke.

Johnny throws him a scrub brush. "Today we're removing the graffiti. Everyone ready?"

I stretch my arms above my head and bend at the waist. Time to kick some serious graffiti butt and prove to Johnny he can't prevent me from making my aunt proud.

CHAPTER TWENTY-THREE
LOVE LETTERS AND LAWSUITS

Water sloshes from the bucket Emma and I carry en route to the far end of the property. Armed with brushes, gloves, sponges, and a bottle of industrial-strength graffiti-eradicating spray, we tackle the garage door. I glance over my shoulder. Johnny is scrubbing a section next to my father. He spoils the scene from Tom Sawyer playing in my head. I prefer being mad at him for lazing around while we do his dirty work.

"Pretty cool of Aunt Donna, right?" Emma brushes her hair from her eyes with the back of her wrist.

"Yeah. I love her even more now. I guess the cat's out of the bag. Did any of what they told us about her mission and what we stand to inherit sound familiar?"

She sighs. "I'm feeling crappy because of how little I paid attention to what she was saying, to be honest. 'Brooklyn, blah, blah. Rental units. New construction.' She may have told me everything, but I was probably too busy rearranging the contents of her apartment in my mind to absorb any of it."

"You shouldn't feel bad. I'm sure she valued your

companionship far more than any potential interest in her business you may have shown." I resume scrubbing, only to rest the brush on the sidewalk. "Oh, speaking of who knew what about Aunt Donna, I have news. My mother filled me in a little on her beef with her aunt a few days ago. It was over the fact that Aunt Donna bought another building on the Upper West Side but kept it as a rental property instead of converting it to co-ops. So today's revelation wasn't exactly news to me. But I still doubt my mother told me the full story."

"Interesting." She scowls. "Ugh. Speaking of parents, here comes my dad. Sorry to abandon you, but I'm not in the mood to talk to him."

Emma brushes past Uncle Curtis without acknowledging him. The woman sure can hold a grudge. I count myself lucky for surviving our little tiff.

Uncle Curtis dips his sponge into my bucket and wipes it across a small section of a red letter 'n' on the garage door. I hand him the bottle of solvent.

"Thanks. Never thought I'd work on the chain gang."

I stare at him, hoping he'll detect the irony behind his joke. He *is* the guy who stole money from his daughter's trust fund. He remains oblivious, scrubbing the paint at a vigorous pace.

"So, Lauren, I got off on the wrong foot with this Johnny character. And I don't think I've helped my case ever since. Simone says you and Johnny seem to get along pretty good. Would you put in a good word with him for me?"

He lifts his shoulders and eyebrows, adopting a pathetic, hopeful pose better suited to a six-year-old begging for a second serving of cake. Next thing I know, he'll be offering me half his Halloween candy in return for the favor.

"I'm not sure I can help you, Uncle Curtis. If you can make a good case for why you should be Aunt Donna's heir, have a chat with Johnny."

"Yeah, maybe I should. You see, I really need to win. There's no way I will ever get Emma to talk to me again unless I pay her back the money I borrowed."

Clever choice of words, Uncle Curtis.

He pauses his scrubbing efforts. "So, maybe her mom didn't take everything when she left like I said she did. Truth is, I did something stupid."

I swipe over my section again with the sponge. "Not that I'm saying I'll intervene on your behalf, but you're not exactly convincing me I should, either." Without looking at him, I douse the garage door with another coating of the spray.

"Yeah, I get how you might see it that way. The thing is, a buddy of mine told me about this sure-fire investment. I was nearing my retirement, and I didn't mind the idea of my investments yielding more income for me so I could retire somewhere nice.

"Well, I sunk everything I had into the scheme. And then some. Then my buddy's friend disappeared with the money. I had to sell the house in Rego Park and move somewhere cheap. That's why I'm in Vegas. My place is nothing fancy, not the sort of place where Emma could be comfortable. But it's what I can afford on my pension."

"Have you tried finding a job?"

"Who wants to hire a sixty-two-year-old man? No one. So that's my deal. I don't need all of Donna's money, but a little would be nice. I could reimburse Emma, upgrade my lifestyle a bit. I was thinking you and I could be partners. Whaddya say?"

Daniel, Aunt Simone, and now Uncle Curtis have each asked me the same question, yet none has mentioned how they could help me. Not that I want anyone's help, but I definitely don't want to align myself with anyone who doesn't want to help me.

I hold the sponge at my side. A trickle of water drips onto my calf, tickling my skin. Bending to wipe it away, I say, "I have no idea how they're going to choose an heir.

I've committed to following the rules, which include working independently. Now that Johnny has revealed Aunt Donna's mission, I doubt we could help each other, anyway. We no longer have to discover her secret. All I can tell you is should I win, I will not neglect my family. I don't know the liquidity of her estate or how generous it would allow me to be, but if I can share it with each of you, I will."

My attention wants to be anywhere but here with Uncle Curtis. My eyes wander down the street, fixing on another person I'd prefer to avoid. "Oh, look. Johnny's holding a stack of pizza boxes. I guess it's lunchtime." I silently thank Johnny for giving me an exit from the conversation.

Uncle Curtis responds to the call of free pizza like shoppers pouring into a store first thing on Black Friday. I'm not ready to be in close quarters with Johnny yet. I set a goal of stripping the rest of the paint from the lower left quadrant of the garage door before I take my lunch break. Amazing how tempting a task involving noxious chemicals and elbow grease is compared to dining with him.

Being alone gives me a chance to unpack what my mother, Johnny, and Juan have dumped on me. We're not competing for a fortune. We're interviewing for a job. And, if buildings full of junkie squatters and gang graffiti tell the full story, it's not a glamorous job.

Given the amount of work she has done today, Aunt Simone doesn't have the stomach for the gig. An hour and a half of manual labor in a neighborhood to which she shares my mother's allergy exceeds her sensibilities. All she has done is swipe a section with a wet sponge, spritz it with the chemicals, and step aside, gossiping with anyone within earshot while her twelve-year-old son scrubs away the paint.

Nor would she be happy having to spend down the estate to maintain a stock of affordable rental units. Her eye is on a prize large enough for her to afford the aspirational lifestyle she bought for herself with money her husband doesn't earn.

Uncle Curtis might not shy away from the gritty task at hand, but he has two strikes against him. Obvs, he embezzled from Emma's trust fund. Worse, he confessed that his motivation stemmed from his ineptitude with investing money.

I can disregard Stew as a viable candidate. He has Gerald's money to play with and no leadership skills. Besides, stepping into Aunt Donna's shoes would demand too much from a guy built to make permanent dents in a couch cushion.

What about my brother? He's going through a rough period. He needs a job. I can't hold him responsible for the drug he helped to develop failing or for him losing his job.

But Daniel rejected the family business long ago. Real estate never interested him. Neither did our great-aunt. This is the guy, after all, who declined a research position dedicated to a humanitarian cause. Instead, he chose a higher salary to manufacture a miracle diet pill. Both decisions paint him as more interested in money than in helping people.

My mother is a strong contender, especially with her career in real estate. It's easy to imagine her managing the construction of a new building and filling it with— And filling it with apartment owners, not renters. She would convert each building into a co-op or condo faster than you can say contract of sale.

My cousin Emma isn't motivated by money. Sure, she's swimming in the stuff and knows how to spend it. But I remember our conversation about doing something for the love of it. She helps her friends organize their exhibitions, store displays, and closets because it fills her with a sense of purpose and happiness. What she brings to Aunt Donna's mission is her selfless nature. But what is missing for Emma is a passion for Aunt Donna's mission.

Which leaves me, the self-titled real estate lady. I love real estate, but I have yet to discover a talent for selling it. I also haven't found the opportunity to develop my hypothetical talent.

Becca lives contentedly in Mrs. Ramos's apartment despite it being small and shabby. Like most people, she doesn't need a fancy-schmancy apartment. A tiny studio with a relatively low rent and nothing special to recommend itself feels like home to her.

My family's nemesis, Leon, doesn't understand the value of a home beyond its listing price. I've scheduled a showing of his sub-million-dollar apartment for my clients, the Johnsons, next week. A quality listing like his shouldn't languish on the market. It remains unsold because of his disinterest in trying to sell a home with a lower price point.

What do my dreams of landing multi-million dollar listings say about me? Am I also motivated by greed?

Aunt Donna's mission resonates with me. To provide a good home for people without robbing them blind sparks a passion within me. I contemplate whether providing affordable housing, rather than aiming to be a high-end broker, is my calling. Help people rather than use them to line my pockets. I'd feel like Charlie Bucket being chosen to take over Willy Wonka's chocolate factory if I won.

Hmm. Aunt Donna might have found the inspiration for her quests from *Charlie and the Chocolate Factory*. No family members have turned into blueberries or drowned in a chocolate river, at least. My stomach gurgles at the mention of a chocolate river. I guess I have to face Johnny if I want a slice of pizza.

"Well, look who finally decided to join us," my brother says to me when I enter the garage.

Johnny lifts the top of a box, offering me the two remaining slices. Large puddles of orange grease shimmer on the cheese.

I lift a slice by its crust, letting the liquid drip onto the paper below. While patting it dry with a napkin, I take inventory of the occupants of the garage. Except for Emma, they all have taken on the metaphoric greasy sheen of bad pizza now that I've tallied their worthiness of inheriting Aunt Donna's estate.

Scared I'll verbalize my thoughts, I say, "The mildewy smell in here is making me stuffy. I'm heading outside."

I lean against the cinderblock wall next to the last garage door and wolf down my slice. Johnny pokes his head out of the open garage and waves. He probably didn't notice me rolling my eyes, which explains why he walks toward me.

"Hey." He plants his elbow on the wall next to me and leans against his fist.

"Hey."

"You know I was kidding about what I said to you at the dog park."

"Do I?"

Pain streaks across eyes that had been pulling their smolder routine on me a few seconds ago. "I'm so sorry. You caught me off guard. The words just came out. I was trying to mask my disappointment with humor. I totally agree with you. We should remain neutral around each other until we settle the estate."

"And then?" Damn it. The bits and pieces of me I had told to avoid any and all Johnny-related matters return from sabbatical. The collective energy of their tinglings and palpitations forces me to punctuate my question with a flirtatious toss of my hair. I'm pathetic.

He flips up his palms and lifts his brow. "And then…"

I don't finish his sentence. I have to keep my desires bottled up for now.

Thankfully, he changes the subject. "I want to show you something. Follow me."

We walk to the corner and turn right. A pristine brick building covers nearly half of the far end of the block. Unlike the gray tower and its new cousins on the side streets my parents and I had passed on our trip from the subway, this building doesn't have grand aspirations.

"This is where Juan lived when he met Donna. And the building where he lives today. You see what we're doing here?"

I'm in awe. This is where normal people want to live. People who don't earn tons of money. People who will take pride in turning a simple apartment into a home. "Yeah. It's amazing. Perfect. Wow! Aunt Donna was a total badass, wasn't she?"

His cheeks inflate when he purses his lips. I bet he misses her as much as me. With a nod, he says, "Yup, she was."

"So what was here before?"

"An abandoned two-story building. Commercial spaces on the ground level with apartments above. It was disgusting. We had to knock it down and start fresh."

I lower my eyelids, contemplating his words. "Wait a second. You're going to demo the garages, too, right?"

He snickers through his nose. "Yup."

"I'm guessing that spray paint doesn't have a super-powerful ability to resist a wrecking ball."

His eyebrows wiggle at me. "Nope."

"So why are we scraping away the graffiti?"

"There wasn't a single task your aunt wouldn't help with. It takes humility to bring a vision like hers to life."

"Mhmm." I continue to stare at the building.

Johnny taps me on the shoulder. "Lunch break is over."

"You've made it tough for me to find the motivation to return to work now that I know our efforts don't matter."

"It's only for another hour. You can hack it. Please don't say a word to anyone."

"Got it."

Orange buckets, brushes, and spray bottles litter the sidewalk in front of the garages, languishing in the sun while my family extends their lunch break inside. As we approach the open garage, I wonder at the silence. I hasten my steps to reach the garage. My family is gone.

Johnny leans against the doorframe and cocks his head. Empty pizza boxes rest on the case of paint remover. Blue rubber gloves are strewn on the floor. Their box is splayed open like the victim of a deranged murder. I pick it up. A handwritten letter addressed to the two of us scrawls across the inside surface. I know the slant and overabundance of loops of the writing like my own. Years of toting paper lunch bags with my name on them and groaning with each to-do list stuck to the fridge has made me an expert in deciphering my mother's handwriting.

> *Dear Lauren and Johnny,*
> *We have just learned the unsettling news that the two of you*
> *are having an affair.*

My eyes bug out of my skull. "Johnny, it's not good." I hand him the box without reading another word.

He squints, reading through the message. "They're hiring a lawyer to challenge the will."

So Daniel blabbed a story without having the facts to support it. And my mother bought every word.

Sure, I stand to lose my chance of being named an heir if they ask the lawyer to consider me ineligible. But what worries me more is what that could mean for the future of Aunt Donna's mission. Put in charge of settling the will, would my family undo all the good she devoted her life to achieving?

CHAPTER TWENTY-FOUR
GETTING FRIENDLY WITH
THE FRIDGE

I mold myself into the seat next to Johnny on the J train, stunned. My stomach snakes and slithers in my gut, dancing from an overdose of adrenaline.

I've done nothing wrong. I haven't thrown anyone under the bus or gained any advantage over them. They're the ones who've messed up their chances of becoming a benefactor, not me. Yet once again, regardless of my labors or honesty, my efforts earn punishment instead of praise.

I call my mother. It goes straight to voicemail. "Mom, I wish you would have spoken to me directly. You're making assumptions based on something my brother thinks he learned three weeks ago. Rather than listen to my version of the story, which is the accurate version, you took the word from someone who has been lying to you since March. Ask Daniel why we haven't seen Genevieve in months. Or why he had no problem leaving work to take part in the weekday commitments related to Aunt Donna."

I take a breath. I shouldn't have blabbed Daniel's secrets before telling my side of the story. It won't strengthen my case. "I can't help that I like Johnny—"

He flashes me the most brilliant smile when he overhears me. I hold my finger over my lips to shush him. The last thing I need is a smile-shaped distraction.

"But trust me. I would never, ever, *ever* let my feelings for him interfere in the quests. He agrees with me. We are not dating. We have not betrayed any of you nor has he given me any advantage. Think about it, Mom. You actually came into the quests with the biggest advantage of all of us. You knew what Aunt Donna's mission was from the start. So why are you acting like I'm cheating you out of anything? I'm not. I hope we can talk when I get home."

I stab the red button on the screen and stash the phone in my purse. I've never confronted my mother with such conviction. It's... well, scary but also sort of empowering.

"I like you too, you know." Johnny reaches for my hand.

I pull away from him. Touching him again won't solve any of my problems. Correction: *most* of my problems. The problems that matter right now. "At least someone likes me."

He sticks his hands between his knees. "I doubt I'm the only one. They're reacting to a random piece of fresh information. Things will calm down. Especially after they learn how we will settle the will. Do you want to hear how we'll make our decision?"

"I guess," I mumble, slumping in my seat.

"I'll be conducting exit interviews. Alexander and an arbitrator will sit in on them. What we have observed so far will play just a minor role in the decision process. Your aunt wanted each of you to share her experiences to better prepare you for answering our questions. Tell your mother this. We've given everyone advantages that should help you succeed during the interviews."

"So she really did imagine that all of us would somehow manage to present ourselves to be her ideal benefactors? Surely she could have foreseen how vying with each other would lead to petty fights."

"Donna possessed a flaw: her optimism. She envisioned her legacy as a utopia and hoped her vision would be contagious. I certainly caught the bug."

"So I've noticed. Which reminds me, I don't know what exactly you did for her."

"I'm basically a property manager. I keep the apartments rented, handle tenant issues, oversee the staffing of the buildings. And I'm the project manager on the new builds."

"You don't want to take over the whole business?"

"I'm just a guy with an associate's degree in building management. Being a super in Donna's building exceeded my professional expectations. Not that I don't like my current job. I love dealing with the tenants and the oversight of the buildings themselves. As for the money side of the business or managing the entire estate, no thanks. I'm involved in choosing an heir simply to get myself a new boss. Yes, I may have a preference regarding who should become my boss—"

His smile makes my heart purr.

"—but I swear it will not in any way influence my recommendation."

A smile tugs at the corners of my lips. Before I can thank him for both his vote of confidence and his pledge of neutrality, my phone chirps. It's a text from Emma.

"Sorry. Give me a second to read this."

"Go for it."

Emma: Is Johnny the guy you allegedly met in the bar?

My breath catches.
Lauren: Yeah

Emma: Did he tell you it was the wrong time to start something?

Lauren: No. That was me

Emma: Cool
That's what I was hoping

I told everyone you would never resort to devious tricks to win

Oh, thank heavens! I rub a kink in my neck before responding to her.

Lauren: Thanks
Do you hate me?

Emma: Not a chance

If you don't want to go home you can crash with me

Troi wants you to know you can't stay unless you bring Stella

Lauren: Let me see what's up with my mom

If she doesn't listen to reason, me and the mutt will see you in a couple of hours

Emma: Keep me posted

I hug myself. My jitters reduce from seismic catastrophe to massage chair on the vibration scale. Since Emma believes me, maybe everyone else will, too.

And that, more than anything, is what I want. For us all to stop fighting with each other. If people are going to hate me, I want it to be for a real reason. Well, I don't want anyone to hate me. That's the thing. Especially when I'm not at fault.

I prop my elbows on my knees and sink my chin into my hands. Learning more about Aunt Donna, especially her mission to provide affordable housing, has made me happy. But I'm far less stoked about having uncovered the vein of greed running through my family. And for running headlong into the heightened sense of competitiveness it raises in them.

I want to play a part in fulfilling Aunt Donna's mission. I suspect I might even have the skill set and the passion to be an ideal custodian for her estate. But striving to be her heir catapults me smack dab into the middle of my family's nonsense. I can't control their motivations. They may be using me as a tactic to avoid having a spotlight shine on the reasons they don't deserve to inherit the estate. Which sucks for me.

And it begs the question: is fulfilling Aunt Donna's mission worth the misery?

"I'm sorry you and your mom are having a tough time talking to each other. She loves you. It's my dad and Aunt Simone's fault she's mad in the first place. They whipped her into a frenzy after Daniel spilled the beans."

After two awkward nights avoiding my parents in our apartment, I've decamped to Emma's. After lunch, I sink into the pillows propped against the arm of her couch and stretch out my legs. Stella takes advantage of my reclined position, spreading herself across my chest.

Emma says, "And speaking of spilling the beans: you and Johnny? That's so hot!"

I sigh and gaze at the ornate plaster ceiling above me. "It could be, but no." A surge of anger courses through me. I sit up, much to Stella's chagrin. She cozies up to her Uncle Troi. "Which pisses me off. I could be in new-boyfriend heaven right now. Instead, I've chosen to be a nun so as not to let my relationship interfere with family matters. Ingrates!"

Troi twirls Stella's hair between his pointer and middle finger. "Our little Lauren finally snags a sexy man but has to give him up for Lent. Think of what this is doing to me. I'm bored. I need stories about someone's sex life. Stat."

"Go rent a porno. I'm leaving to show an apartment."

"Field trip! We're coming with." He says.

"I can't have you in the apartment with my clients. You'll intimidate them."

"Moi?"

"You know all six feet, four inches of your fabulous self intimidates most people. Besides, I don't want them to mistake you for another interested buyer."

"Maybe I am interested in buying it."

"It's much smaller than this apartment."

"In that case, I'm not interested."

"As I expected."

"Doesn't matter. I have to work."

"What type of work?"

"Boring work."

"Nothing you do is boring, sweetie," Emma chimes in.

He air kisses her on his way to his room. "I have trained you well. Speaking of well trained, Stella, come."

My fluffy ball of strawberry-blond goodness follows him to his room.

"He only likes me for my dog," I sniff.

"We both love you for every reason." She pauses. With her pointer in the air and her eyes sparkling, she says, "Oh, I've got it!"

"Is it contagious?"

"Ha ha. Very funny. No. I have an idea for why *I* should tag along with you."

"And why is that?"

"I can help sell your clients a vision of the apartment done with proper furnishings."

"Nice try."

"I want to help you any way I can."

"And I appreciate it. I need all the help I can get. I'm the world's worst real estate lady."

"I don't agree. Besides, is showing apartments to ultra-picky clients your true dream job?"

"Finding the perfect place for people to live is. Between my three-month-old listing that will never sell for the price the client wants and today's clients, whose budget may not be enough to buy them their ideal home, my frustration level is amping up, though. Not to mention how my income depends entirely on these two clients."

"Just between you and me, I think you would be the perfect person to take over Aunt Donna's business."

I wrap her in a giant hug. "Aw, thanks! I needed to hear that. You'd be pretty darned perfect, too."

"It's not my thing."

"But if someone asked for your help with the designs…"

"OK. I may let it be known to the would-be beneficiaries that my talents are at their disposal. I'll mention it at tomorrow's meeting with Alexander Rankin. You're going, right?"

"I suppose. Did you, or I mean, my mom et al. hire a lawyer?"

"Not yet. Or if they did, no one has told me."

"They don't need a lawyer. Nothing has been decided. They don't have a case. Not that a lack of a case will stop them from eviscerating me tomorrow."

"I'm Team Lauren. If they want to mess with you, they have to go through me."

"What did I do to deserve you?"

"I *chose* to love you because you are all sorts of awesome. Now go sell the hell out of your apartment!"

"I love you, too. Thanks for the pep talk. I'm going to show the apartment so hard, my clients will need protective eyewear."

I'm ready to put in a bid in on the apartment for myself before I walk into the building. The location is glorious. I mean, Central Park is right *there*! The cloistered space between the wings of the building leading to the front door whisks you away from the noise of the street. And the cheerful man in a uniform who opens the door when we approach makes the entrance perfect.

The lobby continues to spread the sense that nothing bad can happen here. I watch the Johnsons' eyes register satisfaction with what they see.

We ride the elevator to the sixth floor. Thick burgundy carpet muffles our footfalls. Unlike the hallways in our apartment building, I can't detect what the neighbors are eating for dinner because I smell only a hint of wood polish rather than garlic and fish.

I extract the key from the lockbox and unlock the door. We follow the pristine hardwood floor through a small foyer. The kitchen is on our right. I would marry the refrigerator. Seriously. Mrs. Johnson beats me to it, though, introducing herself to the mammoth stainless steel appliance with a delighted gasp.

I leave the two lovebirds to their flirtations and begin a romance of my own with the professional-grade stove. Mr. Johnson fondles the futuristic faucet through the pass-through into the dining room. He and his wife make eyes at each other across the marble countertop. Yeah, they're falling hard for the apartment.

The bathroom possesses the same sex appeal as the kitchen. We locate the sweet spot in the living room my mother had mentioned. Standing hunched over at the lower right-hand corner of the window, we glimpse the verdant tree line of Central Park.

"You promise this unit is in our price range?" Mrs. Johnson asks.

"The price is a little above yours, but the apartment has been on the market for seventy-three days without a price drop. I think we can bid near the top of your budget. We'll

189

leave ten thousand or so to make room for counteroffers."

Mr. Johnson scratches his head. "If it's been on the market since March, I don't understand why our previous broker didn't show it to us."

"They didn't market the unit widely. I stumbled on it after another broker mentioned she had attended an open house here last month."

His eyes spark. "We may not face a bidding war, then. Honey, should we place a bid?"

His wife falls against his shoulder, gazing at him with a radiant smile. "Yes. Let's."

What I wish more than anything (well, except for the seller to accept my clients' bid) is to run home and thank my mother for sharing the listing with me. I couldn't have gotten this far without her. But then there's the little problem of me not being ready to look her in the eye to defend myself.

CHAPTER TWENTY-FIVE
FAMILY UNDER A MICROSCOPE

"He shouldn't be in the room." My mother points to Johnny with a finger stiff and sharp enough to gut him.

He sits alone in the far corner of the boardroom at Rankin, Rankin, and Gould three days after my family discovered our secret. He scoots his chair forward and back a nervous inch or two on its wheels. Alexander is at the head of the long conference table. Scattered around the table are my parents, Aunt Simone, and Daniel. Separated by empty seats, they are islands in a wooden sea. Emma and I sit in a pair of chairs against the wall on the opposite side of the room from Johnny. He is barely visible behind my father.

Alexander places his palms on the table in a power move. "I've asked Mr. Skeegs to be here. Are we waiting for anyone else?"

My mother swivels her head to take inventory of the attendees. She turns toward Alexander. "Curtis returned to Vegas on Sunday. Simone, where's Stewart?"

"He decided not to come. Brock had to work, and I

191

didn't think this would be a healthy environment for my impressionable, younger son." Her voice breathy, she plays the role of a victim trying to protect her family.

Alexander says, "Let's begin, then. I want to express that I and the partners have always had reservations about the manner in which your aunt wanted to settle her estate."

My mother mimics his pose, slamming her hands on the table. "You should have stopped her. This game of hers is against the law."

"It isn't. And she, being of sound mind and body, had every right to decide the fate of her holdings. While she placed a good deal of trust in Mr. Skeegs, he was never to be the sole arbiter of the will. A court-appointed arbitrator and I will evaluate each of you according to Mr. Skeegs's interpretation of Ms. Piccolo's conditions. The process of selecting an heir has not, for all intents and purposes, begun."

"Then why have we been dashing around the City like a bunch of fools, forced to involve ourselves in meaningless or unpleasant tasks? My husband and I are very charitable people. We give our money. Volunteering is for people without the means to give. And removing paint in a burnt-out neighborhood…" My mother sits back in her chair, satisfied she has said enough.

Aunt Simone raises a finger to speak. Alexander gives her a nod. "Sending us to a blighted neighborhood in Brooklyn to do manual labor in no way indicates our abilities and ambitions for managing her wealth."

He takes a sip of water. "I hear what you're saying. Your aunt was a generous, community-minded person. How she ran her business and spent her time reflected her character. I respect her wish to have her legacy maintained similarly, but it is tricky for us to comply with her wish. Each of you is a unique individual. We can't expect you to be exactly like your aunt.

"She hoped that, by spending a few days involved in activities that reflected her, your similarities to her would come to the fore. She didn't want us to judge you until you could better understand both who she was and the importance of continuing her legacy."

"What was Aunt Donna's relationship to—" My brother points accusatorially toward Johnny. "—him? Were they *lovers*?" The acrid, teasing tone he uses makes the hair on my neck stand on end.

Johnny chokes on a cough. Alexander fixes on him, an embarrassed laugh escaping his nose. "Johnny?"

Johnny holds his hands in surrender. "Definitely not. She was my boss. Nothing more."

"Daniel, what are you implying?" my mother asks.

"I wondered if kissing Johnny was the prerequisite for inheriting the fortune. Or maybe that's what my sister believed."

I lean forward to wheel my chair toward the table, but Emma holds me back. She taps the air downward with her fingers, reminding me to lower the heat. "One thing has nothing to do with the other." I coil with defensiveness.

Daniel toys with his phone while I suppress my rage. He holds his phone to the center of the table in victory. "I did a little research last night. Johnny and Lauren graduated from the same high school."

Everyone in the room — me included — gasps.

Daniel leers at me. "How long have you two been plotting to take over Aunt Donna's estate, hmm? Did you begin after she died, or did you plan your coup ten, twelve years ago?"

Johnny holds his breath. Emma shakes her head at Daniel. Alexander appears to be calculating the square root of the total weight of the furniture in the room. And the rest of my family would devour me if they were lions instead of people.

I can't let Daniel's discovery hang in midair, undefended. I leave sweaty handprints on the arms of my chair when I press myself to my feet. "For the record, I hated Johnny in high school. He made me fail a test, and you know how much that pissed me off."

My mother can't help but nod in agreement. My father throws me an encouraging smile.

"I hadn't seen or even thought about him until the day Aunt Donna died. Total coincidence. We ran into each other in Central Park. He was walking his dogs. Including Stella. She peed on me." Emma erupts in a fit of giggles. I give her a less-than-sincere lethal glance through the edges of my narrowed eyes. "So yeah, ten years after I graduated from high school, I still detested Johnny with every fiber in my body."

Alexander faces Johnny. "You should have revealed that you had prior connections to a member of the family. I agree with the Piccolos: your connection to Lauren may render you unable to be an impartial judge. Can you confirm whether there is a developing interpersonal relationship between you and Ms. Bent?"

Johnny's chest rises with his breath. "I spent time with everyone. Stew, Daniel, and I got to know each other while we were at Luna Park. And I spoke at length with Curtis, Zara – I mean, Mrs. Bent, Simone, and Emma on the subway ride home from Coney Island and while we scrubbed the paint at the Brooklyn property. I developed interpersonal relationships with all seven of Ms. Piccolo's potential heirs."

"How lovely." My mother does not add an accent to any syllable. Her face mimics her sarcasm with minimal movement and dull eyes. "But here's my question: how many of us did you kiss?"

"Um, only Lauren. And the kiss wasn't premeditated. I didn't intend to interfere with any of this. We had a moment. OK, maybe two."

"*Two* kisses?" My mother's rage fills the room. I check my face for burns after she trains her eyes on me.

I stutter, "Yes, but—"

Johnny interrupts me. "I was totally in the wrong both times. And Lauren let me know it. She understood the conflict our attraction posed, and she made it clear that letting anything develop between us would be an ethical breach. I agree. I admire her for choosing you over me.

My mother leans forward to speak, but Alexander interjects. "Lauren, has Johnny presented an accurate description of the situation?"

"Yes." My eyes widen, daring anyone to challenge me.

He continues, "I do not think the kisses in any way compromise Lauren's position in the deliberation process. But I have decided to dismiss Mr. Skeegs from taking part in the proceedings from this point on." He extends his hand to Johnny. "Thank you for your help."

Johnny rises and shakes Alexander's hand. He threads his way between the wall and the incensed occupants ringing the table. I purse my lips, avoiding his eyes.

When the door closes behind Johnny, Alexander speaks again. "Are you satisfied as to the fairness of the settlement process now?"

"Certainly not. He's tainted everything, hasn't he? We will sue him." My mother gathers the support of her sister and son with a bounce of her head.

Alexander spreads his hands, palms up. "I'm sorry, but what exactly is your case?"

"That he prevented us from inheriting our aunt's estate."

"But he hasn't. We haven't begun to settle it."

"It has been three months since Aunt Donna died, and we're no closer to learning who inherits what. Lauren, look at the mess you've gotten us into," my mother says with exasperation.

I want to disappear or to behave with grace, but the seething bubbles of anger inside me propel me out of my chair. "I can't believe you, Mom! I'm your daughter. Just two weeks ago, you told me I deserved to be a benefactor because I shared Aunt Donna's sense of decency."

"Had I known your little secret then, the conversation would have gone quite differently."

My father puts his hand on my mother's. "Zara, you're being unnecessarily harsh to Lauren. Our children don't keep secrets from us, nor do they aim to hurt or deceive us."

I nod fervently, only to reconsider. "One of them doesn't. I've lived in the shadow of my brother for twenty-eight years. Nothing I've done has ever been good enough for you compared to Daniel. But which of your children chose to go into real estate? Who spends more time with you?"

My mother rolls her eyes. "Oh, Lauren. You and your brother are so different. That brain of his was made for science, not real estate. He works for such an important pharmaceutical company, developing medicines to cure humanity of their problems. And with a fiancée to care for, he can't come home to see us as often as we'd wish."

Daniel flashes me a warning signal across the table. I shake my head, holding my jaw clenched.

"His pharmaceutical company is being sued for hundreds of millions of dollars for its role in the opioid addiction crisis. He was developing a diet pill. Hardly the stuff of medical miracles destined to save the world, is it? I suppose he hasn't given you a recent update on his employment situation. Or his relationship status."

"You're being dramatic, Lauren. I asked Daniel about what you implied in your message. He explained that he took late shifts on the days he needed to be with his family. Genevieve couldn't change her schedule to join us."

"If you're judging me for kissing Johnny, I think you all should be judged for who you really are, too. Daniel lost his job and his fiancée. Everyone should know you plan to convert Aunt Donna's rental units to co-ops if you inherit her buildings, Mom. And that Uncle Curtis actually lost his money on a bad investment, not because his ex-wife emptied their bank account. Aunt Simone isn't hiding any secrets on par with her brother, but she did beg me to help her win because she can't afford her apartment or Marc's school. You are all motivated by greed, not by loyalty to Aunt Donna."

My parents and brother talk heatedly amongst themselves. Emma asks me for more details about her father. Aunt Simone's eyes change from meek to conspiratorial. I fly through my memory banks, desperately trying to guess what she might say against me. "I know something else about Zara," she whispers.

Everyone grows silent. "It's the reason she and Aunt Donna had their fight. She staged a coup with her co-op board fourteen years ago. When she discovered that Aunt Donna didn't put an empty unit up for sale, instead renting it to a new tenant, my sister and the co-op board took Aunt Donna to court."

The room buzzes. My relatives become warriors, attacking each other like the cats at the climax of *Millions of Cats*. My mother verbally assaults her sister. Daniel defends himself to my father. Emma leaves a hostile message on her father's voicemail. Alexander takes notes.

I heave a sigh. While I hate the energy of the room, relief rushes through me when I dispel the pressure of being the lone bad guy.

Aunt Donna would hate this. Her nieces and nephews have proven we can't live up to her standards, but is it worth turning everyone against each other in order to find the least undeserving relative?

I approach the table and clear my throat. "Someone has to put an end to our battles. Examining each of us under a microscope has created an impossible solution. No one in any family could survive this level of scrutiny. Aunt Donna devised a horrible way to name an heir. I'd like to present a solution. What I propose to Mr. Rankin is for him to split the estate three ways between Uncle Curtis, Aunt Simone, and my mother. Period. Personally, I believe bringing the family back together and restoring the peace would be the best way to honor Aunt Donna's legacy. I would rather walk away with nothing than continue to endure the insanity you have wreaked."

I retrieve my purse from under my chair and exit the boardroom. My finger is too jittery to press the elevator button. I mash the button with my fist and put my hand on my belly to quiet it while I wait to exit the building.

I exhale when the doors close. Alone at last! Until perfectly manicured fingers bend around the edges of the elevator doors before they fully close. "Lauren?"

CHAPTER TWENTY-SIX
THERE'S ONLY SO MUCH A JAUNTY BOW CAN DO

"Lauren, wait up!"

I step aside to let Emma enter the elevator, but say nothing to her.

She squeezes the breath out of me. "You're a rockstar."

"Not hardly. Unless throwing a tantrum worthy of a rockstar counts."

She shakes her head vehemently. "Listen to you. I'm reeling from everything I heard during the meeting, and I'm ready to go nuclear on my dad and my aunts. Meanwhile, you've been carrying around the knowledge of all of it except for your mother's coup against Aunt Donna without breaking a sweat. How have you managed not to suffer a nervous breakdown?"

I shrug. "I guess I trusted the system and figured the truth would come out. And it did."

"By trusting the system, do you mean you trusted Johnny?" Her tone is teasing.

I take a second to absorb her question. Trying to reconcile my feelings for Johnny with the boardroom maelstrom I've just escaped sets me off-kilter at first, but eventually, clarity seeps in to calm my brain. I suppose learning to trust Johnny lies at the crux of everything. If I didn't trust him, I would still hate him, and I certainly never would have kissed him.

But trusting him as a representative of Aunt Donna's wishes might also explain why I ignored Uncle Curtis and Aunt Simone's pleas for me to help them win. Or paid no attention to my mother's promise to convert rental units into co-ops. Johnny and the arbitrators would uncover the truth without my help. Well, up until everything exploded a few minutes ago and I had no choice but to say something.

Aunt Donna knew my mother had sued her and that Uncle Curtis had ransacked Emma's trust fund. She knew that Aunt Simone was living above her means and wouldn't be interested in following Aunt Donna's mission. She could have cut the three of them out of her will. But she didn't. Which means she trusted the system, too.

I wait until we're on the sidewalk to answer Emma. "Aunt Donna trusted Johnny. Getting to know him has brought me closer to her. He wagers her optimism prevented her from anticipating the mess we're in today. The way I see it, a person who pivoted from acquiring wealth for herself to providing affordable housing for others would focus so much on the good, she wouldn't have suspected her family to be rotten to the core."

"Do you think we are?" The way she contorts her lips gives me the impression she has already answered the question in the affirmative.

"No." It surprises me to answer with such ease, considering how I just eviscerated members of my family a few minutes ago. "Everyone could have been waiting for Aunt Donna to die so they could inherit her money, but in the interim, you loved your father. I love my mother despite the current situation. Aunt Simone hasn't kicked Stew out of her house yet, has she? That's how she expresses her love for her son. And all this love has to count for something, right?"

She wrinkles her nose. "You're going to make me forgive my father, aren't you?"

"Nah ah. I'd still be pretty cheesed if I were you. But I bet you'll forgive him soon enough."

"Maybe. How 'bout you and your mom?"

"I want to go home, but not yet."

"What about Johnny?" Emma says his name with a nasal, singsongy tone.

"What about him?"

"Now that he's not part of the will settlement process, you're free to date him."

My heart doesn't leap at the mention of his name. I can't tell whether it's because my family trampled my heart into submission or whether I am subconsciously as greedy and scheming as the rest of them. Did I really fall for him or was I using him without realizing it?

I should call him to tie up our loose ends, whatever they are. One thing is obvious, though. If we are meant to be together, I can't bring a new boyfriend home for dinner with the folks if he's the guy they're suing.

I decide not to follow Emma back to her apartment or go to the office. I need to get this Johnny thing squared away. I text him to invite him to lunch. He suggests I head to Brooklyn to tour the completed building around the corner from the garages.

The clatter of the J train takes the edge off the sense of isolation encompassing me. While it sounds dramatic, my entire world has turned upside down. Which is stupid, because as messed up as my family life is, at least I have my career.

My phone rings while I'm descending the steps from the subway platform at my stop.

"Hi, Mrs. Ramos. Good to hear from you!"

A gust of anger blasts through the speaker of my phone. "What did you do to my apartment?"

I brace myself against a post, taking a panicked inventory of the recent encounters I've had with her home. Last I checked, I'm not pyrokinetic. Since I haven't been to her co-op in a week, I assume it hasn't burned down.

"I beg your pardon?"

"Your renter. She turned everything pink."

Phew! Call off the fire brigade. "Her belongings are pink. When she leaves, they'll go with her. I told her not to move your things. Please allow me to apologize on her behalf."

"Well, she's packing everything now. Didn't seem too upset when I told her she had to move out. She said she was going home to Oklahoma."

Crap. I've lost Becca as a client.

I correct Mrs. Ramos. "Nebraska."

"So long as she leaves my apartment, she could go to Mars for all I care. But that doesn't help the wall situation."

"What wall situation?"

"They're pink."

"You mean the posters? Or did she leave marks on the walls by removing them?"

"No. She painted the walls. I can't live with pink walls. She — or you — has to pay to have them repainted."

My fingers ache from gripping the phone. I'm less upset about losing Becca than I am about her violating the terms of her rental. But perhaps her transgression won't matter.

My inner real estate lady bursts onto the scene. I tug the hem of my blazer with my free hand and straighten my back. "The walls may not need repainting. A fresh coat of paint, regardless of the color, will help the apartment show even better."

"Oh, about showing the apartment. The pink walls had me so upset that I forgot why I called you in the first place. I'm not selling my apartment. My trial run of living with my sister made the decision for me. That daughter-in-law of hers would be the death of me if I stayed a day longer. Please take my apartment off the market."

Dread lumps in my gut. So long, commission. So long, two-thirds of my clients. That just leaves the Johnsons. Too bad Leon hasn't contacted me about whether his clients will accept our bid.

With my career in tatters, I can't expect a happy ending for the Johnsons. Losing the Ramos listing could be the sign that I should abandon my dreams of being a successful realtor. Should the Johnsons not close on a new home in the next four months, I promise I will walk away from anything to do with real estate.

Even though I haven't shed a tear today, an itchy, buzzy sensation infects my chest and face like what followed a massive crying spell when I was a kid. I can't face Johnny until it passes. Shaking out my arms, I try to restore normalcy before confronting him.

Without my mother's running commentary obliterating my own thoughts, I survey the neighborhood as I walk. From my mother's point of view, it's a wasteland. But she's wrong. The neighborhood pulses with life. People hustle in and out of the shops on Broadway. I wonder whether they rent apartments from Aunt Donna.

When I pass the garages, which bear the silver polka dots from our cleaning spree in their fields of graffiti, I focus on the air above them. I fill in the space. Bricks and glass materialize. As do images of nosy ladies peering through windows onto the street and a mother standing over the shoulder of her kid practicing the piano. What are the chances my mother and her siblings will build homes for them if they inherit the estate?

I growl to myself, hoping to scare away the alternative image forming in my mind. The desire to witness the future my aunt had imagined come to life gnaws at my gut.

I turn onto the side street. The last time my aunt's

legacy filled me with optimism was walking on this block with Johnny. Was it only three days ago? I drag my feet toward the building.

"Lauren!" Johnny waves at me. He's still in his navy suit, the one he wore to Aunt Donna's funeral. I'm glad he was already in his seat when I entered the boardroom this morning. He wears that suit way too well. I may have thrown myself at him given the chance. And that would not have improved matters, to say the least.

I avoid his offer of a hug by extending my hand. He looks at me through quizzical eyes.

"You hungry now, or do you want a tour of the building? I can take you to my favorite coffee shop over on Broadway if you're hungry."

"I'm ready for lunch." Whatever had plagued me on the train has left my body. A single minute next to Johnny, absorbing his calm, and the nonsense I endured earlier falls away.

We sit on opposite banquettes of lime green vinyl in the back of the narrow coffee shop. I crane my neck to read the listings on the chalkboard behind the counter when the server comes to our booth.

"The meatloaf is good," Johnny says.

"I think I'll go with a turkey club."

"Another fine choice. I'll have the meatloaf."

When we're alone, I say, "Look, Johnny. I'm really sorry."

His eyebrows spike with worry. "About what?"

"About my mother. My family."

He relaxes. What had he expected me to say?

"Don't apologize for your family."

"Even if my mother sues you?"

"I hope she doesn't, but it wouldn't involve you."

"How could it not? I'm stuck inside their massive, tangled trap. I'd give anything to escape it. None of what went down would have happened if I hadn't kissed you."

"If you hadn't kissed me, then you really would have

something to apologize for." His eyes sparkle as his grin broadens.

With the chaos exploding within my head, I need to move past his comment and the way it stirs my body to life. "Things went downhill after you left. Did you know that my mother and her co-op board sued Aunt Donna?"

"Yup."

"How could my aunt not hold that against her?"

"It was just business to her. Once upon a time, she invested to grow wealthy. She changed her perspective and hoped your mother would, too. She never lost hope for her niece."

"Who won the lawsuit?"

"Your aunt. There are still ten rental units in your building."

I lift my hands from the table when our server brings our food. "I'm embarrassed to admit to how little I pay attention to the building where I live. Shows you what a crappy real estate lady I've turned out to be."

He plants his elbow on the table and props his chin in the palm of his hand. "Why do you call yourself a real estate lady?"

"Because that's what my mother is. I want to be like her."

His chin rises from his hand to point at me. "Well, you've mastered the wardrobe."

I self-consciously tug the oversized copper-colored satin bow at the neck of my blouse. I wear the uniform with pride, but I suspect my outfits are little more than facades, no different from the false fronts of the buildings on the main drag of an old frontier town.

"Turns out a jaunty bow alone doesn't git 'er done. I don't think I'm cut out to be a realtor on the Upper West Side."

"You'll find a whole lot of real estate beyond your neighborhood. Would you consider changing your title from real estate lady to Brooklyn baroness?"

"I withdrew my name from consideration. It makes sense for them just to divide the estate equally between my mother, aunt, and uncle."

"We'll see." His eyebrows quirk when our eyes meet.

"What does that mean?"

"Nothing."

I stab the mound of coleslaw on my plate. "It's not like you have a say in it."

"Or will be around to see how it turns out. Unless…"

"Hold on. Where are you going?"

"Nowhere. But I've tendered my resignation. I'll stay long enough to help Juan find his footing, but once the will heads to probate court, it would be best for me to be out of the picture."

I drop my fork on the plate with a clatter. "But this is where you belong. You remaining involved is probably the only way Aunt Donna could have imagined her mission continuing, by you helping her heir or heirs."

"They'll be fine without me."

"I can't be so sure. They'll screw it up royally."

"We'll see." His smug smile reappears.

"What are you, the Cheshire Cat?"

"I have faith everything will turn out fine."

"I hope you're right."

He takes my hands in his. Chills zoom the length of my spine. "One good thing about the situation is no one could object to us being together," he says.

Butterflies join the chills. Make that an evil motorcycle gang of butterflies who leave skid marks on the lining of my stomach when they peel out. I pull my hands from his.

"Maybe it's the crazy aftermath of today talking, but I'm not in the right place to start a relationship. Especially with you."

If I spend another second peering into the melting brown pools of his eyes, I will drown in a sorrow equal to his. I slide out from the table. With tears in my eyes and without a backward glance, I leave him behind.

CHAPTER TWENTY-SEVEN
COMFORT POODLE

The passengers on the subway car glance nervously at me when I heave an earth-shattering sigh. I've just walked away from everything I want. The other riders are lucky I'm only sighing. If the floor wasn't a sticky, disgusting Petri dish, I'd be lying prone, pummeling it with my fists and shrieking like my Aunt Shirley at her rich sister-in-law's funeral.

The rational part of my brain puffs on a cigar, pleased with my self-sabotaging efforts. It knows nothing good would come from either situation. Despite the pleas of my heart and every square inch of my body harboring a Johnny addiction, leaving him behind will make my life a lot easier than giving in to my yearning to be with him.

I admit to myself that the more I've learned about Aunt Donna's business, the more running it appeals to me. And I may be the lone Piccolo to share my aunt's vision. But I don't have the stomach for the family drama. And with me at the center of the storm, there is but one logical solution: to extricate myself from the mess.

So no more Johnny, no more quests to inherit Aunt Donna's estate. I've done the two tasks necessary for restoring order. When will my life reflect the fact that I've done the right thing?

I open the front door of our family's office. The bells above it jingle. My mother peeks over her shoulder while feeding pages into the copy machine.

"There she is!" My father greets me with a hug.

"Hey, Dad."

"Did you eat? We have leftover pasta from lunch. Can I warm it up for you?" my mother asks.

"I had a sandwich, but thanks."

Jitters course through my gut. That my mother's first instinct is to feed me bodes well. She must be a fan of my solution for settling the estate. Should I ignore the proverbial elephant in the room and enjoy the peace rather than discuss the events of the last few days?

My mother drops a stack of copies onto her desk and wheels her chair over to mine. "Well, that was a revealing meeting, wasn't it?"

I audition a few responses in my head. When the least snarky thing I come up with is, "Aunt Simone's taste in clothing always leans toward revealing," I opt to remain silent.

"I can't believe your brother has been hiding his life from us since March. The poor dear. Well, at least we know the story now. Between you and me, I never truly warmed to Genevieve. And talk about living a secret life: what a revelation about your uncle. He should have come to your father and me before sinking his life savings into a scam. We would have stopped him. He could not be more upset over what he did to his daughter. I'm ready to loan him the money to pay her back."

"So you're not mad at either of them?"

"Why would I be? They're family. Things happen. We have to help each other when things go awry."

She willingly glosses over everyone else's transgressions. My breathing becomes shallower, constricting my chest. "You blamed me for ruining everything."

My father hovers over my desk, reaching for my mother's hand. "The entire way home, your mother could talk of nothing more than how bad she felt for what has happened between the two of you these last few days, honey."

My mother's eyes widen, and she nods her head. "That's right. Oh, Lauren. Please forgive me. I was so caught up in my anger toward Johnny, I couldn't think straight."

I'm tired of fighting, but I'm not ready to put the incident aside. "I understand how emotional the situation is for you. But Johnny isn't to blame. You shouldn't be mad at him."

"He should have recused himself when he learned you were Donna's great-niece. And he shouldn't have kissed you. Didn't he think about how it could harm you?"

For a moment, the problems regarding Aunt Donna's estate fade away. I picture myself a dozen years younger, waiting for my date to the junior prom to pick me up. My mother fretted and paced, perhaps imagining she was sending me into the deep, dark night with a convicted pedophile. I resented her protection then, but I can appreciate her motivation today. As it turned out, my date was a world-class tool.

My mother may not be the best at showing her love for me, but if I'm paying attention to the details, I never fail to notice it. Like a shooting star, its glimmer will always cut through the darkness.

I wonder if my mother also has chafed at the heir-naming process and the antagonistic spirit it has raised. I wouldn't be surprised if she hated Johnny the minute she met him. Like mother, like daughter. And when she suspected he might corrupt me, she parented me like the mother of a teenager, using emotion rather than logic to make her point.

I press my palms together. "Can we pretend none of this ever happened?" My phone rings, but I decide to

209

ignore it.

"Oh, I hope so." My mother wraps me in her arms. The vanilla and coffee-infused floral scent of her Black Opium perfume soothes away layers of hurt.

She returns to her chair. "Lauren, honey, nothing made your father and me prouder than your decision to follow our footsteps into real estate. Business has not been great for us lately. The slower things become, the more concerned I am about your future. I would hate for you to find yourself stuck in a job that couldn't sustain you.

"If the lawyers take your marvelous advice and split the estate between Curtis, Simone, and me, everything will change for all of us. Imagine the opportunities your father and I can provide for you by incorporating your aunt's properties into our business."

My mouth grows dry as I try to envision myself in my mother's version of the future. But were I to criticize her plans, it would destroy our détente.

My phone alerts me I have a message. It's from Leon. I reel backward when I listen to it.

"Mom, Leon countered my client's bid with one that's ten thousand above asking price."

"He did? Perhaps he has another offer on the table and wants to start a bidding war."

"I doubt it. He said my clients have to pay for what I did to him."

"What did you do to him?" My mother listens to the tone she used. "I'm sorry. I'm still keyed up from this morning. I didn't mean to accuse you of anything."

"I haven't a clue." I really don't.

"Then let me handle Leon. I have a few things I need to say to him."

My father chuckles to himself before returning to his desk. I fight with myself. Professionally, I should stop her and make the call myself. But I don't have the fight in me.

I sink into my seat. "Um, if you think I should call him, I will."

"Oh, no, sweetie. It will be my pleasure." She dials his number with a glint in her eye. When he answers, she speaks in clipped phrases in between whatever it is Leon is saying. She is in full-on momma bear mode, defending me to the death.

"My daughter most certainly would not steal your client," she barks at him.

She claps her hand over the phone and uses her eyes to ask me to confirm her statement. I assure her with my hands I did nothing of the sort.

But something nags at my conscience. I pull out the paperwork from the open house where I met the Johnsons. Reading it, I gasp.

Gus and Leon are partners. I wave at my mother, worry wrinkling my brow.

"I need to take a call from a client. But we're not done." She hangs up, her eyes questioning me.

"Mom, I think he used to represent the Johnsons. They never told me who their previous broker was, and they swore they parted ways on good terms. They left because he only sent them to see his company's listings, all of which were far above their budget."

She crosses her arms. "Sounds like Leon."

"But that means he also never showed them the one listing he had that would have been perfect for them: the listing on which they put in an offer."

"Oh, Leon. He gives our profession a bad reputation. If he thinks I was mad before, he has no idea what is coming next. Let me fix everything for you."

The gulp of air I take in makes the bottoms of my lungs ache. "No, Mom. This is my mess. I'll handle it."

Her eyebrows spike upward, not in doubt but with concern. "You sure? I don't mind taking care of him."

"Yes. I'm sure."

Her willingness to protect me fortifies me for the call. How blind am I that I don't always notice how much she loves me? Her love and support and exactly the reasons

I've chosen her over Aunt Donna twice in my life.

I duck into the kitchenette to make the call. "Leon, this is Lauren Bent."

He begins to bark in my ear. Funny that a man known for stealing clients and listings is losing his mind when he thinks the same thing happened to him.

I cut him off. "You're free to believe whatever you want, but I called to give you my side of the story. The Johnsons approached me because they were frustrated with both the lack of attention you showed them and with the unaffordable units you selected for them. I explicitly stated to them when we met that I would not take them on as clients unless they spoke to you first. I insisted they give you a chance to do right by them."

"They did speak to me."

"And did you listen to them? Did you show them properties in their price range after your conversation?"

He sighs. "Well, I—"

"Yes or no?"

"No. But I planned to."

I throw back my shoulders. "Why hadn't you shown them the apartment on 95th Street?"

"I didn't think they'd like it."

I want to bash the phone against my forehead in frustration. "Would you agree that at least the listing price would have appealed to them more than the two units you sent them to see?"

"Everyone comes to me with a low budget. They sell themselves short. It's my job to make them understand it's worth spending a bit more now to avoid regretting choosing a home that's second best."

"No, Leon. It's not your job to cause financial hardships for your clients. What astounds me more than you not showing the Johnsons an ideal listing is that you continue to do a disservice to the clients whose home the Johnsons wish to purchase. Here is how things are going to go. You will present the Johnsons' offer to your clients.

They — and they alone — can decide whether our bid is to their liking."

"You're just like your mother. You're a first-class b—"

I cut him off, grinning like a loon. "Leon, that is the nicest thing I've ever heard. Make sure the next thing you say to me is equally nice, that your clients have either accepted the offer or have a reasonable counteroffer for my clients. Goodbye."

When I walk into the office, I throw myself against my mother, giving her a squeeze. "Thank you for offering to go to bat for me. You gave me the courage to take care of Leon."

"And?"

"And he will share our offer with his client."

"Good for you, sweetheart! Richard, isn't she terrific?"

My father grins. "You make us so proud!"

"Thanks! I needed something to go right today. Did I tell you that on top of everything else, Mrs. Ramos delisted her apartment?"

"Oh, Lauren. You deserve better." My mom's tone is as soft as the way she caresses my hair while I rest against her shoulder.

My father leans to the side of his desk. "Why doesn't that surprise me about Mrs. Ramos? Well, you gave it your all, and that's what counts."

"A paycheck would be nice..." I inhale sharply.

Even with everything back to normal with my mother, I'm still frustrated. Not only have I lost both my listing and my one rental client today, but also my clients' bid is the hands of a vindictive realtor. Oh, and I told the man who makes me go weak in the knees we're over before we even began. At least I have wonderful, supportive parents.

A bottle of wine and a lapdog are upstairs, calling my name. If getting my buzz on while stroking Stella's silken curls doesn't dispel the rest of my storm clouds, I don't know what will.

CHAPTER TWENTY-EIGHT
WHAT WILL HR SAY?

We return to the scene of the crime — the boardroom of Rankin, Rankin, and Gould — three weeks later, but things are different this time. More Piccolos have shown up, for starters. Eight of Aunt Donna's relatives plus their spouses take seats around the table. Johnny didn't make the guest list.

Alexander and the arbitrator came to our apartment last week to interview my mother and me. Her interview lasted twice as long as mine. While I waited for my turn, I drowned out their conversation by blaring Green Day through my headphones in my bedroom. I didn't have much to say during my exit interview. I mean, why bother? They already knew my point of view. I wasn't up for an encore performance as the family martyr and scold.

I've abandoned my real estate lady wardrobe since our last family meeting. It makes sense, given that I no longer aspire to be a real estate lady. I don't know what I want to be when I grow up. I doubt I will stray far from real estate, but my heart is no longer in the grind of unloading overpriced units on the Upper West Side.

Despite Emma and Troi's pleas to help me replenish

the gaps in my closet where blouses with bows once hung, I am working with what I have at the moment. My mother's eyes spun in their sockets when she realized I planned on wearing jeans to today's meeting. I've decided a blazer over a T-shirt, paired with my best jeans, fits the new me. I consider it a victory for both of us she didn't say a word about the outfit and that I didn't run back to my room to change to please her.

Alexander pours himself a glass of water from the pitcher in front of my mother, who then offers some to my father, brother, and me. An air of civility breezes through the room.

"Good morning, and thank you for coming in today. An independent arbiter and I have completed our deliberations regarding the settlement of Donna Piccolo's estate. It was our task to comply with the wishes of your aunt while following the law. After much consideration, we have determined how best to divide her estate in a fair and just manner according to her wishes."

"Should we have brought representation of our own? We won't stand for any nonsense and personal bias." My mother tugs on the lapel of her blazer with authority.

Even though she and I have been getting along, I still clench, bracing for another dustup.

"Let me read through the full settlement before you make any judgments, please. You may find, when given the full scope of the terms of the will, that things are not as you imagine them."

My mother's hands, which she holds together in a fist, slip from the table into her lap.

"Let me start with your aunt's personal estate. She leaves equal shares of her home on West 69th Street to her nieces, Zara Bent and Simone Heller, and her nephew, Curtis Piccolo."

Aunt Simone mouths to my mother, "How much?"

My mother oscillates her wrist, splaying her fingers apart. "Two mil?"

215

Uncle Curtis smiles, but Aunt Simone bobs her head from side to side, unsure of her level of satisfaction. Uncle Brock places his hand atop hers.

"Excuse me, Alexander," my mother says. "Could I be the listing agent for the unit?"

"No. We advise you to select a neutral party to handle the sale. Continuing on with the personal estate, in addition to the apartment, each of the three of you will receive two-hundred-fifty thousand dollars in assets."

My mother juts her jaw forward and nods. Uncle Curtis beams at Emma, who responds with a frosty stare. Aunt Simone still doesn't look pleased with her inheritance.

Alexander clears his throat, and we return our attention to him. "Donna leaves one-hundred-fifty thousand dollars each to her great-niece, Mavis Davis, and her great-nephews Daniel Bent and Stewart Kline."

Emma grimaces. I assume it's because the lawyer used her given name, not because she wanted to inherit more. Stewart pumps his fist in the air. Daniel remains stoic. My stomach jumps and squirms with disappointment. Aunt Donna didn't leave me anything. But didn't I suggest I should receive nothing?

"Mr. Rankin, why didn't my son, Marc, receive a similar inheritance?" Aunt Simone whines. My mother elbows me, hoping I'll complain about him omitting my name from his list, too.

"If you recall, given the problems Donna encountered with bequeathing money to a minor—" We stare at Uncle Curtis. He turns toward the door, perhaps seeking a different scapegoat. "Combined with the lack of interaction she had with Marc and his age, she explained in her video that his share would be passed down to him from his mother."

Aunt Simone purses her lips. Uncle Brock makes notes on a pad.

"These settlements comprise the whole of Donna Piccolo's personal estate. Which brings us to the matter of her business holdings. Her development company, Community Development Trust, owns the building on 97th Street, the two properties in Brooklyn, and has shares in the co-op on 108th Street. Your aunt leaves Community Development Trust in its entirety to her great-niece, Lauren Bent."

The room becomes a giant vacuum, preventing us from drawing another breath. I'm uncertain whether I heard what I think I heard. I lower my gaze, avoiding the eyes boring into me from around the table.

"In addition to the buildings, the company has set aside assets to pay for the completion of the new development and to cover all taxes, fees, and general upkeep and maintenance costs along with the company salaries for the properties for the next twenty years. Income from the rental units will provide for unforeseen operating costs and a salary for Ms. Bent."

A roomful of accountants hacking away on adding machines would be quieter than the whirring of the calculations going on inside the heads of my relatives. They stare at me accusatorially. I'm still numb from the shock.

Aunt Simone raises her hand. Lightning flashes in her eyes. "Lauren is now worth millions. I don't see why she gets to sell the buildings and pocket the money all for herself. Especially given the whole incident with Mr. Skeegs. Don't the rest of us deserve a share?"

I'm beginning to hate Aunt Donna. Why did she leave me her fortune? I don't want to spend the rest of my life grappling with guilt or worse, dealing with my irate relatives.

Alexander bats his hand at her and continues to speak. "Your aunt had very specific conditions regarding the future of her company. Conditions she assumed would be difficult for some of you to honor. Her search for an heir wasn't about making one relative richer than the others. She sought — through the quests — to find the family member or members who would be best suited to comply with her demands.

"The heir is not permitted to sell any of the buildings for another twenty years. The rental units in the buildings on 97th Street and in Brooklyn must remain rental units, and their rents must be set according to a specific percentage of the tenants' income. Simply put, Ms. Bent cannot convert the buildings into co-operatives or condominiums or raise rents or do anything with the intention of increasing profitability of the properties until the twenty-year period ends."

Aunt Simone's wrists flick backward in a gesture of surrender. My brother leans back in his chair, his face a study of disinterest. To them, and perhaps my mother, as well, this portion of the inheritance could not be more undesirable, thanks to its conditions.

I'm in the opposite camp. Had I inherited an estate defined solely by its monetary value, I would be lost. It's not money I desire. What I need is a sense of purpose, an opportunity to help people. And carrying out Aunt Donna's mission fits me like a wet suit. Not in the "encase me like I'm a disgusting hunk of sausage" way, but in the "my goodness, your bespoke suit brings out the color of your soul" kind of way.

My mother drums her fingers on the table. "What about the rental units remaining in the building on 108th Street?"

"The fate of the units is for Ms. Bent to decide."

My mother's mouth widens into a grin. My father's eyes catch up to her plans, sparkling with dreams of me asking them to list all ten apartments. I might not agree to sell any, but I'll let them have their dreams at the moment.

Uncle Curtis leans forward. "So I'm to understand that inheriting Community Development Trust may be more trouble than it's worth?"

"If you consider an estate that is not and cannot be liquid or significantly profitable for the next twenty years to be trouble, then yes."

"I suppose I have no arguments with the division of the estate." Uncle Curtis scans the room, enlisting the rest of the family to join his assessment.

Stew nods. "I'm cool."

Aunt Simone confers with Uncle Brock before facing me. "Lauren, sweetheart. I hope in twenty years if you do liquidate the estate, you won't forget your family."

I picture having to endure my aunt hounding me more than Stella does when she's hungry — which is to say constantly — for the next two decades. I seriously consider contesting the will to avoid such a fate. But the mission gives me the courage to accept.

"Mr. Rankin, thank you for putting your faith in me. If I can become half the woman my great-aunt was, it will be a monumental achievement for me. I can't say what I'll do with the properties in twenty years, but know this: family means everything to me. I promise I won't let greed make the decisions for me."

"No one is better suited to continuing Aunt Donna's mission than my cousin, Lauren. Congratulations!" Emma kisses the tips of her fingers and waves them at me from across the table.

The news begins to sink in. I am stepping into Aunt Donna's shoes. This is the future I am meant to embrace.

But I can't do it alone. Only one living person can guide me. My legs pump nervously while I wait for the meeting to end. I need to make a call.

Stella, the little slut, uses her full arsenal of tricks to command Johnny's attention and demonstrate her delight in seeing him. I wish I could twirl for him and lick his face.

Um, that came out wrong.

Johnny and I sit awkwardly beside each other on a bench in Riverside Park. He breaks the silence first. "So she left it all to you."

"I'm having a hard time believing it."

"You deserve it."

I shrug. "I'm not sure I agree, but I adore the idea of carrying on what she started."

He wears that confident smile of his, the one that fueled my hatred of him in high school. I don't mind it anymore. "Her system for picking an heir worked."

I guess I spoke too soon. "It sucked a whole lot, too."

"All of it?" His eyes are pulling their annoying smoldering routine on me.

I shush my heart when it thumps wildly.

Be cool, Lauren.

I can't pull off being coldly indifferent (to borrow a phrase I learned from Troi) toward him. "Maybe not all of it."

"The Wonder Wheel was pretty awesome." His eyebrows dance above his infernal eyes. I can't prevent myself from slipping into their vortex.

My body thrums with the memories from the Ferris wheel. More than my recall of our first kiss is forcing me to lean toward him, though. Johnny is the antidote to my family. He doesn't overreact. He doesn't try to impress anyone or think only of himself. He nudges me to be better. Because of him, my dreams evolved and came true. I could love a man like Johnny.

But evaluating his merits as a potential boyfriend is not why I wanted to meet with him today. I need him for reasons that have nothing to do with him repeating the trick he does with his tongue on my upper neck, right behind my earlobe.

He reaches for my hand. I push it away with a laugh. "No hanky-panky, young man. I've called this meeting to discuss business. I need a partner to ensure the company's success as I carry out Aunt Donna's mission. My aunt trusted you to assist her, and I know of no one more qualified to continue to serve in the role of right-hand man than you."

"Can we do this—" He cups my cheek with his palm and draws me toward him. His lips alight on mine, and every cell in my body hums. "—if we work together? I don't want anyone to call HR on me for breaking company policy."

Damn it. I can't resist him.

"Does the company have an HR department? I'd hate for them to receive a report about the boss doing this with her employee."

En route to bringing him in for another kiss, my fingers detour, combing a shock of brown hair from his eyes. Pressing the hair to his scalp, I help myself to another delicious smooch. His lips flatten against mine and part. My heart leaps with joy. Stella whines and slithers her head between us.

Johnny pulls away from me with a laugh. "Obviously, HR has gotten word of what's going on between us." He plants a kiss on her head. She wags her tail, curling her butt toward her head.

"And what is going on between us?" I walk my fingers across his thigh to reach for his hand.

He flips his palm upwards to welcome my hand. "You tell me. You're the boss."

"So you accept my proposal to return to your position at Community Development Trust?"

"I do indeed."

"In that case, since we will be working *very* closely with each other—" I inch my leg toward him until it's touching his. "—I can see the merits of developing a bond that extends beyond the office. What I suggest is that we strive to forge such a bond purely for unselfish reasons. I mean, it gives me no pleasure in having to—" I graze the bare skin on his arms with my fingernails. He shudders. "—do this. Or this—" My fingers reach his neck. I slow the pace. His jaw pushes upwards with my stroke. He sucks a breath through his open mouth.

I whisper in his ear, "And I am definitely thinking only

221

of the business when I do this—" I lean across his chest and find his lips with mine. Oh, yes. My new job definitely agrees with me.

CHAPTER TWENTY-NINE
HARD HATS WEREN'T DESIGNED
FOR KISSING

"Ow!" I rub my cheek when the brim of Johnny's hard hat collides with my face. "They didn't take kissing into consideration when they designed these, did they?"

"I may be going out on a limb here, but I doubt much kissing goes down on the average construction site." Johnny removes his hat and tucks it under his arm with a laugh. He puckers up, ready to give it another try.

I pat the bright yellow plastic helmet on my head. "I'm keeping this sucker on. What with the hat hair of it all."

He smiles, undeterred. With a surgeon's precision, he avoids the brim of my hat and engineers contact between our lips, warming me against the early November chill.

Our hard hats and the setting provide an incongruous pairing for our make-out fest. Unless you consider an idle backhoe, a bored backhoe operator, and a vacant lot in Brooklyn to be sexy. Who am I to say? When it comes to fantasies, to each their own.

While I can prattle on for days regarding the thrills of

dating Johnny, this vacant lot is equally capable of sending shivers along my spine. We're breaking ground on the new apartment building today.

I boned up for the event by watching a slew of groundbreaking ceremonies on YouTube. Speechifying was big at a lot of events similar to ours. But I figured renting a podium and sound system was a little over the top given the size of our guest list.

The crew who removed the debris from the demolition of the garages formed a fifteen-foot-long pile of dirt in the middle of the lot. Officially, we're not breaking ground today. Everyone who joins us for the event gets to toss, rather than dig, a ceremonial shovelful of dirt.

My parents and brother emerge from a rideshare car. They're only ten minutes early. Something must be wrong.

"Oh, Lauren. I'm sorry we're late. Your father." My mother says nothing else. She shakes her head with despair, making her lips shudder like Jell-O.

I widen my eyes. "You nearly missed it. We were ready to pack up and go home."

My mother's face sags.

"Ah, Mom. I'm joking. You're early. No one else is here yet."

"Phew. Your father will be the death of me. You know what he did this time?" She doesn't wait for my reply. "He stopped in the office just as we were leaving, made a phone call, and then — you won't believe it — began to brew a pot of coffee. A full pot! He forgot we were on our way to Brooklyn. And our driver was waiting for us out front the whole time."

My father takes a defensive step in front of my mother. "My call generated a new to-do list for me. I thought, 'No time like the present.' I was ready to get to work. But then my tie slipped into the sink when I filled the coffeepot. I realized I was wearing it for a reason. And that reason was to be with my daughter on her very special day. I love you, Lauren, and I'm so proud of you!"

My father's hug drives home what he said. I imagine my Aunt Donna is here with us today, too. I hope she'd be proud of the progress I am making. I sure am.

"Thanks, Dad! It means everything to me for you and Mom — and your new roommate — to be here with me."

Daniel gives me a fist bump. "Pretty cool stuff going on here, Lauren." He has become less of a pill than he used to be. Behold the humbling power of moving into the family apartment! I hope he finds his purpose someday soon. He deserves it.

A black Bentley glides to a stop in front of the lot. The telltale designer red sole of a black suede boot as unsuitable for a construction site as a hard hat is for kissing plants itself on the ground. Red lacquered nails press against the top of the doorframe, and Emma rises from the car.

She runs toward me to give me a quick peck on the cheek. With her arm wrapped around my shoulder, she says, "Lauren! Oh, my god! How amazing does this look without the garages?"

"Girl, yellow is *not* your color." Troi, pinching the brim of my hat, jerks his head upward with disdain.

I bat his hand away. "Oh, you brought *him*."

Emma waves her hands like an umpire calling a runner safe. "No. Nah, uh. Not today, you two. Kiss and make up, will you?"

He and I vocalize our air kisses at a volume loud enough for Aunt Shirley to hear in Rego Park.

I reach for Emma's hand. "How was Vegas?"

"It was a good trip. Dad's new place is great. I could see visiting him every so often."

"Excellent!" I turn when Johnny calls my name. "I'll be back in a second. I have to make my rounds."

Juan and Manny, the two former squatters who my aunt hired to help clean out the building around the corner, are chatting with Johnny. They'll both join the construction crew for this project. Johnny and I haven't told Juan the news yet, but we plan to hire him to be the super of the new building.

I've learned that my aunt not only had a sixth sense about buying properties, but she also had a way of recognizing the potential in people. She gave Johnny a chance, something I, for instance, wouldn't have done in the old days. And Juan is quickly becoming one of my favorite people. His work ethic, sharp mind, and even sharper wit make him my second favorite employee.

The red plastic handle of a shovel blurs when I stare at it without blinking. A pale brick building shimmers into existence in its spot. On the walkway leading to it, a young girl pulls the arm of a man with shopping bags slung on his opposite shoulder. Next to him, a woman pushes a baby carriage. An older man holds the door when the family enters the lobby.

Johnny and I watch the neighborly act while we plant annuals in the cool dirt below a row of shrubs. He abandons his plot to wrap his arm around my waist. My body adjusts to the contours of his like a river to the shoreline. I belong next to him, providing affordable housing for many families. The Beccas and Mrs. Ramoses of my former life fade away. Like when a mirage breaks apart, revealing itself to be nothing more than light and sand, I can barely conjure my silly dreams of selling multi-million dollar properties. I—

"Lauren!"

I snap out of my daydream when my cousins call my name. "Hey, Stew and Gerald. Thanks for coming. You both were able to take the day off from GameStop?"

"My manager wasn't going to let me at first, but after much pleading, he changed the schedule to help me." Stew elbows Gerald in the ribcage. Gerald cautiously extends his elbow toward Stew to reciprocate.

"And the apartment?"

"We're still deciding on the decor. Neither of us had much furniture or stuff. I'm sleeping on a futon on the floor, but Gerald's back went out the first night, so he had to buy a mattress and frame. When the apartment's ready, we're going to throw an epic party. You two will come, right?"

"Johnny and I wouldn't miss it. We're in the mood to go to a party. Especially since your mom decided not to throw a housewarming party for herself."

Stew holds his finger to his lips. "Don't tell her I said so, but I don't think she's as proud of her new house as she was of the last one."

"Upper East Side, Upper West Side, it's a difference of one word."

Our building on West 108th Street lacks the glamour of the home she left. I sold her a three-bedroom apartment for an insanely low price, helping her to escape a huge mortgage and put aside the funds to keep Marc in his private school. And now she lives only two floors away from her dear sister. I don't know why the two of them appear ready to clobber me whenever I mention this convenient little perk of Aunt Simone's new home.

Johnny waves. We're ready to go. I lead my cousins toward the pile of dirt. Eleven shovels, all but two crowned with a hard hat, form a line in the dirt.

I gesture to the rest of our guests to join us. "Why don't you stand behind a shovel with a hat? And for the photo op, we ask for you to wear your hat. Yes, Troi, you included."

Johnny and I go to the opposite side of the dirt pile, facing my family and friends.

I stand on my tiptoes to whisper in Johnny's ear. "You want to speak first?"

"Do I have to?" He scrunches his face like a recalcitrant twelve-year-old.

"No."

His arms crossed against his chest, he says, "Then I will."

"You're an odd duck, Johnny Skeegs. And I love you!"

"I love you, too!" He flashes me the contented, confident smile that once irked the pants off of me. Now the pants come off when… Sorry. Got a little distracted by my handsome boyfriend.

Johnny clasps his hands together. "OK. Before we get to flinging around dirt, Lauren and I want to say a few words about why we're here. We've had a rough journey to reach our groundbreaking, starting with losing Donna. I never expected I'd work for someone with as selfless a vision for solving the pervasive problem of unaffordable housing. I could not have been luckier to be the guy Donna called the day the plumbing went berserk in her building on 97th Street and then for her to invite me along on her journey. She put her money where her mouth was, increasing her holdings to provide additional units to rent. And nothing could make me prouder than to have been by her side to realize her mission.

"This site represents her final project. And while she isn't here to share the excitement, I think bringing her vision to life with you today more than offsets her absence. Most of all, watching the future of Community Development Trust unfold in the hands of her great-niece is the best way to honor her legacy. It's extraordinary to work for two different women who committed themselves to making the world better. And on that note, I'll hand things over to Lauren, the most amazing woman I know."

The depth within his brown eyes reflects the truth of his words. It never crossed my mind I'd find someone who believed in me so fiercely.

My emotions sweep me away. I would love to sneak away to the office around the corner for a little alone time with the man who brings out the best in me. But I can't go rogue now. I have to stick to the plan.

"Um, wow. I don't know what to say except that I will spend the rest of my life trying to be a woman of my great-aunt's caliber. Her deeds inspire me, and I hope this is the first of many opportunities I will have to make a positive impact on the lives of New Yorkers. So, everyone grab a shovel, and let's get the party started."

I hand the backhoe operator my phone and run to the other side of the pile of dirt. Hats on heads, shovels in hand, we pose for the camera and fling dirt before popping the corks on the celebratory bottles of Champagne.

Emma and I clink our glasses together. She leads me to a back corner of the lot, checking over her shoulder to ensure we will be alone. "Guess what? I'm going to be a stepmom."

I choke on my Champagne. "Wait, what? How does that work?"

"When your husband's girlfriend has a baby, you become a stepmom, right?" Her smile can't hide the hurt in her eyes.

"He didn't."

"He did. And he thinks the right thing to do for his child is to marry her mother."

"Oh, hon! What can I do to make you feel better?" I rest my chin on her shoulder, the joy of the day dissipating in an instant. "What happens next?"

"He's giving me the apartment in the divorce and has even offered to pay the taxes and fees on it until it sells. At least Troi and I aren't homeless yet. But I will need a realtor soon. Do you know any?"

I glance across the lot at my parents, who are hugging Johnny like a favorite son. They will die when I hand them the listing of a lifetime.

Emma's news unsettles me. No sooner does my dream come true than her world comes crashing to the ground. So much has changed since I ran into Johnny and his dogs in Central Park seven months ago. Then, I imagined a future built on matching fabulous people with sensational properties. What would fulfilling that dream have brought me? Hefty commissions, sure. And a certain amount of adulation from Lauren wannabes. I can't help but believe my search for approval, especially from my parents, had as much of an impact on preventing my dreams from coming true as anything else.

Despite my protests, Johnny and Aunt Donna introduced me to a new dream. Perhaps it's not so different after all. I still match fabulous people with their dream homes. But I do it for them now. Doing so makes me happier than selling a penthouse apartment on Central Park West ever could. And having Johnny at my side? Well, that's the biggest — and most wonderful — surprise.

So my dad is right about how a planned route doesn't always take us where we're meant to be. Sometimes life sends you on a detour. My advice: take it.

I give Emma a parting kiss at the door to the Bentley. Helping her to find a new dream is top of my list. Stew and Gerald walk toward the subway, and my parents watch the approach of their driver on her phone like children stalking an ant with a magnifying glass.

I entwine my fingers in Johnny's when we're alone. "If you want, we could build a mansion for ourselves on this lot."

"You wouldn't dare!"

"Not a chance. A big, fancy house isn't my fantasy. This—" I sweep my hands first toward the lot and then point at him. "—is the stuff of my fantasies."

His eyebrows wiggle lasciviously. "I gotta hear more about your fantasies. You ready to head home?"

"Only if you promise to wear your hard hat when we get there. And—"

I grin, leaving the rest to his — and my — imagination.

THE END

Reviews are one of the most crucial tools an author can use to introduce her books to new readers. I would be so grateful if you could post a review of *Splitting Heirs* on Amazon, BookBub, and/or Goodreads. Thank you!

SNEAK PEEK OF

LAST RESORT

Book 2 of the Empire State of Mind series

CHAPTER ONE

I cradle the bottle of Champagne as if it were a colicky infant who had just fallen asleep in my arms. "Brandon and I had planned to drink the Bollinger on our tenth anniversary," I say.

Aunt Zara peers at the label. "Was 2002 a good year for Champagne?"

"So he said. He paid at least one thousand dollars for the bottle at auction."

Troi wags his finger at me. "Emma, pour it into plastic cups. Anything he values doesn't deserve the Baccarat."

"But we're drinking it; not him. Besides, the contents of the wine cellar and the crystal are mine now."

"And so is forty-five point seven million dollars." Aunt Zara's eyebrows perform a celebratory dance. Her arms and legs should join the dance since she brought my apartment to contract today.

My cousin Lauren claps her hands, her eyes as wide as her smile. "Two million dollars of which is yours, Mom. I can't believe you and Dad sold the apartment in only seven months. But then again, you're early for everything."

"I don't dawdle, you know," she says.

Lauren shakes her head. "Oh, I know, Mom. I know."

Troi fixates on the unopened bottle of Champagne in my arms. He slaps a plastic travel mug onto the marble kitchen counter. "Fill'er up."

I examine his cup, bemused. "If you insist. I'm sticking with the crystal. The last thing I need is to leave a foul taste in my mouth on purpose. I'm done with the bitterness." My last sentence may not be the complete truth, but I'm willing to repeat it until it becomes true.

"Then let's drink!" Troi grabs the bottle from me with the gentle touch of a sanitation worker flinging trash into a garbage truck. He removes the cage with equal haste.

I wince and reach for the bottle. "Allow me."

A hologram of Brandon swaddling a bottle of Champagne shimmers in my mind. I can't count the number of bottles he has opened for me or how many times I've laughed at his schtick.

With the towel wrapped around both the bottle and the cork, I follow each step of his pantomime, starting by mimicking the placid, almost distant expression in his face while I twist and push the cork. I coax it from the neck of the bottle with care to avoid a bubble-flattening explosion. Before I banish the hologram, I copy one last gesture of Brandon's: the punch line. Without having heard the trademark pop, my guests laugh with surprise when I present the cork. I give my brow a haughty lift and adopt a French accent. "It is done."

I lower my head, hovering my cheek a few inches above the cool marble countertop to compare the level of wine I pour into each glass. I hand glasses to my aunt and cousin and give Troi his sippy cup before claiming a glass for myself. "Let's toast Aunt Zara and Uncle Richard! Without your tireless efforts, I'd be stuck in limbo, waiting for the apartment to sell. My life can't begin until I move, and thanks to you and Uncle Richard, now I can."

Lauren clinks her glass to ours. "Too bad Daddy couldn't make it today. And Johnny, too. He sends his congratulations from the construction site in Brooklyn."

At her mention of her boyfriend's name, Lauren floats away to her happy place.

Aunt Zara clucks her tongue. "Your father isn't a fan of Champagne. But given the chance to raid Brandon's Scotch collection…"

I shake my head. "Like Brandon, the single malts have left the building. But we may have an unfinished bottle of Johnny Walker Blue. I'll definitely save it for Uncle Richard."

Troi retracts his chin, a guilty grimace plastered across his face. "Um, we *had* a bottle. Sorry."

I rub his shoulder. "Don't apologize, sweetie. I'm glad you enjoyed it. Drink away. It will make packing easier. Not to mention that a dwindling supply of booze will reduce the square footage requirements of our next home."

The topic of moving makes my nerves jangle. Eight weeks before I close on the apartment, I still haven't decided where I'll live next. Living in limbo while waiting for a buyer has suited me. Limbo protects me from acknowledging that I need to plan my future. Which is the scariest bit. I've never *not* had a plan.

Last Resort and all books by
Diane Michaels are available at Amazon.

AUTHOR'S NOTE

The inspiration for *Splitting Heirs* came to me in the early fall of 2019. I had the urge to write a mash-up of Puccini's comic one-act opera, *Gianni Schicchi* (and now you know where I came up with the name Johnny Skeegs!) with a story about people on a quest similar to that in either *Charlie and the Chocolate Factory* or the movie *It's a Mad, Mad, Mad, Mad World*. After writing the first two chapters, I had to put it aside at the beginning of November when my job as a harpist went into overdrive.

Two weeks later, I lost my father. The man who, after reading the couple of f-bombs I dropped in my first novel, had jokingly threatened to wash my mouth out with soap, was no longer there to hold my hand, impart wisdom, or make me laugh.

The world stopped, or at least it should have. But while I mourned, life continued. Before long, I had to jump back into the insane schedule that comes from being a harpist during the holiday season. Being busy, instead of distracting me, left me desperate to do something, *anything* to ease the grief.

I've never found the time to write in December, yet the second I earmarked the minuscule pockets of spare time I had to writing, the words flowed, healing me. I finished writing *Splitting Heirs* in mid-January. My editor sent me her notes at the end of March 2020, another moment when I again felt like I had lost my funny.

This novel sprang to life during a personal crisis and entered the public phase of its life during a worldwide crisis. One thing I've always understood as a harpist is that the arts heal us. Nothing would make me happier than to know that *Splitting Heirs*, which is something of a love letter to New York City, may make any difficulties you may be facing a little easier to bear.

ACKNOWLEDGEMENTS

Danielle Stockdale of Keen Eye Editing was the first to read my manuscript. Through her guidance, I shaped *Splitting Heirs* into the book I had dreamed it could be.

Thank you, Phyllis and Kirsty, for the mounds of encouragement to keep polishing my manuscript.

I am eternally grateful to the members of the Band who have enthusiastically supported each of my releases and reminded me why I keep writing.

When the worst happens, it's so easy to feel isolated. But when grief can be shared, the burden eases. Each step of the mourning process, I have found the most comforting companion in my sister, Heidi. I couldn't have survived without you!

Kevin, who patiently listens to my undecipherable musings when I uncover a conundrum in my manuscripts, is my absolute favorite person with whom to shelter in place. You make the space between these four walls a place I never want to leave.

And to all of you, my readers, I thank you for taking the journey with Lauren, Johnny, Stella, and the Piccolo family. Happy reading!

ABOUT THE AUTHOR

Diane Michaels is a harpist and author. She balances her fondness for ice cream with an enjoyment of working out and walking in the woods. When she is not spying on the world from behind her harp to collect ideas for her next book, she and her husband make up stories and songs about and for their miniature poodle, Lola. To keep up with my book news, I invite you to subscribe to my newsletter. Visit DianeMichaelsBookandHarp.com for your exclusive backstage pass.

Made in the USA
Columbia, SC
20 July 2020